∞

THE TRANSFER PROBLEM

Adam Saint

Deixis Press

First published in 2022 by Deixis Press
www.deixis.press
ISBN 978-1-8384987-5-7

Cover design by Libby Alderman
paperyfeelings.co.uk
Typeset using Adobe Garamond Pro

∞

THE TRANSFER PROBLEM

Adam Saint

Deixis Press

∞

To Julia

CHAPTER ONE

June 13

Ethan curled his fingers around the edges of the armrest. Its tarnished metal corners bit into his flesh. The girl in the neighbouring seat looked at him with compassion, sympathy and worldly understanding. She shuffled her teddy bear across her lap and stretched out its hand towards Ethan, but quickly withdrew it when her mother glanced over from the aisle seat.

Ethan willed his head to turn and stare out the window. Fluffy clouds were smeared out of focus by the faintly gelatinous plastic of the inner window, pocked and scratched by countless hours of use. The thunderous pounding of his heartbeat inside his head drowned out rational thought. He struggled to slow it down, to grapple with the fear and to stuff it back down deep inside. Concentrating on the constant susurration of the aeroplane engines restored some tranquillity. He squeezed his eyes shut until stars sparked behind his eyelids.

A feathery touch against his clenched fingers. Ethan jerked and looked down at the armrest. The teddy bear had stretched out a tentative paw to pat his hand. The girl looked at him bashfully. Ethan ventured a smile. It seemed to work. And then he remembered the message on his phone and the smile drained out of his face.

Ethan was not scared of flying. On the contrary, the rigid laws of fluid dynamics, the metallic tang of technology, even the sense of being compressed into a metal tube breathing frigid, musty air – it all appealed to him and gave him a sense of well-being. He would happily trust himself to the physics of flight and the physical nuts and bolts holding the aircraft together. It seemed like a more certain existence than the random happiness and despair of human relationships.

What scared Ethan was the message on his phone, freshly delivered in flight: They're waiting 4 u at hthrow.

If the flight never ended, he would be happy. Like jumping off a building, it wasn't the falling but the landing that would hurt.

His phone beeped with another message: Engage air protocol. IWS

This message panicked him in a completely different way. It was Anna: that alone was appalling. But of course, it was also impossible for it to be Anna: that meant he was going mad, which was also scary. And the 'air protocol' itself? He knew it was the logical choice – the equipment was bubblewrapped in his hand luggage; the software was freshly updated. But contemplating that plan was scariest of all. Better not to think about it. Better just to let the sequence of steps of the plan unfold before him.

With muffled excuses, Ethan levered himself to his feet and crabbed sideways into the aisle, squeezing past the girl and her mother, retrieving his bag from the overhead locker and walking at a studied, slow pace towards the rear toilets. The plane was a new Airbus design – a wide body aircraft designed to cram in as much human cargo as possible. Most of the seats were occupied: families united in isolation as they flicked through the channels on their TVs and listened to their headphones; business executives shifting sweatily in crumpled suits as they prodded at their laptops; tourists staring out of the window or reading creased magazines. A comfortingly eclectic mix of people, all practising the uniquely human skill of ignoring fellow travellers in a confined public space.

Fiddling with his satchel, Ethan almost collided with a flight attendant walking up the aisle. He recoiled and stammered an apology and tried to edge around her. She stood impassively, blocking his path.

"If you could return to your seat, sir, as the captain has switched on the fasten seatbelts sign," she said.

Ethan shot a pleading glance at her. It slid straight off.

"I'll be quick," he said, "I'm feeling sick."

As he said it, he realized it was true. He felt a roiling in his guts, the blood draining from his face. The flight attendant softened imperceptibly – or perhaps she was worried about cleaning any potential mess.

"OK. Go on then, quickly," she said.

Ethan squeezed around her and trotted to the back of the plane. No heads turned to look at him – everybody was straining to hear the sonorous voice of the captain explaining that they were soon to land at Heathrow. He yanked the curtain across the doorway to the rear galley, stepped inside the rear toilet and slid the bolt shut.

The bathroom had barely enough room to carry out the vital functions for which it was designed, let alone major feats of electronic engineering. Ethan placed the satchel in the scooped-out surface that passed for a sink and pulled out a long, unwieldy package swathed in bubblewrap and trailing a tangle of brightly coloured wires. Under it was a folded schematic of the plane and a laminated instruction sheet. He extracted a laptop from the bubblewrap and put it and his phone on the edge of the sink. Then he set to work with the first part of the task – deftly detaching the various screws and bolts that held the laptop together.

The Airbus was entirely fly-by-wire. Every command from the cockpit was converted into myriad electronic impulses that propagated minuscule adjustments to all the control surfaces of the aircraft. The cabling that made this possible formed an intricately branching skeleton submerged beneath the plane's metal skin. Individual wires snaked along the wings and tail and were bunched together into broader skeins that combined into hefty insulated ropes. By a quirk of design, the whole assemblage – the broad spine of electrical cables – passed only a couple of feet below the floor of one rear bathroom.

It took Ethan about ten minutes to assemble the pieces of 'air protocol'. When he had finished, he tried to step back and admire his construction, but there was no room. He contented himself with leaning back over the toilet and craning his neck around. He could see a jagged hole in the floor – lino rolled back to reveal thin metal plates painstakingly unscrewed and folded back. The laptop was attached to a trail of wires snaking into the hole that led to a long black cylinder wrapped around a trunk of insulation, like a shiny piece of lagging around a hot water pipe.

The cylinder was a transducer. Electrical signals running through the trunk of cables induced tiny corresponding eddies of current in the copper coils – the faintest tremors of electronic vibration. Similarly, pulses of current in the copper coils induced signals in the cables. This ghostly back and forth could read the messages being passed through the cable and replace them with new ones.

The greatest vulnerability in the whole plan was the only purely mechanical device. Ethan propped up some loops of string and springy wooden strips against the door and slid it open. He glanced up and down the aisle and stepped outside and gingerly pulled the door closed. Just before it slid shut, he tugged on the trailing end of a piece of string and tossed it back through the narrow gap into the bathroom and jammed the door completely shut.

There was a clatter of tumbling wood and the bolt slid home and the Engaged light flickered on. To the casual observer, the bathroom was occupied, although it would only take a couple of determined kicks to smash down the door.

Ethan felt curiously calm. The enforced concentration on minute, intricate tasks had settled his thudding heartbeat. Heralded by a gentle ping, the cabin intercom switched on. As Ethan lurched back along the aisle, a reedy voice delivered various weather forecasts followed by profound good wishes to passengers embarking on or returning from vacation or business trips. Finishing with a gentle entreaty to remain safely seated and belted, the voice signed off. The intercom clicked and then pinged again. Passengers resumed their conversations and arguments or slid their headphones back into place. A toddler started to scream and its mother hastily ripped open a pack of sweets. They tumbled out of the bag and onto the floor and the toddler stopped screaming and started laughing. Finally, Ethan reached his row and shuffled across into his seat with a weak grin at his neighbour. As he prodded at his phone, she studied him intently for signs of panic.

"Oh, is that a flight simulator?" she asked, "I like those."

Ethan nodded. He poked at the icons on the screen. The view wavered and windows popped up with various angry error messages. He flicked them away and tweaked some settings. The girl was still talking to him.

The phone hung completely for a few seconds and then a green 'connected' icon blinked up and the screen started to fill with coloured schematics.

"Oh, look, I can see where you are! Is that the sky? Is that the sea? It looks pretty."

The link between his phone and the aircraft telemetry had stabilised. The screen showed a stylised view of their current location, with dotted purple and yellow lines curving into the distance showing their current heading, air speed, wind direction and other incomprehensible vectors. Risking a glance up from his phone, Ethan scanned the cabin. A thin shaft of early dawn sunlight picked out a man snoring majestically, oblivious to sidelong glances from passengers nearby. The air was cold and stale; the mood bored and scratchy with impatience.

It was time to test the connection in the other direction: influencing the plane's controls rather than simply reading them. Under the girl's watchful gaze, Ethan slid a finger cautiously across the screen. Another cohort of error messages popped up all over the screen. They multiplied as fast as he could swipe them closed. Eventually, the flow of new errors slowed to a trickle and another green icon started to blink: avionics control established.

Ethan wiped his hands on his shirt. They were clammy with sweat. There would be no escape once they landed at Heathrow. He would never be heard of again. There could only be one plan: flee, find Robert or Anna, work out how to fix things. And step one of that plan needed him – needed his full attention. Needed his abilities free of emotion, unclouded by judgment or doubt. He stretched and flexed his fingers – a concert pianist preparing for a virtuoso performance, soaking up the anticipation of the audience with a mannered display of unconcern and languid grace. Or perhaps a jaguar lying in a branch, extending one limb and then another in turn to admire the flash of sunlight on claws. His fingers tingled in anticipation – time to do something nobody had ever done before.

"Oh dear, sorry. Naughty Budgerigar!"

Ethan barely had time to wonder why the little girl's teddy bear was called Budgerigar before the screaming started. Budgerigar's paw had pressed down firmly on the down arrow. The grid of purple vectors slewed sideways across the screen, numbers in a digital display tumbled downwards and then started to pulse red. Messages flashed up on screen, shouted that they were urgent, and then just as abruptly were gone.

The background whine of the engines shifted in tone, rising smoothly but rapidly to a shriek. Matching the change in noise, the cabin started to tip forward. Ethan's satchel slid along the floor until it bumped against the seat in front and, as if in competition, acceleration pushed it firmly back towards him.

Ethan's mouth was dry – the arid cabin air seemed to empty it of all moisture. A vertiginous sense of unendurable height or depth was crushing his head from the inside, pressing behind his eyes. He was floating suspended in infinite space, unable to contemplate the awesome void. Blackness leaked into his vision, leaving just a sense of his phone's screen glimpsed at the end of a dim tunnel. He could still hear a voice screaming. He hoped it wasn't his.

"There you go, Budgerigar. Do it like that," said the girl, peering over his elbow. Budgerigar's paw had moved from the down arrow to the up arrow. "Is that better?" she asked Ethan.

"That's better," he replied. He found that he was able to speak. He could see the screen. He could see what he needed to do. Under Budgerigar's watchful gaze, he tightened his grip on the phone and dragged a finger over the control icons.

The rest of the cabin was in confusion. Drinks had spilt over chairs, passengers and their computers. Food landed on the floor and was trodden underfoot. The source of the screaming was a large man with a scrawny beard and prominent tattoos on his forearms; he was travelling with an elderly woman who took his hand and coaxed him back into silence. In the back row, a young couple, previously strangers, found themselves clasped together in an awkward embrace.

As the engines returned to their normal whine and the cabin tipped back to approximate horizontality, the frenzy subsided. Flight attendants glided along the aisles and tended to their customers. There were mutterings about turbulence. A fleshy white man began to explain authoritatively about sudden air pockets to his neighbours in an unnecessarily loud voice.

Ethan was dimly aware of the ebbing panic and the continued skittish mood. He tapped nervously at the phone, checking each of the controls, nudging the vectors a degree here, a degree there, and allowing the plane's fly-by-wire to translate his commands into appropriate instructions to the various moving parts.

A voice crackled over the intercom: "Ladies and gentlemen, we apologise for the slight turbulence you have been experiencing. We are currently investigating some issues with the flight avionics, so if we could ask you all to return to your seats and fasten your seat belts …"

Ethan cut out this voice and all the others. He spared a brief smile for Budgerigar and its owner and then plunged into the details of his flight simulator. He widened the cockpit view until a dotted diagonal curve revealed the entire path to Heathrow. Only twenty minutes flight time left. He pressed on a glowing yellow rectangle, another nearby runway. It looked a bit shorter than the Heathrow runway but it would have to do. He flicked away some irritating warnings until at last the dotted lines tore away from Heathrow and realigned on the new runway.

"All electronic items switched off now, please," said the flight attendant.

Ethan glanced up from his screen. The flight attendant loomed over him, one hand resting carelessly on the armrest.

"He can't, he's flying the plane," said the little girl next to Ethan. "Budgerigar is helping him."

She lifted Budgerigar up with both hands, presenting him to the flight attendant. Budgerigar waved a paw weakly at her.

"It's just a computer game, dear. The captain is flying the plane. Oh, it's you." She stopped and squinted at Ethan, seeing him properly for the first time. "Are you feeling better?"

"I'm still a bit sick," muttered Ethan. But the flight attendant was not interested in his answer. She gazed over Ethan's head and down the aisle. "If it makes him feel better," she said to the girl, apparently deciding that she was Ethan's guardian, "let him play his game. And make sure he's not sick again."

The girl nodded wisely and the flight attendant swished past to find other victims.

The next few minutes were so full of activity that it was difficult afterwards to sort events into a coherent order. He remembered engine noises shifting crazily up and down the scale, desperately searching for equilibrium. Sickening plunges turned his stomach over as the entire aircraft dropped vertically and then surged forward, like a rubber ball bouncing down a flight of steps. Then tilts from side to side that sloshed the blood inside his head, threatening to bring back the nausea, setting his fingers tingling, breath coming short and sharp, struggling to focus on the tangle of lines on the screen in front of him.

At some point, the screaming started again. There were sobs as well. Panic gnawed at the superficial calm the flight crew were straining to enforce. The couple in the back row appeared to be proceeding rapidly towards a consummation of their brief relationship. A tall white-haired man pronounced prayers in a gravelly stage whisper until he was angrily shushed by other passengers.

Ethan mainly remembered the grid of yellow and purple lines spiralling around, dividing into smaller grids, branching and merging. He remembered steering the aircraft along the gently curving paths, adjusting the vectors and then compensating for his clumsy adjustments.

Crackly announcements from the captain hushed the cabin and led to a disappointed clamour when she stopped. Ethan ignored them.

The plane bumped and buckled as it plunged through the layer of clouds. Ethan lifted the flap covering his window and risked a quick glance out. The ground loomed out of the mist, much closer than he had expected. Lights twinkled, but of course he could not see the runway directly in front of the plane. He had to trust it was there.

A clatter of feet alongside – a man and a woman in uniform racing back along the aisles, stumbling as the plane dipped and decelerated, so that they were swimming uphill. Altimeter showing one hundred metres. Stall warnings flashing on his phone's screen. Shouts and knocks as they reached the rear toilet and bashed on the door. The screen covered with red warnings. Fifty metres. Too late, remembering the undercarriage. Was the runway there? It had to be. A screeching crash as they kicked at the door and it buckled. Hands reaching around the door. How had they worked it out? What would happen if they disconnected him now? Twenty metres. Whistle and trundling roar of wheels extending and catching the air. Angry shouts. They had opened the toilet door. But it was too late. Too late. One metre. Zero metres.

Ethan's last thought: How did I let Anna talk me into this?

CHAPTER TWO

May 19

Anna thought she would scream if Ethan and Robert didn't stop discussing cricket statistics. She might have really done it, thrown her head back and filled her lungs and let go with a lusty full-bodied shriek, except for the nagging suspicion that they would simply pause and then resume their discussion without paying her any further attention.

Instead, she picked up a sugar cube between finger and thumb and dropped it into Ethan's drink. It hit with a satisfying plop and sank slowly to the bottom. She picked up another one and repeated the operation. She had a third sugar cube poised above Ethan's glass when his fist closed around her hand.

"I think you've made your point," he said. The glass of red wine was effervescing gently.

Robert sniggered. "What you're meant to say is, 'aren't I sweet enough already?'" he said.

"Or you could maybe avoid that pathetic cliché altogether?" said Anna. "And talk about a proper sport, instead of your precious cricket. Like tennis, or baseball."

Robert and Ethan were both staring at her now. Their conversation on the relative merits of Australian fast bowlers of the 1970s ground to a halt. Anna's aim was achieved. She grinned at them.

"Think maybe you'd better pay some attention to your girlfriend," said Robert.

Ethan stirred his red wine with his index finger. The bubbles subsided. It may have been her imagination, but Anna thought she could smell a sweet, fruity aroma coming from the glass.

A burst of raucous cheering from a group of shiny-suited City gents crashed into the momentary silence at their table. Anna, Robert and Ethan were perched on shiny orange chairs around a tiny orange table in a winebar on a side street at the fashionable interface of the East End and the City. The plastic chairs were moulded into daring curves that were painfully stylish – literally so; the only way to sit on them without experiencing agony was to perch on the very edge. Anna and Ethan were still at the early stage in their relationship where it mattered where he chose to take her out for an after-work drink. This bar must have conformed to Ethan's idea of where a high-flying City banker took his girlfriend, but from the way he kept glancing abstractedly at the surrounding mass of people, he was no more comfortable there than Anna or Robert.

"Yeah, I guess I must be pretty crap at this if I'm getting relationship advice from you," said Ethan at last.

Anna laughed. "You're not doing crap. You're doing very well. For someone who's never done it before. I mean, you've got to start somewhere. That might be a pretty low somewhere, of course."

"Careful Anna," said Robert, "you can't just pluck this young man's virginity and then toy with him like that."

"Robert, do you have to be so crass? What have we been discussing about boundaries?" said Ethan. Anna could see that he was growing anxious. He hunched his shoulders and his lower lip started to extend into a pout. She decided it was time to rescue the situation.

"Ethan, tell us what you're up to now. It's so much more interesting than my little job," she said.

Ethan accepted the change of subject gratefully. "Well, it's true," he said, "my job involves the manipulation of razor-thin momentary pricing discrepancies in financial markets to accumulate profits, whereas all you're doing is saving the world."

Anna laughed, a chuckle deep in her throat, mirthless, an acknowledgement that the joke had been made rather than an appreciation of it.

"I don't think my academic work counts as saving the world. It might save a few mice. I don't think I'll ever get to work with something more complex than that."

"That sounds intriguing. You can't leave us hanging on like that," said Robert.

"Please don't tempt her," said Ethan. "Once Anna gets going, you won't be able to stop her."

"Nothing wrong with having some genuine passion for what you do."

"Anyway, it would blow your old hacker mind if you even tried to understand what Anna's doing in her lab."

"OK, well, instead, let's go and have a look at it," said Robert. He leaned in with eyes wide and gleaming and slapped his hands on the table. "Come on, rather than sitting here, let's go and have a look."

"No, absolutely not," said Ethan, "this is another of your mad ideas. Anna's lab will be locked up anyway. Absolutely not."

∞

Thirty minutes later, Ethan, Anna and Robert were crouched outside the crumbling rear façade of the biology department of University College London. The Victorian redbrick building backed onto a narrow alley. A ragged line of plastic bins was propped against rusted metal railings that ran along one wall. Torn refuse sacks bulged from the tops of the bins and spilled over the rest of the alley, filling most of the awkward wedge of space between the adjacent buildings. Rows of black windows gazed sightlessly down – Ethan glanced up anxiously at the opaque glass, straining to make out shadows that might be figures staring down at them.

This was worse than the time Robert had tied him to the railway tracks. Ethan had said no then too; he always said no to Robert's ideas, but it never seemed to make any difference. It was about two years after their mother died, so Ethan would have been eight, Robert eleven. One of those endless afternoons, steeped in the mouldy decay of their grandmother's house, hiding upstairs and conferring in whispers so as not to trigger one of her migraines. Even then, Ethan did not want to visit the disused railway station. He hated the twisted mat of weeds climbing the walls, the faint web of cracks in the concrete floor, the splintered edges of the broken railway sleepers. Everywhere the ravening disorder of nature reclaiming its own.

Somehow, they had ended up climbing the low wall at the end of the garden, creeping along the track as it followed a gentle curve that swept into the station. They stood on the tracks between the platforms, the tops of their heads level with the floor, and Ethan shivered in the oppressive silence.

"I've got an idea," said Robert, with an air of sudden revelation. "Let's play a game. Let's pretend it's a real railway station and robbers have tied you to the tracks. Then I'll come and untie you and rescue you just in time before the train comes."

It turned out that Robert had a ball of twine in his pockets. Ethan lay down gingerly on the clammy ground and Robert methodically tied his hands to one sleeper and his feet to another. As Robert heaved on the knots, pulling them tight, Ethan's fingers started to tingle. He shifted from side to side, trying to loosen the twine biting into his ankles and wrists. It had sounded like a fun game when Robert was explaining it to him but, lying on the weeds and grass with random splinters of wood jutting into his back and his arms and legs yanked uncomfortably in opposite directions, he struggled to remember what the point of this game was.

Suddenly, Robert stopped and gazed into the distance along the track behind Ethan. He raised one hand to his forehead to blot out glare from the sun and squinted as though trying to make out something in the distance.

"What's that?" said Robert.

"What?" said Ethan, craning his neck to follow Robert's gaze.

"I thought I heard something … no, no, that's impossible."

"What's impossible? What is it?"

"This line is meant to be closed. There aren't meant to be any trains. Oh no, can you feel it vibrating?"

Robert laid one hand gently on the metal track, still staring past Ethan. Ethan struggled against the twine. Could he feel the track trembling? He thought he could. He thought he could hear the faint thrum of an approaching train transmitted through the track, ripping past the weeds and wildflowers growing over the line, shattering the stultifying peace of the station.

"Untie me, quick," said Ethan. He started to gasp and squirm against his bonds. He felt his heart pounding – or was it the beat of the approaching train's wheels on the track?

Robert fiddled desperately with the twine. "There's not time," he said, "I don't think I'm going to make it. Hold still, hold still."

Hot tears pricked the back of Ethan's eyes. He tried not to struggle as Robert picked vainly at the knots. He heard the whistle of air in and out of Robert's mouth as he breathed heavily in concentration, like the sough of wind against the trees lining the side of the line. Why was Robert taking so long? He seemed to be absorbed in one tiny loop wrapped around his ankle. If he would only free Ethan's hands, then Ethan could at least sit up and help him. He tugged again, letting the thin cord dig into his wrists as he twisted and jerked. Nothing. Each move seemed only to confirm how intractably he was fixed to the railway line.

"I'm sorry, Boom, it's no good," said Robert. He looked up and shrieked and threw himself to the side, tucked into the gap under the overhang from the station platform. Ethan braced himself, trembling violently despite his stiffened limbs. His hands and feet were numb, the rest of his skin was tingling. He heard a tiny moaning sound and after a few seconds realised that he was the one making it. The instant before impact stretched to an unbearable climax, his whole body tensed in anticipation.

Then Robert let out a huge guffaw and the spell was broken. His booming laugh echoed around the deserted platforms, desecrating the silence with absurd hoots and splutters. Eventually, he pulled out a penknife and strode back to Ethan, who lay limply on the track feeling embarrassed at the trail of snot hanging from his nose that he could not wipe away because his hands were still tied.

"No sacrifices today, Boom," said Robert as he cut through the twine.

∞

As Ethan stared up at the blank windows and shrugged into the deepest shadows of the alley, he thought that not much had changed. At least

Robert did not call him Boom any more. It had been short for boomerang, because whenever Robert attempted to get rid of Ethan he would come wandering back. But it was many years since Ethan had looked to Robert for protection – now it was more likely to be a panicked call from Robert when he needed Ethan to bail him out of trouble.

"Where's your lab?" asked Robert.

Anna pointed at a window on the third floor. A cast iron drainpipe ran up the side of the building to a gutter that extended horizontally three feet above the window. The drainpipe was fixed to the wall by a dozen small, rusted bolts. The frame of the window was wooden, warped with age and containing only a single frame of glass. In one corner, its ill-fitting shape left a clear finger's width of gap.

"I thought we could climb up and along," said Anna, pointing at the route up the drainpipe and along the gutter to the window, "the window isn't locked. It doesn't even close properly. Easy."

"Well, it does look a bit tricky to me," said Robert, "I mean, don't you think it's a bit melodramatic. You do work here, right? Don't you have, like, a pass or something?"

"Of course, but it doesn't work outside of office hours for a junior researcher like me. And the lab doesn't allow visitors. The whole place is shut up tight."

Robert extended a hand and Anna fished around in her handbag, eventually removing a small white rectangular piece of plastic and giving it to him.

"Hmm, cute picture – you've done well for yourself there, Ethan – and what's this, an RFID chip built in, security is electronic not mechanical." Robert looked up at Ethan and smiled.

Skirting the bags of rubbish, they walked around the corner of the alley to the front entrance. One of the terms of Robert's probation at age fourteen was a total ban on the use of electronic devices. Sadly, the ban came too late to prevent him from perfecting his hacking skills. Nor had its enforcement ever been particularly effective. The university's entrance system was exactly the kind of flashy, superficial hack that appealed to Robert.

Five minutes later, they were sitting at benches before a generic beige workstation in Anna's lab. Serried rows of tables supported racks of test tubes, tiny metal cages, random agglomerations of electrical apparatus, syringes, pyrex bowls and plastic tubing. Another row of desks held monitors, laptops, routers, wires and piles of electronic components.

Ethan knew roughly what Anna did, of course. He left her to explain it to Robert while he explored the darkened laboratory in the shifting light from the one monitor she had turned on.

"Biomathematical learning processes. Using the central nervous system of a living thing, fairly simple at this stage of course, we've been trying ants, worms, the odd beetle when things have been going well." Anna was waving her arms and talking faster and faster, swept up in her passion for her work. "Interfaced with standard computer hardware, running a neural network that multiplies the efficacy of the original brain. We've set them to simple tasks. Facial recognition. Anything pattern based. Aiming for the plasticity of the organic cortex plus the power and speed of electronics."

Robert held his hands up in the air until Anna trailed to a halt. "Okay, so let's assume for a moment that I don't have a doctorate in biology or mathematics or whatever you've got …"

"It's biomathematics with statistics, actually."

"Right. Good for you. So, assuming, as I said, that I'm an idiot … don't interrupt, Ethan" – catching Ethan as he was about to break in with a chorus of agreement – "can I take it that this is some sort of supercharger for the human brain?"

"No, not at all. The computation is run on the electronics, not the brain at all. And it's not a human brain, we're talking something a billion times more primitive. We use the established neural pathways to create learned pattern-recognition skills …"

"Yeah, I got it. Let me try again. You're transferring someone's brain into a computer where it will be really good at solving certain problems."

"Ah, the Transfer Problem," said Anna, with a half-smile at Ethan. She pronounced the capital letters emphatically, "let's not get into that."

"Alright. I'm not even going to ask. Last go. You're running something similar to a brain on a computer so it can solve pattern-recognition problems."

"We're trying to. We're not getting very far. We've made real progress on the interface side, with a non-invasive EEG-based technique for …"

"But look at this," Ethan said before Anna could build up into another unstoppable oration. He was crouched over a stack of circuit boards, picking up each in turn and sorting them into piles. "Your tech is, erm, it's really last year. Or two years ago. You've got, I mean really ..." holding up a rat's nest of cabling "... it's twisted copper, not even fibre optic."

Anna shrugged. "I'm in academia, not high finance. We've already maxed out our budget for the year. We were using some cloud services to top up our processing power, but that worked out even more expensive."

Robert clapped his hands together. "That's a great idea, Ethan," he said, ignoring Ethan's puzzled frown in response. "Let's use your tech. Let's put her pattern recognition on your high finance supercomputers."

Ethan held up his hands in protest. "There's no way I can let you near my work. They'd probably sack me if they even knew you were my brother."

"Not me. Not me. You don't need to let me anywhere near it. Just her," Robert pointed at Anna. "We may only have met this evening – and I don't see why it took you so long to introduce us, by the way, Ethan – but I'm pretty sure she's not got any sort of undesirable background. It doesn't have to be anything to do with me."

Robert smiled wolfishly. Then he could not restrain himself any longer – he leaned back his head and let out a whoop of laughter. Ethan and Anna both shushed him and he looked back down at them as if seeing them for the first time.

"And I know exactly what you can use Anna's pattern recognition for. The patterns that your bank and every other bank spend all their time struggling to predict. The patterns they recruited you to look at and let you build your own kit for and write your own code and put it all on their systems, all so that you might one day get a second or two ahead of the pattern and know what's going to happen next."

Ethan and Anna looked at Robert in bemusement. Anna figured it out first and let out a low whistle of appreciation. They both had to explain it to Ethan. He would certainly never have agreed if he had known it would end with him crashing a plane into a North London suburb.

CHAPTER THREE

June 13

Elstree Aerodrome was a small airfield on the outskirts of London: its runway a tarmac scar squeezed into the patchwork of fields, ponds and triangles of scrubby woodland that formed this corner of the green belt. A dozen two- and four-seater airplanes were lined up on the neatly cropped pasture that abutted the runway. A breeze block and corrugated iron hangar housed several other light aircraft. The combined terminal, control tower and – most importantly – airport café was a squat brick building. Parts of its earlier incarnation as a prefabricated structure were betrayed by plastic window- and door-frames and one wall where bricks terminated abruptly in sheets of wood and breeze block.

The Aerodrome was only accessible down a winding country lane marked by an apologetically drooping road sign appearing to point into the bowels of the earth. It was so incongruously ugly, so ashamed of its architectural shortcomings compared with its bucolic surroundings, that it was inescapably quaint and was regarded by the local inhabitants with a proprietorial affection, especially the pork pies served at the airport cafe. Even the angry buzzing of the aircraft every five minutes as they took off and landed only served as a natural counterpoint to the harmonious sounds of the country: birdsong, chattering of insects, the occasional diesel belch of a tractor negotiating the winding roads.

Early on a Sunday morning, it should have been a scene of relaxed endeavour – perhaps a plane or two awkwardly manoeuvring around the taxiway marked out by loops of rope connected by stakes, or one of the pork pies reheating in the microwave for a customer. Instead, the steel-haired matronly lady running Elstree Aerodrome was facing a scene of devastation and chaos.

A new wide-bodied Airbus had decided to land on Elstree's miniature runway. Its path was marked out by a series of discarded sections of airplane, damaged regions of airfield or similar miniature tableaux of destruction, like a trail of clues leading a detective painstakingly to the scene of the murder.

A broken slab of concrete halfway along the runway marked the point where the plane had touched down. A crazy network of cracks threaded out from the initial shallow crater, zigzagging along the length of the runway until it reached a large wheel, still attached to the jagged ends of metal spokes and black plastic tubing. Strips of rubber radiated out from the wheel, showing where the tyre had exploded and the front undercarriage had collapsed and ripped in half.

The plane had started to slew sideways as it slid along the runway. A deep muddy gouge showed where it had run out of airstrip, although this seemed to be only a minor impediment to its continued progress. The gouge continued in a wide arc to the edge of the field and straight through the tattered remains of a brambly hedge to the neighbouring field, which had now – somewhat against its will – become an impromptu extension to Elstree Aerodrome.

The plane itself was in the adjoining field, turned almost at right angles to the runway and resting on one wingtip at a jaunty angle, as though better to survey what it had wrought. It was decorated with a row of inflatable scarlet emergency slides. They were now sagging and empty, having disgorged their human cargo.

The passengers had formed a disorderly line heading back towards Elstree Aerodrome, spontaneously compelled into airport queueing behaviour by their genetic Britishness. Most had a glazed expression and were drifting aimlessly, huddled in their individual family groups. One woman was trying to limp and look furious at the same time, not the easiest combination to pull off, especially in the middle of a muddy field.

She had spent several minutes at the top of the slide engaged in a heated argument with a flight attendant over whether she had to take off her high-heeled shoes before going down the chute. She had won the argument but then lost the tip of one of her shoes and her dignity, as she rolled shrieking from one side to the other, flapping her arms helplessly as if she could fly away from the plane. Ethan had joined in with the hearty laughter. Now he strained to blend in with the other passengers. Budgerigar and his owner were standing nearby staring up at Ethan awkwardly and with a certain amount of awe.

The flight crew were gathered at the base of one of the slides. Shaking her head and pointing, the captain seemed to be arguing with her team, who showed no sign of leaping into action. Whatever emergency protocols had been drilled into them apparently did not include squelching through a muddy field.

When the straggly line of passengers reached the main part of the Aerodrome, Ethan shuffled sideways into the crowd massing by the building. Ethan did not find it easy to look inconspicuous. He sometimes felt that he was a small, weedy boy trapped in the body of a large, muscular man. He had a habit of stooping slightly to draw attention away from his tall, rangy frame but, of course, this only drew more attention to it. Budgerigar's owner was still staring at him with wide open eyes and her frank amazement was starting to attract attention from the other passengers.

There was a tug at Ethan's sleeve.

"Are you a pilot, or … or an astronaut?" she asked.

"Yes," Ethan said, with an apologetic smile aimed vaguely at the gathering crowd of onlookers, "I'm an astronaut. I just flew down from Mars in my spaceship."

"Don't be silly, you didn't fly a spaceship. You flew our plane."

It was time to leave. Ethan attempted another placatory smile but the audience was starting to grow restive. Muttering and pointing rippled outwards. The knot of passengers around them was coalescing into a mob. The flight crew would soon overcome their apathy and confusion and work out that Ethan was responsible for their unscheduled descent.

Ethan patted Budgerigar's owner on the head and turned to one side, not varying his pace from a steady shuffling walk. He was pointed straight at a hedge – a brambly, shaggy outcropping drawing a ragged line that defined the edge of the airfield.

As his path diverged from the rest of the passengers, he felt their gaze prickling between his shoulder blades. A single infinitesimal dot of sweat traced a meandering path down his back, leaving an icy trail in its wake. The moan of a distant siren broke into the pastoral background hum of birdsong and traffic. A second later, another siren answered the first. Then the two sirens became indistinguishable notes in an orchestra of sirens, weaving in and out in a perplexing absence of pattern.

Ethan kept walking. He expected a hand on his shoulder, a gruff but business-like voice asking him to stop. He kept walking. The hedge varied from thick to impenetrable. Ethan picked a clump of tangles through which spots of daylight were visible and curved his path gently towards it. His breath came in short gasps. Springy thin branches whipped at his face, coiled around his ankles, slapped his arms and shoulders. Brambles grasped at him, snagged at his shirt. The bush pleaded with him to stay. He shut his eyes and forced his feet to drag ahead.

Then he was through and suddenly dazzled by shards of sunlight glittering off puddles on black tarmac. A country lane, its surface undulating and cracked, followed the curve of the hedge. Weeds groped around the roughly painted white stripes bordering the edge of the road; a bee hung above a bright pink flower sprouting from the hedge, biding its time. There was no haste here, only a heavy inertia which lay over the faint noises of disgruntled airline passengers and the ticking and rumbling of rapidly cooling aircraft components.

Ethan picked a direction and turned and walked along the edge of the road. His shirt was sticking to his back, but his skin was already puckering into goose-bumps as the sweat evaporated in the breeze. He listened for footsteps running up behind him; he watched for sirens of police cars circling the countryside in search of him. The raspy buzz of a motorcycle broke the stillness. Ethan shuffled to one side as it puttered past him and then realised too late that he should have asked for a lift.

It was time to stop reacting and start thinking. Ethan trudged further up the lane while he collected his thoughts. He had escaped for now. But where could he go? He had to find whoever had helped him on the plane. You know who that is, came the unbidden thought, but he instantly banished it. Let's work through all the possibilities. Anna had to come first. It was Anna who had christened incywincy – the same IWS that had been texting him. Morris had said he was calling an ambulance for Anna and surely that ambulance would have taken her to the closest hospital? It was a slender thread to follow, but Ethan could see no better option. Find out from Anna what had happened – find out, apart from anything else, what had happened to all the money. Maybe they could give it back. Maybe it wasn't too late to undo what had been done.

There was one sensible step he could take immediately. He took his mobile phone out of his pocket, unclipped the back, removed the SIM card and slid it into a zipped compartment in his wallet. Then he disconnected the battery, clipped the fascia of his phone back into place and put the phone and battery into different pockets.

A gentle bend in the road brought a small roundabout into view. The lane sloped down and widened; the scraggly hedge faded into low brush, trampled and trodden into a dirty yellow mat. Three cyclists sheathed in garish pink and yellow lycra were crouched by the far exit of the roundabout, passing a water bottle back and forth. Two were paunchy men in their fifties, with a faint sheen of sweat glimmering off their bald pates and jowly faces. The third was a woman, wiry and angular, with a slender beak of a nose dividing a narrow face.

Ethan set his face into a rigid smile, thrust his hands into his pockets and slowed his pace to a carefree saunter.

"Hi guys," he called out, "look, I don't suppose you could help me out at all. Looking for a train station – any chance you could point me in the right direction, even give me a lift?"

∞

Three hours later, Ethan was standing in front of the main entrance to University College Hospital in central London. Behind him, cars and buses inched along the congested Euston Road, belching fumes and rattling the blackened windowpanes of nearby shops and restaurants. Ethan felt the noise as a constant vibration through his feet.

In front of him rose the glass and chrome façade of the hospital, blank and impassive above the swirling mass of pedestrians squeezing along the pavement and the impotent hooting of the traffic. Sets of double doors led into an airy atrium, decorated with large plants wilting gently in the air-conditioning and shedding leaves on the pastel carpeting. As Ethan stood on the pavement, attempting to loiter inconspicuously near a bus stop, two young men in white coats shouldered one set of doors open and stepped onto the pavement, making way for an elderly man in a thick winter coat who shuffled inside. A security guard smiled and waved the man to a reception desk.

The flow of humanity around Ethan was a solid presence, compressing his thoughts into a panicked useless blob. His breath came in torn, ragged gasps. He was a fugitive, foolishly returning to the one place he knew one of his known associates might be, looking for her, looking for guidance. He had no weapons, no training. More importantly, he didn't have the right personality. This wasn't him. A problem on a computer screen – he could help with that. But problems involving seething human irrationality? Involving persuasion, pretence, even violence? He was the last person for that task.

In the end, though, it was easy. Ethan barged awkwardly through the double doors – they were heavier than they looked, surely not a wise choice for a hospital entrance? – and marched to the reception desk. His sweaty, shifty nervousness was an excellent match with most of the visitors to the hospital and his clothes were no more bedraggled than most, except for his shoes, which were showing the effects of several miles of Hertfordshire country lanes on foot and bicycle and a run through muddy fields, not to mention a plane crash.

"Can I help you, sir?" asked the lady behind the reception desk and then immediately snatched at a ringing phone and leaned away from Ethan to start an animated conversation. He grabbed the opportunity to lean over the desk and read the visitor log upside-down, picking a name at random from the middle of the list.

"Yes, here to see Miss Trelawney," Ethan said, with what he hoped was a winning smile.

The lady nodded absently and tapped at her keyboard. Then she glanced sharply up at Ethan.

"She's in the morgue," she said.

"Of course, the morgue, thank you," said Ethan, rapidly modifying his expression to that of a recently bereaved relative.

"Level minus two. Lift along the corridor and turn right at the end. Sign and print name here please. And I'll need to see some ID."

With a sigh, Ethan handed over his passport and, while the lady photocopied it, scribbled something indecipherable in the guest register. He shuffled away from the desk and concentrated on maintaining a deliberate pace, painfully aware of the lady painstakingly entering his details into her computer.

Ethan entered a corridor, still resisting the urge to turn and look behind him despite the prickling in his scalp and the back of his neck. The lift took him down to level minus two and then he ducked out of the next corridor into, successively, a storage cupboard, a lobby marked as the entrance to the Imaging Centre and – behind a door marked Private – an empty office. He didn't quite have Robert's skills, but it took only two minutes at the computer in the office to locate Anna. He scribbled down the ward and bed number on a page torn from a jotter pad and set off in search of her.

This was so much easier on television, thought Ethan ten minutes later, as he apologised to yet another nurse and backed awkwardly out of the entrance to a ward. By now, James Bond would have knocked a doctor unconscious, changed into their uniform, found Anna, and probably seduced a scantily-clad nurse along the way.

"You want Ward 17A, at the south end of the third floor," a nurse called after him, "this is Ward A17, at the south end of the third floor annex."

After another few circuits of the endless corridors, Ethan stumbled on Ward 17A. A front reception desk was strewn with paper – some sheets spraying out of a partially collapsed pile of beige folders, others propped against a computer monitor and jammed under a keyboard. Two nurses sat behind the desk. One – a young, pleasantly plump woman – smiled at Ethan.

"Erm, I'm here to see Anna Volkov."

"Yes, dear," the nurse crinkled her eyebrows in an expression of sympathetic concern. Ethan could feel cold panic creeping in at the edges of his self-control.

"Is she here? I mean, is she, is she, that is, has she …"

"Yes, Anna is on the ward, dear."

She was still alive. That is, Ethan immediately corrected himself, her body had survived. Perhaps this was the Anna who had helped him guide his plane to safety. Perhaps that had been somebody else. His thoughts were tumbling over each other and the nurse was gazing at him with increasing concern.

First things first: "I need to speak to her. I need to see her right now."

"Well, I'm afraid that's not ..."

"I don't care if it isn't. I have to speak to her right now."

The two nurses exchanged a glance.

"You're quite welcome to see her, dear. It's not that. But she's under heavy sedation. Well, she's had quite a time of it." The plump nurse looked at the other nurse who was flicking through one of the beige folders. She shook her head slowly and looked up meaningfully at the first nurse. Moving over to the desk, they pored over the chart and muttered to each other. Ethan strained to appear as though he was granting the nurses their privacy while simultaneously overhearing their conversation – he caught only a few phrases:

"Seventy-five of pethidine by IV on admission ... another hundred two hours later ... seventy-five after four hours ... renal function improving."

As if on cue, both nurses looked up from the chart and stared at him. He scratched at a fleck of grime on his nose. His skin itched where it had caught on some brambles. Was he blushing? He was fairly sure that secret agents did not blush. Yet it seemed to have the desired effect on the nurses. Their expressions softened.

"She's not waking up any time soon," explained the first nurse, "we had to give her a great deal of pain medication initially, and for several hours while it was continuing, and now she's up here on the renal ward to monitor ..."

"Look, I don't understand, I was there when it happened, what do you mean, when it was continuing, it was over in a second." Ethan raised one hand to his head, wiping sweat across his forehead with a blackened sleeve and leaving behind a trail of grime. Too many variables he didn't understand, too much happening all at once, and he was chasing after it. One step behind. He had to start finding answers instead of questions. He had to jump one step ahead.

"Are you friend or family, dear?" asked the plump nurse.

"I'm, er, friend. Look, can I just see her, please?"

Another long, appraising stare from the nurses – was it his imagination, or were they taking in his muddy clothes and faint sheen of desperation? Finally, the plump nurse swung out from behind the desk and trotted along the corridor. Ethan fell into her wake, as though she were gently tugging him along. He was barely conscious of following her.

A cheap wooden laminate door gave onto a small room, little more than a cupboard. It was dominated by a metal-framed hospital bed surrounded by medical equipment: monitors, intravenous drip stands, trolleys stacked with sealed syringe kits and cardboard tubes lazily ripped open to reveal gauze bandages and pipettes and other paraphernalia Ethan could not identify. But these details were a background fuzz – Ethan focused only on the slight figure lying on the bed.

Anna was tucked neatly under a thick blanket, her arms carefully arranged straight by her side. The hospital gown ended at her elbows and patches of gauze daubed with spots of blood on her lower arms marked a trail of entry points for various fluids. Her face was white, framed by a tangled black mess of hair, which itself nestled in the bleached white fabric of a pillow. She seemed pale to the point of transparency. Her eyes were sunken, nose and cheekbones sharp in a gaunt face. The faint network of scars on her cheeks and forehead – legacy of childhood acne – were visible as threads of lesser white: an imperfection that heightened the impression of general pallor.

Ethan drew a single shuddering breath, gasping as a jolt of pain arced inside his head. He was blinded – for a moment felt he was looking directly at himself, hunched over the narrow hospital bed, stretching out a hand to keep his balance.

Anna was asleep; not only that, she was unconscious. But was this actually Anna? There was no doubt it was Anna's body lying in front of him. Was her mind still inside that body? The person lying in front of him was not the source of the message that had guided him on the plane. Until she woke up and spoke, there was no way to be sure if she was the real Anna. It was a classic variation of the Transfer Problem.

CHAPTER FOUR

January 30

The first seminar was called The Transfer Problem. Ethan had originally decided not to go. Most people didn't turn up until mid-morning; the opening session was a graveyard slot. But then Robert had started clanking plates and glasses in the kitchen – he was sleeping on Ethan's couch for a couple of days in between rentals – and haranguing Ethan with his comical political views, and Ethan had eventually conceded defeat and sneaked out of his own flat for the relative peace of the conference.

Ethan rarely attended academic conferences. He had received a slew of spam emails advertising this one – not unusual, although they were curiously adept at avoiding his spam filters. Then flyers had arrived through snail mail – he remembered Robert, on another visit, holding up the flyer and reading the title of each lecture with mock seriousness, finally breaking into roars of laughter. Eventually, Ethan had accepted the inevitable.

He had arranged his arguments carefully and endlessly rehearsed his little speech setting out the positive impact of academic engagement. It was all unnecessary. His boss had waved it through without a second thought. The bank might have the money for nifty hardware, but they recognised that a lot of the nifty ideas were in academia. Fortunately, unlike the finance industry, academia tended to publish all its results.

Still, it was prudent to keep a close eye on the latest developments. Plus Ethan was a frustrated academic – smart enough that it was worthwhile humouring him. So if Ethan wanted to go to a conference on the latest computer science developments, his bank would happily expense the paltry registration fee and grant him a day's leave.

The seminar conformed to every banker's stereotype of an academic conference. The dusty hall was both cramped and uncomfortably empty. High, thin windows fogged with age and neglect admitted shafts of bright winter sun, sweeping shadows into the corners and the rear of the stage. Plastic chairs were arranged in a rough semi-circle in the front third of the hall, centred on the lectern at the edge of the stage. The rest of the hall was bare, with stacks of plastic chairs arrayed around the edge. As it was a mathematical conference, there were two blackboards and a long, multiple-panel whiteboard set up on the stage behind the lectern. They were covered with half-completed equations, rubbed out, layered over each other, some sideways and others written in small curved gaps, like competing voices in a shouted argument.

Ethan sat in the front row. His rangy frame could not squeeze into the unnecessarily small gaps between the other rows. He was conscious of being the only person in the room without a ponytail, a beer belly poking out from beneath a T-shirt or a life-threatening hangover concealed beneath a black hoodie. At least he had had the sense not to wear a suit.

"… and I'd like to welcome our first speaker this morning, Dr Anna Volkov," said the convenor of the conference, a spry lady with an iron-grey bun.

There was scattered applause from those not checking email on their phones. After a confused pause, a slight, angular woman appeared at the far side of the room and threaded her way through the chairs, moving noiselessly, like a ghost, towards the stage. Ethan's first impression was of her sad eyes, heightened by her pale face, which itself was emphasized by her black clothing. She wore a dark, long-sleeved top, a floor-length skirt and a large, floppy hat with a wide brim, squeezed on top of unruly black hair.

"The Transfer Problem," she began, in a painfully quiet voice, "is a central dilemma in the field of hybrid neural networks. It has been neglected due to its philosophical underpinnings in problems of consciousness, which are historically seen as outside the remit of theoretical computer science, but recent advances in achieving congruence between biological and artificial neural networks have brought it back into prominence. Let us define a set of tensors as follows, first a constraint tensor ..." She turned to the blackboard and fished around for a piece of chalk.

Ethan was intrigued by this diffident but eerily confident speaker. He was vaguely aware of the Transfer Problem; it dealt with the hoary concept of transferring a human consciousness into a machine or a computer. This was often portrayed as one way to achieve a sort of immortality: download your brain into a computer and carry on living in silicon instead of carbon, a digital reproduction unaffected by the vagaries of physical imperfection or accident.

It was a tantalising promise – a scientific advance that would transform human existence. But, in practice, nobody would ever agree to download their brain. Imagine that you receive an offer, a serious offer: a machine would deconstruct your brain and put it into a computer. The computer would be indistinguishable from you, running your thoughts, and effectively immortal. Would you do it? No. Because you, the *real* you, would be lying in pieces on the laboratory floor. The you in the computer might argue vehemently that it was still you. It might believe that it was you. It might even be right. After all, it would have same memories as you, think the same thoughts as you, feel the same emotions as you. Yet there was absolutely no way to be sure that the result of the transfer would be the same subjective consciousness currently lying on the cold steel table about to be cut into little pieces.

That, in a nutshell, was the Transfer Problem. Scientists didn't like it because it shattered all their illusions of majestic scientific advance and destroyed the plots of their favourite science fiction novels. Above all, they didn't like the Transfer Problem because it wasn't really a scientific problem at all. There was no experiment that you could design to tell the difference between the original and an identical copy, between a consciousness that had moved and a consciousness that had been deleted and recreated elsewhere. It was a philosophical problem, not a scientific problem. And yet it stymied a real scientific advance.

"... and the lemma, applying it to the previously defined vector of goals, each of which is a weighted graph of type alpha prime, as defined here"

— Anna pointed vaguely at the whiteboard on the far side of the stage — "proves our first theorem, so that continuity is maintained ..."

Ethan tuned back out of the lecture. He concentrated on Anna's precise hand movements, fluttering with nervous energy as she pointed at various impenetrable scrawls on the whiteboards and blackboards. The Transfer Problem did not have much to do with financial arbitrage algorithms, anyway.

∞

"So why are you here exactly?" asked Anna.

Anna and Ethan were standing at the food counter of the university canteen; Ethan was contemplating the glutinous steaming mound on his plate. The university canteen was a long narrow room with moodily low lighting, apparently to discourage close examination of the food. The canteen staff appeared to have been selected for their hatred of humanity in general and mass catering in particular. A scrawny woman with a dark blue rinse and a pale blue uniform pushed a mop in desultory circles next to the tills, splashing dribbles of soapy water onto Ethan's feet. A uniformed man behind the counter plopped a pile of grey mashed potato onto Anna's plate.

"I'm here mainly for the cuisine," said Ethan.

Anna laughed — a low, full, throaty laugh that was at odds with her fragile appearance. She took her plate of goop and, as though following a prior understanding, they turned and headed towards the far corner of the canteen where an alcove afforded some privacy. They sat at a round formica table on adjacent stools.

"Really, I haven't seen you at any of these before," said Anna, "you don't seem quite like a proper academic. Like, underneath that T-shirt, maybe you're wearing a suit."

"OK, you got me. I'm here under false pretences. I'm not in academia at all. Actually, I work for a bank."

"A banker? I knew it. Ah, you're, like, one of those people who destroy the world for a living?"

"And you're one of those people who's going to create a new world."

"Yeah, a Brave New World, perhaps."

"Oh come on. You're making progress on the Transfer Problem, right?"

"Not that anyone really cares. But yes, we're working on it. Is it relevant to your work in the bank then?"

"No, not at all."

Anna laughed at Ethan's directness – again, it was that low, throaty sound. Ethan was captivated. For once, his self-deprecating wit wasn't only effective in his head – it was being appreciated by another human being. If only Robert had not been crashing on his sofa. He tended to show up at the most inconvenient times.

∞

Ethan had been eleven, first term at big school. Robert was fourteen, but had left home several months previously, and Ethan's life had achieved a sort of precarious normality. He crept out of the house on weekday mornings, inching the front door shut with infinite care to avoid waking his grandmother. If he was lucky, there would be some food in the kitchen – dry cereal or a slice of bread that he could scrape the mould off. If he was unlucky, his stomach would be growling until lunchtime.

When the phone rang, the early morning stillness was shattered. The house was not accustomed to the harsh mechanical noise. The sound seemed to slap the dust off the sofas in the front room that nobody was allowed to enter; it echoed behind the locked doors on the first floor. Ethan grabbed at the phone to answer it, but it was too late. He could hear thumps and creaks from his grandmother's room as she stirred.

"Hello?"

"Yes, is that the Stennlitz residence?" asked an official, kindly voice.

"I'm, er, yes, this is."

"And may I speak to" – sound of riffling through papers – "Ethel Stennlitz?"

"I'll just get her."

It took about five minutes: bashing on his grandmother's door, replying to her muffled queries, guiding her to the one phone receiver in the house. He thought he might actually have to show her how to use it. The conversation was short and his grandmother did not say much, apart from grunting and tssking under her breath.

She put the phone down and stood for a long moment with one hand resting on the phone and her eyes closed. Her breath was short and juddery. Ethan watched her cautiously; she could lash out without warning, a rainstorm scudding across a clear summer sky.

There was no school that day. A ride in the back of his grandmother's elderly car to the police station. Sitting on a bench in a waiting room, gazing at the unlikely sample of humanity washed up there. A cup of tea, dark and bitter, brought by a policewoman with kind eyes. Waiting and more waiting. Ethan strove to make himself small and insignificant, better yet, invisible.

A flimsy Perspex door swung open and Robert and his grandmother walked through. His grandmother strode ahead – she appeared to have forgotten about her limp – and Robert tagged along behind, shoulders slumped, hands thrust into pockets. Neither of them paid any attention to Ethan. They walked straight past the reception desk, through the heavy double doors that led onto the street. As the doors swung shut behind them, Robert glanced round at Ethan and gestured with a flick of his head. It broke the spell. Ethan jumped to his feet and trotted after them.

It turned out that a condition of Robert's parole was that he lived at their grandmother's house. This wasn't Robert's idea – he had lied about his age and spent two days in jail before the system had caught up with him. Nor was it his grandmother's – the judge had simply assumed that Robert's legal guardian would be happy to look after him.

Another condition of Robert's parole was that he have no access to electronic equipment except under strict supervision. Every evening after Ethan had finished his homework, his grandmother took the beige modem for dialling up the internet, unplugged it, and put it in the heavy antique dresser, locking it with an iron key that she kept in her bedside table.

And every night, at about midnight, Robert padded quietly into Ethan's room and took his laptop, tucking it under his arm before wordlessly turning round and padding back out of the room. The first night this happened, Ethan snuck after him.

"What are you doing?" Ethan asked.

"Shut up," replied Robert. He was crouched in front of the antique dresser, his face inches away from the lock as he explored its innards with a set of small metal implements.

"Come on. Tell me what you're doing."

"Shut up," repeated Robert. There was a click and the door swung open. He took out the modem and with quick, efficient movements unwound the cabling and started to plug it back in.

"I'll tell grandma."

Robert stopped and turned to Ethan. "You tell her anything and I'll crush you like a bug."

"So what are you doing?"

"I'm having some fun. Easy way to make money, look."

Robert had set up the modem and Ethan's laptop. He swivelled it round to face Ethan. It was showing the login screen to a bank.

"What is that? What are you doing?"

"Will you stop asking me that? Just shut up and watch if you want to. But quiet. We don't want to wake up the dragon."

It was true. Neither Ethan nor Robert wanted to wake up the dragon. Ethan stifled a yawn and curled up into a little ball against the chill of the dark kitchen. The flickering light from the laptop screen painted geometric patterns on the faded wallpaper and the ochre wood of the kitchen cabinets. There was no sound apart from Robert's distracted breathing and the soft tick and sigh as the fans in the laptop sprang into life.

Ethan gazed at the screen, his eyes dazzled by the white rectangle demarcated by the gloom, like an incandescent lamp burning at the bottom of a well. The kitchen floor was cool and smooth. Another yawn came, too urgent to stifle, and he drifted into sleep.

School suffered, of course. With Robert, there was always a price to pay. Ethan nodded off in lessons; he stumbled through the day, bleary and confused. Their grandmother was oblivious, keeping precisely to her routine of unlocking the modem when Ethan needed it for homework or she wanted to browse the internet and then locking it back into the kitchen dresser and clasping her hand around the precious key.

It lasted about three months. Grandmother woke earlier than expected one morning and saw the phone bill before Robert was able to intercept it.

Ethan came upon her sitting at the kitchen table with both hands resting on a single piece of paper. She was staring at some undefinable point in the middle distance. It was rare that Ethan caught her in repose. Staring up at her face would normally earn a sharp rebuke or a well-aimed slap. If she came into a room and saw him, she would shoo him out or start muttering insults under her breath until he crept out.

A shaft of light through the kitchen window picked out the patchwork of wrinkles at the corners of her eyes and on her forehead but left her deep-set eyes in shadow. Her expression was not sad or angry, although he could see both of those emotions in her face: a crease between her eyebrows set her face in resolve, a glint of a tear tracing a crooked path down her cheek. There was pain and acceptance, and something more. It was defeat, he realized. Her expression was one of complete defeat.

The bill was over a thousand pounds. Robert had blown through the internet usage cap and added a selection of direct phone calls to exotic faraway destinations. The police came that day and took Robert away. Ethan did not get to say goodbye, but he was used to that. Robert appeared and disappeared without warning. There was no point in trying to predict one or mourn the other.

∞

None of this helped when Robert was definitively and undeniably lying on his sofa and a striking young woman was leaning over the cafeteria table expressing an unwarranted interest in the details of his job, life and personal history. Somehow, they ended up at a coffee shop next to the university campus after the end of the conference, squeezed into opposite sides of a rectangular table between two groups of students.

"And after your doctorate?" asked Anna.

"Oh, no, I didn't finish my PhD. By that time I was working about three jobs to keep up and my debts were, well, you'd probably need a PhD in maths to count them. The banks came sniffing around. They were searching for computer science nerds to help shave a few more microseconds from their arbitrage algorithms. All my debts wiped out with their sign-on bonus. It was …"

"I understand," said Anna. "I'd never have gotten through it, except I had some money, inherited, after my mother died."

"Your mother died? My mother too. Well, it sounds weird like that. I just meant ..." Ethan trailed off, cursing himself as usual for his clumsy language.

"It's OK," said Anna, "I know what you meant."

Anna's mother had died when she was three. They had been living in Japan, where Anna's mother was from; her father was Russian. She had been passed between a succession of uncles and aunts and wound up doing her postgraduate study in London.

Although they were both computer scientists, modern academia was so extraordinarily specialised that they shared almost no mutual understanding of their areas of research. Ethan started to explain a little about his work optimising financial algorithms – enabling computers to crunch data and make split-second investment decisions. In return, Anna grabbed a handful of paper napkins and started scribbling networks of lines and boxes, speaking quietly and urgently about brains and neurons and propagation of concepts. Ethan recognised a passion and commitment that he lacked – a true academic absorption in the subject.

Anna flicked her hair back out of her eyes as she stabbed with a pencil at a diagram. The paper napkin tore and she gave a despairing laugh, breaking the spell of concentration. She smiled at Ethan and he smiled back, lost in her dark eyes and wondering how he could have found such a pale, delicate and perfect creature.

CHAPTER FIVE

May 24

Anna looked almost credible with her hair tucked into a shapeless brown cap and her slight frame lost in a set of baggy overalls. These were also brown, except for a broad yellow slash across the chest featuring the logo of the services company to which First Global Bank had outsourced all its office cleaning needs. Anna had cinched them at the waist with a black utility belt. Ethan walked slowly around her, frowning distractedly. Anna stood to attention with mock seriousness under his scrutiny.

"Am I alright?" she asked.

"You'll do," Ethan replied.

"Are you sure? I mean, do they have regular inspections of the cleaning staff, to check that their outfit corresponds to norms of minimum wage Eastern European cleaners?"

"Yes, I'm not defending the bank's diversity strategy – I just thought we might as well take advantage of it," said Ethan, continuing his inspection. Anna's face was an enigmatic blend of Europe and Asia, exotic enough to suggest a foreign origin but plain enough to pass for any one of dozens of faraway countries. And her diffident manner, as though she were always compressing her body into the smallest, narrowest space to avoid attention, fit perfectly. The corridors of First Global Bank bustled with young people, swaggering and entitled. Support staff edged around them, quietly, invisibly, speaking in low tones in whatever languages they could find in common.

Ethan's plan was straightforward. That way there was little to go wrong, he hoped. He could bring Anna in through the front gate to First Global Bank, signed as his guest. He could even use his security pass to get her onto the trading floor. But she could not spend an hour pottering around with their computer hardware without attracting suspicion. She needed a disguise.

Ethan took Anna through the front entrance, past the echoing marble atrium and to the banks of lifts serving sets of different floors. They blended in with the crowds of suited men and women sneaking sidelong glances at their reflections in the polished chrome and glass lift doors.

Voices drifted down from the walkways crossing at artfully geometric angles in the cavernous space above them: braying laughter, impassioned argument. Ethan stole a glance at Anna – wondering, as he did a thousand times every day, why this elegant, self-contained figure chose to invest her time in him. Anna looked back at him with a neutral gaze, then gave him a deliberate wink.

"Don't look so worried," she said.

"This is my normal look. Anything else would seem suspicious."

"Fair point. Carry on then."

The lift reported its arrival with an infuriatingly gentle ping and the suited workers filed obediently out and in. Ethan and Anna rode up to the 40th floor and then ducked down a side corridor and into a large storage closet. On the floor was a pile of brown uniforms, neatly wrapped in cellophane and ordered by size and gender. Ethan grabbed one at random and thrust it at Anna and watched as the rest of the pile slowly collapsed. He bent and scrabbled at the cellophane, striving to rearrange the uniforms in order.

"It's OK, Ethan, just leave them."

"It will only take a second."

"International spies don't stop to tidy up."

"International spies aren't clumsy."

Anna decided to let Ethan finish his housekeeping task. It seemed to calm him down. Meanwhile, she tore open the cellophane and clambered into the brown uniform, pulling the cap over her hair and tucking in a few disobedient curls.

"You look great," said Ethan, finally stepping back from the reconstituted pile of uniforms.

"Oh sure, I'm really working this look."

"You know, we're in a storage cupboard."

"Yes, I had noticed, actually. It does say 'storage' on the door."

"Well, you know what people get up to in storage cupboards ..."

"Do they store things?"

"Oh come on, it's like a cliché, the couple in the storage cupboard."

"Ethan, we're on a schedule and, really, there's not much room."

To illustrate the point, Anna flung her arms around Ethan and leaned into him, planting a kiss on his lips. He stepped backwards and the end of a broom jabbed into his back and fell over, scattering the painstakingly assembled pile of uniforms.

"OK, I get it, let's get back to Plan A."

"Yes, Plan A. My clever disguise."

"What's wrong with it? What's wrong with your disguise? What's wrong with the plan?"

"Ethan, all the way up here, the only people I saw wearing any sort of uniform were the cleaning staff. Your IT department, what do they wear?"

Ethan shrugged. "I've never really noticed. Same as everyone else, I guess."

"Exactly. I could have worn anything, really, couldn't I?"

"But you'll blend in more in that uniform."

"Yes, I get it. I'm more invisible this way. But how much time do your cleaning team spend installing computer hardware? It's going to make that bit of the job harder, isn't it?"

Ethan closed his eyes and pinched the bridge of his nose between his fingers. He sighed and then, after a weighty pause, sighed again.

"OK, you've made your point," said Anna. "You're trying to protect me. Except that your plans are always so painfully unsubtle. Can we get on with it now?"

Ethan was silent. Anna was about to prompt him again when he turned abruptly and peered out of the cupboard and signaled to her – they both swiftly exited into the corridor. Three men, walking and talking rapidly, came around the corner and Ethan and Anna pressed themselves against the wall as they strode past.

"And I'm still not sure why we're not doing this in the middle of the night," Anna asked after the men had turned around the next corner of the corridor.

"I'm not sure why we're doing this at all," Ethan replied.

"Look we've been through this ..."

"... but neural networks for stock market prediction. It might have been all the rage in the 1990s, but nobody thinks it will work now."

"Are you kidding? In the 1990s they were using two-level perceptrons – this is a deep convolution network based on biological neurons. You might as well compare an abacus with a supercomputer. And you think nobody's making money right now on the stock markets with neural network algorithms? Basic ones, nothing like the detailed biological models we're using. Anyway, I asked my question first."

"Why we're not here at night? Well, it's obvious. At night there are enough people around to notice everything that happens, but not enough to stop two people spending hours messing with the bank's hardware from sticking out. Lunchtime, there are loads of people, but everybody is walking around, distracted. Maintenance crews are using the downtime to tune up any systems that aren't working properly. Easiest place to hide: in the middle of a crowd."

As if to illustrate the point, another group rounded the corridor and, this time, Ethan and Anna blended in with them as they walked past the corner and up to the entrance to the trading floor. It was sealed by another pass-protected door but the first person in the group swiped their own ID card to open it and the rest of the group shuffled through, holding the door open for each other, politeness prevailing over any security considerations. Ethan could have used his own ID card to swipe the door open, but he was grateful for any additional confusion to cover their trail.

The main trading floor of First Global Bank took up most of the 40th storey of First Global Bank Tower. The views would have been magnificent, but the architects had decided to surround the edges of the floor with offices, so as not to distract the workers. The only light came from the rows of strip lighting in the ceiling and the lurid glare of computer monitors. It resembled a vast subterranean grotto illuminated by garish flickering lights in clashing primary colours.

This grotto was inundated by keyboards, screens, cabling, desks, chairs, paper, telephones and, above all, people. The furniture was arranged into serried ranks of desks stretching from one end of the space to the other with only a single gap near the centre. But this superficial order disintegrated in the face of humanity's propensity towards messiness.

And there was no lack of humanity here. Humanity sitting at chairs and on desks, gathered around printers as they spat out spools of paper, hunched over monitors and pacing back and forth with a telephone receiver cradled between ear and shoulder. The passageways between rows of desks were filled with collapsing piles of computer printout, discarded sandwich wrappers and stacks of boxes filled with unused promotional material. This left only a slender twisting pathway free of obstacles, filled with yet more people threading their way between their desks and one of the few exits at the far edge of the trading floor.

Anna gradually distinguished different groups within the general mass. There were a few queen bees – although Anna noticed none of them were women – poking their heads out of their offices lined along the edge of the trading floor, scanning up and down the lines of workers, sniffing the air for any sign of crisis and then ducking back into their offices. The bankers on the trading floor fit into an approximate hierarchy. The leaders lounging at their desks, arms spread wide to indicate proprietorial rights over the neighbouring chairs and tables, wearing well-cut suits with loud, clashing shirts and ties; mid-level bankers honking with laughter into their hands-free telephones or gesticulating as they talked, showing to all in the vicinity how valuable and hard-working they were – the suits were louder but the shirts quieter. The junior ranks were more numerous but took up less room, scurrying back from a printer holding a stack of paper or huddled at the corner of a desk chewing listlessly at a sandwich – this layer featured a few women and ethnic minorities. Finally, there were the support staff: wearing uniforms rather than suits, cleaning and fetching and carrying and repairing; most of the women and ethnic minorities on the trading floor fell into this category. Largely ignored by the bankers, it was as though they inhabited a separate, parallel continuum. Anna saw why Ethan had dressed her in a maintenance uniform – it made her instantly invisible.

The overwhelming impression was of youth, excitement and stress: a scratchy, bouncy tension. Stocks ticking up or down by fractions of a penny; deals closing or falling apart. All orchestrated by an omnipresent relentless beat of pure white noise. Every monitor was blasting out at maximum volume. Every phone conversation was conducted by shouting or screaming into the receiver or headset. Computers hummed and wheezed; printers chattered busily as they spat out sheets of paper. Underneath was the bass hum of the air-conditioning, filling the interstices with a negative sound that was indistinguishable from silence except when it ceased, leaving an echoing absence. Stentorian laughter and squeals of excitement provided the top notes.

Swallowing an acid taste of fear, Anna willed her face to show only serenity. She followed Ethan through the maze of desks to a plain metal door set in a blank white partition. The door was fitted with a large old-fashioned lock but left slightly ajar. Ethan shouldered it open in one practised movement and guided Anna through. Behind them, the bustle of the trading floor ebbed and flowed, indifferent to their passage.

Behind the door was another maze. A narrow path was made to feel narrower by the looming cabinets ranked along both sides. The path turned an abrupt right angle after a few feet. Further twists and bifurcations were partially visible behind a crazy tangle of cabling draped along a metal grid suspended from the ceiling and spilling down in long awkward loops. Small halogen bulbs shed a dim blue light that did little more than sweep the shadows into the corners. More light came from tiny LEDs set into the cabinets – blue, orange and green pinpricks blinking in obscure patterns and casting a multi-coloured glow.

The cabinets contained racks of servers: identical shallow steel boxes stuffed with circuit boards and wiring, innards spilling out carelessly – stacks of soldered chips connected by loosely knotted loops of copper wire. Hard drives chittered and whirred. Tiny metal fans whined intermittently as they pushed gobbets of humid air away from the chips soldered onto the circuit boards and into currents that swirled up into slatted metal vents set into the low ceiling.

The door clicked shut behind them, muffling the sound of the trading floor. The layers of white noise blended into a soothing hum; the space was dark and warm and vaguely womb-like. The twisting passages disguised the fact that the entire maze was squeezed into an uncomfortably small space, an organic jumble that seemed to have been grown rather than assembled.

Ethan led Anna around one corner and along another gap to a rounded terminus, a gentle bulge where racks had been awkwardly pushed back to clear a makeshift room. There was a small wooden table with slender curved legs and a slightly bowed fragile surface patinated with an intricate fractal network of faded yellow lines. A chrome and leather office chair was pushed up against the table. Piles of paper were stacked on the chair and the floor. The table was empty except for an empty sandwich wrapper.

"Morris's office," explained Ethan in a whisper.

Anna nodded, as Ethan seemed to expect some sort of response.

Ethan pointed into a corner, where the racks of servers bumped against the outer wall of this curious space. A single thick cable, liberally wrapped in rolls of black insulating tape, sprouted from a wall panel and rose in lazy coils.

"Main optical cable comes in there. Up from the basement. The exchange is about half a mile behind us – we have a direct link from there, underground, terminated in the basement where the main servers are located …"

"The main servers? What the hell are these then, if they're not the main servers?"

"Oh, this is just our little nest, for the algorithmic arbitrage team." Ethan patted one of the server racks near him, then laid a proprietorial arm across it. "They keep threatening to move us all into the basement; they say it might be worth a few more nanoseconds. But we're not so keen to move down there. Especially after we've built all this up here. Every week it seems like we're adding something new, we'd never be able to fit it all in here, except that Morris keeps it all ticking somehow.

"The physical racks are grouped into logical volumes, each one operates as a single parallel unit. That's mine there. All based on standard processor types, although we've got some ASICs running over there, and the chip design team have given us a bunch of their bespoke product to speed up some of the more critical calculations. I guess this is all pretty obvious for you."

"It's amazing. How many processors have you got running here? There's more power in this room than in my whole department."

"Well, I can't really say, you know, it's proprietary information, our competitors don't know how much we've built here …"

"You mean you have no idea."

"OK. I have no idea. I'll ask Morris. I think someone mentioned last week that if we merged all the processors we'd have the third largest parallel supercomputer in the UK. Is that enough for you?"

Anna's flashed a quick, wolfish smile. "Why don't you keep watch while I get to work?" she asked. Ethan shuffled back to the entrance under her watchful gaze before she started work.

Anna tipped a small pile of USB drives onto the floor, sorted through them with a finger, and then picked one to insert into the USB slot of one of Ethan's servers. She grabbed a keyboard, mouse and monitor from a stack in a cardboard box and plugged them in too. Then she pulled out a small contraption from her bag, an articulated chain of metal links, about one foot long, much wider in the middle than at either end, threaded with spools of wire and gnarly accretions of chips, transistors and other electrical components. More strange components followed. Anna spread them on the floor and bent down to examine them, turning them over and nudging them into a precise arrangement that presumably meant something to her.

Ethan imagined he could hear Anna's breath whistling through her nostrils as she concentrated on assembling her work and integrating it with First Global Bank's systems. There was a familiar tickle at the back of his mind: the dawning realization that other people's misbehaviour was about to get him into trouble. Usually, it would be one of Robert's elaborate schemes that collapsed, leaving Ethan blinking in the harsh glare of reality and explaining to the victims that their money, reputation or personal information had vanished.

Anna could plug into Ethan's protected section of the network. But how could he connect from there into anything useful without arousing suspicion? There was a clank and a muffled curse as Anna dropped something on her foot. First, Ethan would have to conceal whatever it was that Anna was building. From the sound of it, that might be enough to cause its own problems.

The door opened, letting in a shaft of light and the noise of the trading floor. A stooped figure stopped at the entrance, as if sniffing the air, and quickly pulled the door shut. The humid half-darkness reasserted itself.

"Hello, Morris," said Ethan.

"Hi, hello there, Mr Stennlitz," said Morris.

"Ethan, please."

"And you've decided to pay a little visit to the cave, then?"

"Well, actually, I'm installing some new kit, nothing really."

Morris's brow creased in concern. He was a short man with a flabby frame and stumpy arms and legs, but he moved in rapid, furtive darts and his fingers were nimble and deft whenever he handled delicate electronics. There was not a hair on his head, although his beard was lavish, and this heightened the effect of his furrowed forehead.

"Ho, then, new kit, new kit, only the power outputs, I mean I was just looking at it and we're getting close – is it hooked into the main circuit breakers? – that is, I assume it's within your server shard, so then …"

"Look, I don't think it's going to draw much power, it's really …"

"Don't think it's going to draw too much, don't think? Don't you know? Have you got any calculations? Every day there's a new piece of kit. Nobody tells me. I'm working to balance the load and the numbers are refusing to settle down and then I see some new bolt-on and then I see somebody's been fiddling around, fiddling around when everything was neatly arranged …"

Morris's grumbled faded into the background noise of mechanical whirring and buzzing as he edged along the passageway in a shuffling, rolling gait, heading towards Ethan's bank of servers. Ethan hurried after him, desperately trying to think of something to say to forestall his progress. He succeeded only in propelling Morris onward and they rounded a corner and collided with Anna.

There followed the customary British ritual of mutual apology. This involved reciprocal protestations of shame and embarrassment of increasing volume and ardour and the frenzied gathering of dropped papers, empty plastic wrapping, screwdrivers, screws and other sundry items. Ethan suspected that Anna had arranged the collision as a distraction.

Morris suddenly became convinced that a small screw had fallen onto one of the circuit boards and was about to roll into the blades of a whirring fan, thereby precipitating a disaster of a magnitude so awesome that he could not bring himself to describe it, but merely muttered "So then, let's have you," over and over as he fished about in the server with his stubby fingers. Ethan and Anna waited patiently until with an exasperated snort Morris desperately yanked a tiny power lead out of the fan and it coughed into silence.

Morris peered over Anna's shoulder at a square metal box tucked neatly into a corner formed by two racks of servers. A thick skein of cables curved up from the box and punched into the wall panelling, held in place by hefty plastic cable ties fixing it to vertical metal struts.

"Well, it's going to take me a while to get everything straight here, isn't it?" he asked.

"Oh, I'm sorry about the …" Anna gestured at the neatly packaged machinery, "about the, er, the mess."

Morris stood and gazed at Anna's work, cocking his head to one side and absent-mindedly rubbing the nearest corner of the steel trellis-work that held the servers in place, as though straining to sense the overall disturbance in the harmony of his kingdom. He clicked his tongue a few times and abruptly shook his body, as if dispelling a painful thought.

"You're from the cleaning crew? Since when did you install our IT equipment?" he asked.

Anna fixed Ethan with a significant gaze and lifted one eyebrow.

"Er, it's OK, Morris," said Ethan. "It's a new initiative, a diversity initiative. She's had special training. She knows how to put it together."

Morris ignored Ethan and continued stroking a finger along a metal frame.

"I see you've hooked into the main data cable for Ethan's shard," he said.

Anna nodded obediently.

"But no other data cables, we couldn't allow that anyway, you understand?"

Anna nodded with increased vigour.

"But what's all this power cabling? What are you planning to draw here?"

Anna's nodding was now in danger of flinging her head off her shoulders. Fortunately, she stopped in order to reply.

"It's OK, I've put in 100 Amp circuit breakers and a decoupled power supply in a redundant module equipped with ..."

"... double power terminal blocks," finished Morris, "yes, I see. All very clean. But that's a lot of kettles you're planning to boil." He hitched up his trouser legs and squatted in front of Anna's contraption and extended a single finger towards it.

Ethan coughed and took a step, holding out his hand but suddenly reluctant to clasp Morris's cold, clammy digit. Morris sensed his confusion and withdrew his finger and rose ponderously to his feet. He smoothed his jacket and glanced awkwardly at Anna and Ethan.

"So, then, I guess it all checks out. I'll be keeping an eye on it though."

"Yes, of course, Morris. I have no doubt."

∞

Ten minutes later, Anna and Ethan were crouched in an internal conference room on a sub-basement level. Ethan plugged a laptop into the conference room data cable and logged in to his private workspace, firewalled off from anything sensitive in the bank. He called up his internal network and paged through until he reached the new connection. Then he swiveled the laptop to Anna and handed over control of the keyboard.

Ethan watched Anna type; her fingers moved swiftly, chains of commands building up painstakingly. Ethan was used to watching others driving the keyboard – a legacy of his months following Robert. He watched as Anna manoeuvred around the stark interface her machine presented, tweaking settings and firing up individual components. She built a tunnel through Ethan's workspace – using his remote login credentials, they would be able to access her machine from any computer in the world.

"I'm hooking it up to all the publicly available information sources," said Anna, "Bloomberg, Reuters, anything the bank has a general subscription to."

"OK, good, hurry up now, we're almost out of time."

"I'm locked out of your trading account. I'm locked out of the financial systems. I'm locked out, out, out."

"Yes, of course. That's what I said. You're in the child-safe portion of my private workspace. Any more sandboxed and you'd need a bucket and spade." Ethan shifted from foot to foot. This was messy and getting messier. He wanted clear, bright corners, the regular, predictable flow of computer code scrolling up the screen. Not this eerie young woman hooking up her unpredictable biological machine. It was all locked down, he reminded himself. Anna was an academic researcher – prodigiously talented with computers, but not with criminal hacking. He had enough experience to recognize expertise with illicit electronic entry – he was, by proxy, an expert himself. And Anna did not have the skills to break out of the sandbox.

"OK, I understand, but there must be some corner of the systems we can use. Oh look, here's something, what's that?"

Ethan peered at the screen. Then he laughed.

"That's our petty cash account, for our team."

"Is there anything in it?"

"Yes, let's see. There's six pound and eleven pence."

"And you have full permissions to use it?"

"Sure. I mean, it's part of the bank, obviously, one of their accounts. I can't transfer anything into it myself. Finance will add something for our Christmas party, I guess."

"Can you transfer out?"

"I can do pretty much anything else with it. But, Anna, it's petty cash. What use is six pounds and change?"

Anna looked up at Ethan as she carried on typing. Her face was ghostly in the wan half-light of the conference room. Her face split into a wide smile. She shook a stray strand of black hair away from her forehead so she could stare boldly at Ethan.

"But we can use it to buy and sell shares, right? With whatever tiny bit of money there is in it. My machine won't just have access to all this information, it won't just be able to learn how the stock market moves, it will be able to invest in it and make money?"

"Oh, sure, you're plugged right in to our brand new instant settlement blockchain-based infrastructure. All the financial markets are right there, zero delay, hyper-efficient, vast sums of money flowing automatically, exactly how we arbitrage hedge funds like it, with lots of juicy profit waiting to be made. And all you've got to lose is the six pounds in the petty cash account."

"OK, the petty cash account," she said. "It's a start. Now, to the lab. It's time to do some brain surgery."

CHAPTER SIX

February 14

My mother was born in Japan. She moved to Russia in her early twenties."

Anna paused and toyed with some of the steak on her plate. Ethan loved serving her steak. He loved the way she sliced it into strips and then chopped each strip into uniformly-sized cubes and then formed the cubes into a mound on side of the plate. Only once the heap had been assembled into a perfectly symmetrical cone would Anna contemplate putting any of the cubes into her mouth. By this time, the juices flowing from each chunk would have started to congeal, the tiny streaks of fat to harden. Undeterred, Anna would select one lucky cube and pair it with a suitably shaped portion of vegetables, before quickly swallowing the whole package, as though unwilling to be witnessed in the act of mastication.

Anna was speaking in a low voice, staring down at her plate. A single candle in the middle of the table flickered, painting shadows into the hollows of Anna's eyes and along the line of her cheekbones. Ethan had been aiming for cosy intimacy; Anna had quickly veered into raw confessions.

"What was she doing in Russia?" asked Ethan.

"It was a student exchange programme. Not that Japan and the Soviet Union were on great terms then, what with conflict over the Kuril Islands ..."

"Well, of course, I was just about to mention the Kuril Islands."

"Sorry, Ethan, I've spoilt all this. And you've been so sweet."

Anna waved at the scene around them. The lone candle cast crazy shadows on the tastefully whitewashed walls and the stripped wooden floors; gobbets of wax dripped from it onto the polished black glass of the table, measuring out the minutes until it leaned too far and toppled over. Flowers were squeezed into a tall, narrow vase – bright red and yellow petals crushed together in awkward embrace. Ethan had served their meal on his best plates, pale blue china faded in places but scrubbed to a translucent sheen. The cutlery sparkled. Quirky jazz music issued from tiny speakers lodged in niches in the ceiling.

The overall effect was spoiled by a large pile of luggage and assorted bric-a-brac heaped into a corner of the room. Robert had left the same day that Ethan had met Anna, the day of the conference. His comings and goings were unpredictable, ineffable. Ethan had learnt to accept them as he accepted a sudden thunderstorm or a rainbow. As if to compensate for his sudden disappearances, Robert rarely left entirely. He usually contrived to leave small tokens of appreciation, such as personal effects, clothes, computer hardware, books or – in one memorable case – a sheaf of paintings, oil on canvas, ragged around the edges where they had been crudely torn from the frame, rolled up and bound with twine, and of extremely dubious provenance. These presents came with strings attached. Ethan invariably received instructions to send them on to unpredictable destinations at irregular intervals. Robert's presence would gradually ebb away, leaving one or two discarded remnants. Eventually, Ethan would throw them away, raging at himself for being unable to quash completely his feelings of guilt at this petty abandonment.

Anna was polite enough to ignore this heap of detritus. In a way, it only heightened the clinical cleanliness of Ethan's flat. She had recently become familiar with its nooks and crannies – not that these were anything but neatly swept niches. The meal was prepared with all Ethan's customary precision, but underlying that was a creative flair, a spike of anarchic risk-taking that seeped around the edges of his rigid organization. Take the drizzle of pomegranate seeds that had inveigled their way into the recipe. Logically, they didn't fit with the rest of the meal. They certainly disturbed the pattern made by the other ingredients tidily arrayed on the plate. And yet they were there, and somehow they worked, turning a humdrum meal into something a little unusual.

Anna was careful not to underestimate Ethan. Their relationship had survived the first three weeks. The first night, when she had not been sure whether his gauche sincerity was just an act. Feeling herself drawn in despite her best intentions, her resolve unraveling. And why not? He was attractive, in a sort of rumpled, accidental way. She had agreed to see him again. Several more dates followed, nights at her poky flat, a weekend morning in his apartment. And now the first full-throttle, no-holds-barred evening at his place. No furtive giggles at a stolen few hours to be turned into anecdote later. This was the rollercoaster ticking gradually to the top of the slope and pausing before its plunge. And Ethan was fully aware of this, she knew it, despite his air of total obliviousness.

"It's OK." Ethan said. "It's just, you're not exactly forthcoming about how you got here. Your background, I mean. I know it wasn't easy for you, when you were small."

"Yes, it wasn't. I don't mean to hide anything from you, really. Let me try to explain."

Anna sorted her tiny cubes of steak into a line and popped them one by one into her mouth as she told her story. Her mother had been old when she had Anna, in her late forties. Her life had been difficult as a single mother, but then it had never been easy. She had lost her parents early in life, applied herself at school, leaving her with a clutch of academic qualifications but no friends. The opportunity to go to Russia had seemed like a rare stroke of luck, but by the time Anna arrived she was living in a small apartment in a modernist block on the outskirts of a city in Siberia that Ethan had never heard of.

Anna's childhood seemed to have been unremittingly bleak. After watching her mother succumb over many years to the disease that ate her up from the inside – she didn't give any details, but she painted for Ethan a clear picture of a cancer left untreated to ravage its host – Anna was shuffled around various state institutions until ending up at a school in Moscow. It was another apparent slice of good fortune that turned sour.

While she had excelled academically, she bridled against the strict regime. After falling in with a crowd of libertarian computer geeks – they sounded to Ethan more like anarchist hackers – she had scraped together a small nest egg in cryptocurrency that financed her transfer to London.

"And you arrived here knowing nobody?" asked Ethan.

"I had a few contacts – friends of friends. The university found me a place to stay, well, you can see it's not much, but I didn't really care, as long as it was a basement flat …"

"A basement flat? I guess Moscow has lots of tower blocks, so you fancied a change?"

Anna paused and looked down.

"Basements are cheap. I'm a student, not a swanky banker, you know."

"Did you say swanky banker? Because you were mumbling a bit."

Anna grinned at him as she skewered another cube of meat and put it in her mouth. She chewed slowly without breaking eye contact and while somehow continuing to grin.

"You're always quizzing me about my dull little life. What about you? Why aren't you a dull little academic too?"

"Actually, I am quite dull. One of a million maths PhDs stuffed into a windowless room counting out money for banks. There's rows and rows of us. Whole phalanxes, like a clone army, stored in jars overnight like a, like a big jar storage place."

"A jam warehouse?"

"Yes, or a pickle factory. That's where I work, really."

"Well, I've never heard a bank compared to a pickle factory before. Or a banker to a soldier. But I guess maybe that's how you see it, given your background."

"Oh," said Ethan, suddenly deflated, "how did you know about that?"

Anna nodded at the shelf in the kitchen. Neatly swept and dusted, of course, it held a variety of anodyne ornaments: a vase filled with cut flowers; a small, silver picture frame lacking a photo; a carved wooden statuette of a giraffe. Around the neck of the giraffe hung a pair of tarnished dog tags. The name and number stamped onto them was not visible from the table where they were sitting, but Anna must have inspected them earlier. They were Ethan's sole reminder of his time in the army.

It had started, like many of Ethan's more intense life experiences, as one of Robert's jokes. Ethan had finished school and plunged spiritedly into a career of staring morosely through the cracked windowpanes of his grandmother's front room into the slanting rain. He watched individual drops trace crooked routes down the glass, betting with himself which would win the race. By the time the raindrops reached the window sill, he had forgotten which one he had supported. The hours merged into days; the days into weeks.

Robert was missing, presumed happy. Every so often a postcard would drop through their letterbox, featuring a picture of a far-off tourist scene and a few scribbled lines of anodyne tourist-speak: wish you were here; weather is fine. There was never any personal information – even his location had to be painstakingly reconstructed from the picture on the front of the postcard and the blurry postmark. Ethan suspected Robert was actually living in a small flat nearby and had a vast pile of postcards featuring different global landmarks.

And then there were the other letters. These bore Robert's unique imprimatur, even more clearly than the handwritten postcards. The first one had been pleased to inform Ethan that that there was space to attend a forthcoming lecture at the local sexually transmitted diseases clinic entitled "Are condoms enough? Advice on promiscuity for the young gay man." This had caused some lively debate with his grandmother – she still had the habit of opening all post that arrived at the house, regardless of who it was addressed to. Ethan insisted that he had not contacted the clinic to request a space, but an uneasy air of suspicion shrouded their relationship until the second letter arrived.

This had been more of a package than a letter. Enclosed were two tiny sample pots of paint and a swatch of fabric. These, the accompanying card explained effusively, were completely free, just a taste of the exciting home transformation possibilities offered by TransFinite Furnishings. The card went on to thank Ethan's grandmother for her interest and suggested some convenient times for TransFinite Furnishings' local agent to visit in the comfort of her own home and start the conversation that would lead to vistas of interior design hitherto unimagined.

After this missive, it was clear that Robert was behind it all. Ethan and his grandmother waited with a mixture of fear and sniggering anticipation for the next offering. It duly arrived a week later – a catalogue of patent remedies for baldness addressed to Ethan – and then there was a gap of several weeks and two arrived at once, followed by others at highly irregular intervals, until they merited little more than a raised eyebrow or a snort at something particularly outrageous or inventive.

It was during the depths of Ethan's post-school depression that another suspicious large brown envelope flopped through the letterbox. His grandmother took a cursory look and flipped it straight to Ethan without a glance. There was a glossy brochure featuring pictures of young men and women in combat fatigues crouched in helicopters, smiling grimly into the stiff breeze as they prepared to shoot their weapons or jump to the ground or do something similarly vigorous and decisive.

The accompanying letter thanked Ethan for his recent visit to the army recruitment centre – an in-person visit, Ethan noted, meaning that Robert must have put considerable effort into this prank – and confirmed that an appointment to deal with the remaining formalities had been made at a local army base.

The tone of the letter – somehow both lofty and matter-of-fact – and the cheery pictures of young busy people stirred Ethan's soul. He turned away to stare through the window into the drizzle but his gaze drifted back to the letter and its bland assurance that he would be present at 11.40am next Tuesday with his passport and other sundry documents.

As it turned out, Ethan was not a good soldier. However, he was excellent at pretending to be a good soldier and this, as far as the army was concerned, seemed to be a perfectly acceptable alternative. The routine, the constant drills, the obsessive need for every shoe to be polished until it sparkled, for every crease to be starched into perfection, appealed to Ethan's need for order. He gratefully surrendered to the needless repetition.

And yet he also bridled against the strict regimen. It was not the petty details that chafed; it was the big picture. The code of honour, the sense of higher purpose, the devotion to a cause: all of these Ethan could simulate, but none of them could he feel in his heart. Although his superiors were unaware of his inner misgivings, they sensed that although Ethan passed every test and completed every drill, he would not graduate to be a leader or perform feats of bravery in combat. Ethan thought that, ultimately, war was a fairly unimaginative way to resolve a dispute. It was also chaotic and, worst of all, tended to result in people getting hurt. While he enjoyed the intricate manoeuvres involved in stripping his rifle, reassembling it and firing it at a target, he could not imagine pointing it at another living human being. Just thinking about the mess made him shudder.

Ethan's numeracy and facility with computers did not escape the notice of the army. They were content to recruit foot soldiers with a taste for violence, but it was computer operators that they really craved. He was transferred to signals intelligence for a series of intensive courses. There was some talk of transfer out of the army to work on submarines or aerial unmanned drones.

Ethan had not joined the army to spend his time tapping at a keyboard. He accepted the offer of sponsorship through a mathematics degree. The head of his unit, an affable lieutenant, signed off the relevant paperwork, even though it was clear that he was unlikely to return.

It was a stage of his life that marked the transition between aimlessness and success and he chose not to dwell on it. Anna's casual reminder discombobulated him. He started to explain a few basic facts, stumbling over details. Anna reached across and placed her slender hand over his clenched fist.

"It's OK. I'm not really interested in whatever games you played with guns and knives and other boy toys. I can see you're not a highly-trained killer."

"Yes, you can always see what I am. You, on the other hand, are a complete mystery to me."

"Except, of course, that you're a lady-killer. That sort of killer, definitely, with those sad eyes of yours."

"Now you're just deflecting. Whenever I get close to something, you go off at a tangent. This meal was meant to be, well, a way to really communicate."

"Deflect, hmmm, yes, that's what I'm doing," said Anna. She stood and smoothed down her skirt. Leaning over the table, she took Ethan's head in both hands. Delicately, she positioned his head at a slight angle. Ethan felt her warm, moist breath on his cheek and then her teeth gently nibbling his ear.

"OK, well, I suppose this is a sort of communication."

"Yes, that's exactly what this is," said Anna in a muffled voice. Ethan could think of worse ways to be deflected.

CHAPTER SEVEN

June 13

"How long until she wakes up?" asked Ethan.

The nurse shrugged. She looked at the other nurse. The other nurse shrugged.

Suddenly, Ethan wanted to be outside the room, outside the hospital. There were no answers here, not until Anna woke up. His skin itched from caked sweat and dirt; his head was buzzing with exhaustion and confusion. It was probably not a clever idea to be loitering about the bedside of one of the few people who could be traced to him when about the only thing he knew for certain was that he was being hunted.

"Look, can I, er, see her medical records?"

It was a clumsy question and the nurses stiffened and exchanged a quick glance.

"I'm afraid that's confidential," said the senior nurse.

"Yes, of course, of course. I'm a bit overwhelmed. I better let her rest. Could I just have a moment alone with her?"

The nurses exchanged another information-rich glance and then silently consented, backing out of the tiny room but leaving the door wide open.

Ethan leaned over Anna, watching her chest slowly rising and falling under the thin hospital blanket, scrutinizing the details of the room, the labels on the cupboards, anything that could give him some clue as to what had happened to her. Sheafs of computer printout were stacked on a shelf – filled with rows of numbers that meant nothing to Ethan and might relate to a completely different patient. Boxes and supplies were piled everywhere – the room obviously doubled as an overflow storage closet – and it was impossible to pick out what might be relevant. There was a small metal filing cabinet next to the bed. Ethan leaned forward to obstruct the view from the corridor and surreptitiously pulled the top drawer. It was locked. At last: something interesting.

The nurses were muttering to each other as they pretended to check on the other patients while monitoring Ethan. He risked another glance downwards – the cabinet was a basic system: a primitive wafer lock securing a vertical plunger bar. Ethan was not a hacker with the credentials of his brother, but this was not a major impediment. He steadied himself with a single slow breath, then quickly leaned down, tipped up the cabinet to a 45 degree angle, poked around the bottom corner for a small hole, inserted his finger and wiggled until he felt the bar move inside and the mechanism click as it released. Then he rotated the cabinet back onto its base, coughing once to cover the metallic clang as it landed on the tiled floor.

He pulled gently on the top drawer and it slid open. A wallet, a small black diary, a mobile phone, some coins and a set of keys. He flipped open the wallet: a credit card, a library card, a university membership card, others hidden behind. He heard a slight noise behind him, grabbed the diary and slid the drawer shut in one movement as he turned around to face the older nurse.

Ethan made muffled excuses and walked quickly out of the ward. The nurses clucked over him sympathetically. He lurched past them with head bowed and retreated into the corridor. Heading for the hospital exit, once again he wandered aimlessly. Hallways and stairwells and passages and rooms were all indistinguishable, safe and bland in neutral colours painted on shiny clean tiles.

Ethan paused outside the entrance to an unmarked rear stairwell. It looked worryingly similar to another staircase he had come down a few minutes previously. He was going round in circles. This was not allowed. He was not a big fan of spy films, but he was fairly sure that the protagonist, when engaged in a daring flight from the authorities, did not simply get lost. Actually, it struck him, many of those films featured long circuitous car chases at high speed through foreign cities, yet the hero always reached his destination without any detour. Ethan shook his head. Now he was not only lost but also distracted.

Abruptly, he slammed shut the exit from the stairwell he had just opened, turned around and sprinted back up the stairs. He swung round the corner of the stairs and collided with a short, wiry man with a deeply creased face.

There followed a chorus of mutual apologies, which reached a peak and eventually subsided into awkward silence.

"Are you looking for something?" asked the man.

"Yes, the exit. It's a bit of a maze here, isn't it?"

The man nodded.

"Could you point me the right way, do you think?"

"I can do better than that. I'll take you there."

They traced a route that took in several more stairwells, corridors and junctions – all marked with numerous signs that did not betray any clue as to how to escape from the building. Eventually, a set of swing doors took them through to the lobby. The man fell into step beside Ethan, taking almost two steps for each of his long strides.

"Do you want a taxi?" asked the man.

"Yes. I really do appreciate your help," said Ethan.

"No problem, I'll show you to the taxi rank," said the man.

They continued side by side through the sliding glass doors and to a line of three taxis huddled in a short bay beside the dual carriageway. Ethan suddenly understood that he would have to think of a destination. With that, came the knowledge that he already knew where he was heading. He had found Anna, but this had resolved nothing. There was only one name left on his list: Robert. And while Robert was largely itinerant, he did currently have an address, which Ethan knew, largely due to their recent activities.

Ethan's guide held open the door of a taxi as Ethan clambered in – he had never mastered the art of climbing into the back seat of a taxi without appearing ungainly.

"OK, well thanks again," said Ethan, after he had told the taxi driver where to go. The man was leaning into the taxi, his creased face grimaced against the constant din of the traffic.

"Oh, no problem," replied the man, "I hope you find what you're looking for."

"Goodbye," said Ethan, gently closing the door so that the man had time to withdraw.

As the taxi merged into the traffic, Ethan saw the man standing at the kerb, waving. Strange behaviour, thought Ethan. But then, so much human behaviour was strange, it was probably not worth dwelling on.

After a halting ride through the clogged London traffic, the taxi drew up outside a grim 1970s maisonette. It was inserted between two respectable late Victorian villas, like a blackened tooth in an otherwise healthy mouth. The breezeblock walls were faded to a dingy polluted grey. The window frames were cracked with peeling paint; the windows streaked with grime. Next to the front door was a large metal intercom peppered with more buttons than seemed feasible for the size of house.

It was no use. Ethan could see that straightaway. This was not living accommodation for Robert; it was a cut-out, a convenient location to receive mail and to write on forms that required an address. He probably visited at least once a week, more if he was using the place for a particular purpose. But Ethan was sure he was not living here and that there would be no clues leading to his real location.

Nevertheless, Ethan went through with his plan. He pressed the correct button on the intercom and, when there was no reply, he pressed all the other buttons. The door buzzed and he pushed it open and entered a corridor. Striding to the end and down a flight of carpeted stairs, he reached a tiny hallway. The entrance to apartment 1A was an unprepossessing brown door. The lock was rudimentary. Robert would have viewed it as equivalent to no lock at all. Ethan was not surprised when it swung open to his gentle push.

Inside, there was a single room. It was empty and clean. Not the emptiness and cleanliness of an abandoned room – it was like a decommissioned operating theatre. Every surface was wiped clean. There was no furniture, apart from a single deckchair propped open in a corner. A bare lightbulb hung from the ceiling. Even the thin white wire from which the lightbulb was suspended was free from dust or dirt. The overall sense was not of absence, but of an oppressive negative presence that had the power to remove all traces of human existence.

Ethan took a single pointless circuit of the room, finishing at the small window set high in the wall to reach floor level outside. He stared out but could see only a pair of black polished boots standing by the front door. He removed the pieces of his phone from his pocket, reinserted the SIM card and reattached the battery, and waited for the phone to reboot.

After a short pause, the phone beeped. A single text message flashed up: THEY'RE RIGHT BEHIND YOU. IWS.

Ethan spun round. Framed in the doorway was the odd man who Ethan had met in the hospital.

"What are you doing here?" asked Ethan.

"I could ask you the same thing," replied the man.

"This is my brother's place. I've come to visit him. But that's none of your business. Why did you follow me here?"

"We've been following you for a while, Mr Stennlitz. At first, we thought you were simply incompetent. Then we thought that you were extraordinarily devious and merely pretending to be incompetent. When you doubled back in the hospital and bumped into me, for instance. Then we came to the view that, in fact, we were right the first time and you were incompetent."

The man stepped to one side and several uniformed police officers came into the room. With barely a cursory glance at Ethan, they started to unpack forensic equipment and don gloves.

"You won't find anything here. He's not stupid enough to leave any trace."

"I expect you're right, Mr Stennlitz," said the man, with an apologetic shrug, "but we do have to go through the motions."

CHAPTER EIGHT

May 26

Anna told Ethan to keep watch at the door to the lab. He suspected this was merely to stop him peering over her shoulder and asking distracting questions. It was her own lab after all. But apparently there were innumerable rules about what experiments you were allowed to perform and she was busily breaking most of them. He stood in the doorway and looked out every so often down each end of the corridor, but he was just going through the motions. Most of his attention was on Anna. Even though she was crouched over her bench and most of her movements were too small to see from a distance, it was still fascinating and faintly creepy.

Anna's first job had been to catch a spider. The spiders were housed in a large glass tank in a corner of the lab. A few twigs and leaves were scattered on the floor of the tank – a flimsy effort to introduce an authentic habitat for the occupants. But the main obstacle to the harmonious co-existence of the spiders had been their disturbing tendency to eat each other. Accordingly, separate glass partitions had been set up inside the tank, so that each spider had its own space to crawl around.

Catching a spider involved coffee, although it was not the spider that drank the coffee. Anna dispensed her coffee from a vending machine in the corner of the lab – free access to unlimited coffee was an inalienable right of all science researchers – and downed it in a single practised draught. Then she rinsed out the cup, dried it with a paper towel, removed the lid from the glass tank and lowered the cup into one of the partitions. The denizen of that partition promptly scuttled into a far corner and settled into a crouch, ready to pounce on any prey or make further efforts to flee, as appropriate. Aided by some coaxing with a pencil and numerous clucking and sighing sounds – these were probably more for the benefit of herself than the spider – Anna guided the spider into the cup and triumphantly lifted it above her head as she transferred it to the main bank of apparatus on her lab bench.

"How are you going to do brain surgery on a spider anyway?" asked Ethan, pacing up and down next to the door.

"Very carefully," replied Anna.

"No, seriously, I mean, they must have such tiny brains, couldn't you pick something a bit smarter?"

"It's true that this particular species has a little less than a million neurons. But spiders are quite intelligent. Think about the complex behaviours they exhibit. They build webs; they hunt prey; they have complicated mating rituals. And they have eight eyes; in some species those eyes are as acute as human eyes. We have enough trouble integrating two images, imagine the processing needed to integrate eight images covering 360 degrees."

Ethan was starting to regret bringing up the subject, but he did not have much else to do, and it was rare to see Anna so talkative. She was crouched over the spider which was now encased in a tiny black box, but her intricate movements did not stop her from chatting.

"OK, they are smart after all. Eyes in the back of their head. How do they fit all that brainpower into such a small body?"

"That's actually a good question."

"At last, I'm appreciated."

"And the answer is that they have some trouble squeezing it all in. Spiders are arthropods right, not insects?"

"Yes, just because I'm a mathematician doesn't mean I'm a complete idiot."

"That means their bodies are split into two sections, not three, which gives more room for their central nervous system. Effectively, in many spiders, including this one here, their brains fill most of their body, even stretching out into their legs."

"And I suppose that makes it easier to get to their brain right? Makes it more accessible."

"Exactly. The main problem we've had is that they tend to explode."

"To explode?"

"Explode. Makes a terrible mess. Their insides are under pressure, held tightly packed by the exoskeleton. You poke in a needle and it all spurts out. Not much use."

"So how do you do it?"

"As I said first up, very carefully. We use very thin electrodes, inserted into the legs and gain access via there to the central nervous system and the brain."

"Is that what you're doing now?"

"No, I'm immobilising it and pinning it into place. All the really tricky work is done robotically."

Anna pushed back on her chair. The wheels squeaked as it rolled across the linoleum. She swivelled round at the same time, so that, in one practised movement, she landed opposite a large bank of monitors on an adjacent bench.

"Now we can really get to work," she said. She punched a button on the keyboard and then sat staring at the monitor. Ethan watched in expectancy. Anna continued to stare at the monitor. Then, she extended a hand to the keyboard, hesitated and then withdrew it.

"I can see you're a key part of the process," said Ethan.

"This is far too delicate to be left to humans. The software is running right now. It's just calibrating. That will go on for a while. The actual download won't take long, but, as it's a destructive transfer, we'll simulate it a few times before actually running it."

"Measure twice, cut once?"

"Something like that."

"And where will the spider be at the end of all that?"

"There will be a spider in the box at the end of the process. But its brain will be so much jelly threaded with electrodes. May still be some function there – it's hard to ask a spider how it's feeling. There will also be some function in the rest of the system. A copy of the spider? The original spider? Hard to say. That's your Transfer Problem, right there. In any case, that's the bit we can squirt through the VPN tunnel into the bank."

"Giving it complete control of our petty cash account."

"Which is more cash than a spider can normally lay its hands on, after all."

"And until then …"

"We wait. That is, you keep guard and I'll monitor the software. Sometimes it needs a nudge."

Ethan was happy to wait and keep guard. He looked out again into the corridor. It remained dark and deserted. Dusty windows set high in the wall were fitted with slatted blinds that let in parallel stripes of yellow streetlight that crisscrossed on the faded plaster of the opposite walls. There were doors set into the corridor at regular intervals. All were identical, thin wood painted white with a panel of safety glass set into the middle. All were closed.

A faint hum permeated the corridor – a relic of traffic noise from the roads outside or an artefact of the power lines or some other internal system, it was hard to identify. There was also an occasional ticking sound from the radiators and, more rarely, a deeper creak that originated from deep within the building as it settled and shifted.

The lab itself was shrouded in gloom, apart from the glow of the single monitor and the blinking of LEDs from other pieces of equipment that Anna had roused to participate in their conspiracy. This illumination cast an uneven pallid glow over the room, with some edges and corners highlighted in stark colours and others shrouded in deep gloom.

It was hard to imagine that this was an ordinary workplace by day. The odd angular machinery; the hints of function and form; the spider tank dominating one corner: it seemed to Ethan more like a crazy scientist's cave, home to malign experiments that would unleash havoc upon the world.

It was a place that made Ethan feel at home. Inevitably, it reminded him, with its aura of diabolical intent, of Robert's room at their grandmother's house. Naturally, Ethan was strictly forbidden from entering Robert's room. But, when his brother was safely absent, Ethan was in the habit of disabling the multiple anti-trespass measures – a strand of hair glued with spit between the door and the doorframe, the laptop webcam set to record on detecting movement – and sneaking in. He would lie on the bed and imagine that he was fearless and impetuous, until the ripe smell of teenage boy drove him out or he started to worry that he might get caught.

One night, late in the evening, he had been sorting through the pile of computer magazines on Robert's bed, when the door opened and Robert and a girl had walked in. They were hugging each other around the waist and walking on tiptoe. They had intended to sneak up the stairs avoiding any inconvenient confrontations with Ethan's grandmother. Instead, they had unwittingly surprised Ethan.

The girl was dressed in a black lace diaphanous dress and chunky black boots. Her deep purple make up was streaked into clownish patterns and her long wiry hair was matted down. Robert was also distinctly soggy.

Ethan stared at the couple and they stared back at him. Robert was the first to recover his poise. As ever, his reaction was the opposite of what Ethan might have predicted.

"You're spending too much time here, brother. Time to get you out on the town. Look" – after a break to check his phone and swap messages by various clandestine means – "there's a little thing going on tonight, not far away, I was going to skip it, some nasty types there, but maybe it'll be fun. You're coming with us."

Ethan was not sure about the sound of 'nasty types', but Robert did not entertain the possibility of argument. He had already turned to one side and was whispering to the girl still hanging on to his arm. They both looked at Ethan and the girl shook her head slowly. Robert nudged her and she shrugged in assent.

Within a few minutes, Robert's companion, who was called Beth, had supervised Ethan's transformation into a respectable partygoer. She followed Ethan to his room and walked straight to his wardrobe and pulled out some clothes. Then she pulled out some more clothes and finally she simply emptied the entire contents onto his bed. She stood staring at this collection of school clothes and hand-me-downs in silence for several seconds. Ethan thought she might simply give up, but her face slowly cleared. This might be a challenge that would put off lesser mortals, but for her it was clearly a chance to demonstrate both a talent and a zeal for fashion. Robert watched over proceedings from the corner of the room, sitting astride a chair turned the wrong way round so he could lean forwards and rest his head on his folded arms, with an avuncular smile that Ethan found extremely irritating.

Beth started to sort the clothes into a few distinct outfits. Ethan was handed one outfit and told to try it on. Beth's cool, appraising tone reminded Ethan of his few visits to the doctor, and he almost stripped off in front of her as though for a medical examination. Fortunately, instinct preserved him from this embarrassment and he retired to the bathroom to change.

He assumed that on his return they would be ready to sneak back out of the house. Instead, Beth commanded him to turn around several times, exchanged a knowing glance with Robert, and pronounced his transformation inadequate. Another outfit was selected and Ethan was despatched to try it on. This procedure was repeated several more times, until Ethan was on the verge of mutiny and even Robert looked a little downcast. For Beth, the journey had become more important than the destination. She started to give Ethan tips for each outfit: how it might co-ordinate with his other clothes; what matched his eyes.

Only when Ethan and Robert were both fidgeting and bored did Beth pronounce herself satisfied. This signalled the start of a long-practised operation – sneaking silently out of the house. They crept down the stairs – Robert painstakingly pointing out each creaky tread to Beth. From the front lounge, the hall light cast anyone walking along the hallway into a sharp silhouette, so it was necessary to crouch down into an awkward shuffling gait to reach the front door. Robert, Beth and Ethan moved in single file, Robert in the lead. He unlatched the door and ushered the others through it, closing it silently behind them.

Waiting for the bus was an unromantic way to celebrate their hard-won freedom. Unfortunately, they had no choice if they were to reach their destination, which was – as far as Ethan could tell – at the wrong end of town.

The bus deposited them at the entrance to an industrial estate. A wide curving slip road led to a square surrounded by warehouses. Brown weeds sprouted through cracks in the tarmac. There were no cars parked outside – the space was open and bare, with the warehouses squatting against the swirling wind. The buildings featured a variety of brick, corrugated iron and steel-framed constructions. Robert steered them towards an anonymous warehouse. It featured one small metal door set in an otherwise blank brick wall. Tiny windows were set at roof level, but they were all covered by cardboard. A tiny trickle of light leaked around the edges of the windows and door.

Robert knocked on the door and it was opened by a pasty youth wearing dark sunglasses.

"What's the password?" he asked.

"Oh, shut up, Reg. It's me. You probably couldn't see that wearing those stupid glasses."

Robert sauntered past Reg with Beth and Ethan in tow. Reg shut the door behind them. Ethan could hear a dull throbbing through the floor and walls. They were in a small room with people sitting around the edges smoking, talking and engaging in more intimate forms of social intercourse. On the other side of the room was another door. Robert heaved it open and pushed them all through.

They were greeted by an overpowering profusion of noise, light and sweat. The main inner section of the warehouse was dominated by a haphazard pile of speakers at one end. About two hundred people were dancing in front of the speakers. Others floated around the edges, buying drinks from a makeshift stall set to one side, or clumped together in groups talking or arguing or watching. Dance music throbbed a percussive beat. A rank of disco lights on one of the speakers stabbed random rays of colour into the open space – there seemed to be no other source of light.

Robert and Beth drifted to a clump of people Ethan recognized from school. Most were older than him. Robert perfunctorily introduced him to the group and then drifted off with Beth to the dance floor.

Nobody spoke to Ethan and he lacked the courage to strike up a conversation with anyone else. He stood at the edge of the dance floor and tried to pretend that he was busily engaged in appreciating the music or was moving from one close group of friends to another and only alone on a very temporary basis.

This was a fairly exhausting charade to maintain and Ethan was relieved when after about half an hour the police arrived to break up the party. The music abruptly stopped, arc lights came on and the occupants of the warehouse were all corralled into one corner by a dozen police officers.

"Bit of a shame they broke it up, isn't it?" said a girl standing next to Ethan. She was thin and gawky with mousy-brown hair and a gap between her front teeth that was curiously appealing.

Ethan was not sure how to react. Secretly pleased that the painful party experience was coming to an end, he just grunted noncommittally.

"You're Robert's brother aren't you?"

"Yes."

"I'm Mindy."

"Hello Mindy."

"Don't worry, they won't arrest us."

"OK, that's good to know."

"Unless you've got any drugs on you. They'll probably search us all and then let us go, if we don't have any drugs. You don't have any drugs on you, do you?"

"No."

Mindy nodded thoughtfully. It was hard to tell if this was the answer that she had been hoping for.

"Hey, what's going on here," said Robert. He had emerged from the crowd behind them, sticking his head between theirs and squinting suspiciously from one to the other. As usual, Ethan had not heard him approach.

"Hi, Robert," said Mindy.

"Yeah, whatever, Mork," Robert replied. Ethan winced and felt a burst of sympathy for Mindy.

"Ethan was just talking to me," said Mindy. Ethan did not remember telling her his name.

"Not any more, he isn't. Little brothers have to go home now, with their big brothers."

Robert took Ethan by the elbow and guided him away. As they left, Mindy leapt past Robert and clasped Ethan's hand in both of hers.

"Bye, Ethan. Nice to meet you."

Ethan felt her put something in his closed fist. He slid it into his pocket. Examining it later in the privacy of his room, he uncrumpled a piece of paper with a telephone number written on it.

It turned out that Mindy had the single essential characteristic that Ethan needed in a girlfriend: namely, she was willing to be his girlfriend. As a bonus, Robert was instantly and implacably opposed to their relationship – this spurred Ethan to dial the number on the piece of paper when he might otherwise have ignored it. Robert complained about Mindy all the way home on the bus, calling her 'Mork' and accusing her of being irritating and pointless, until Beth complained that he was talking about this girl quite a lot and perhaps he should spend some time talking about her.

Mindy's quirky features and slight frame could also be seen as attractive – especially to a teenage boy with no points of comparison. After a few weeks, though, her slightly over-cheerful tone started to grate. She was also keen for Ethan to try one of the pills she took most weekends, telling him it would loosen him up. Ethan did not like the sound of the surrender to chaos and disorder that was implied by 'loosening up'. Nor did he like Mindy in the dreamy, fidgety state that she subsided into after taking her pills.

These nascent irritations were rendered irrelevant the next time that Ethan snuck into his brother's room. It was a Saturday night. His grandmother was out for the evening – playing bridge with friends – and Mindy had slunk off some hours previously claiming overdue schoolwork. Robert had not been seen for at least a day, which was not unusual during the weekend.

Ethan returned from the corner shop – he had scraped together enough change to buy a loaf of bread and some cheese and was fairly proud of having both the idea and the practical experience to make a cheese sandwich – and slammed the door behind him. The bang echoed into silence. He stood for a moment absorbed in the stillness and emptiness of the house. Then he decided to take advantage of it.

He deposited his groceries in the kitchen and stole up the stairs, trying not to disturb the tranquillity with his own footsteps. He opened the door to Robert's room. Inside, Mindy was lying in Robert's bed with the sheets pulled up to her neck. Her eyes were closed, but she was not asleep.

"What are you ..." started Ethan, but then he trailed off.

"Oh god, sorry," said Mindy. "Look, I was just ..."

"Just what? Get out, get out of here."

"Yes, I'll get out. I'm going," said Mindy. Ethan stood at the foot of the bed; Mindy was still lying in it, still with the sheets pulled up.

"Well, go on then," said Ethan. Mindy nodded but did not move.

Ethan walked to the side of the bed and ripped the sheets off. Mindy lay underneath completely naked. She suppressed a tiny squeal, then staggered to her feet and grabbed her clothes from a pile in the corner of the room. Ethan heard her stumbling down the stairs, stopping to pull on her shirt and jeans. Eventually, the door slammed. He continued to stand at the foot of Robert's bed, staring at the shallow depression left by Mindy, taking in the unexpected mix of her perfume and his brother's less salubrious fragrance.

Mindy did not call and Ethan made no effort to contact her. She vanished from his life as inexplicably and completely as she had arrived. Robert's vague disdain for her ebbed away in her absence and Ethan never mentioned the episode to him.

∞

"Are you asleep over there? You're meant to be on guard," asked Anna.

Ethan returned to reality and his assigned task. The corridor was still deserted; the lab remained shrouded in gloom. Anna was crouched over the spider tank, peering into its depths.

"It's all under control here. How's the calibration?"

"Done," said Anna, standing and rubbing her hands together vigorously, "I've run the simulation three times, set it to higher sample rates than I've ever used before. It'll create a data dump that we'll have trouble holding, let alone using – it'll need a whole lot more iron to run than we have here."

Anna bounced slightly from foot to foot as she spoke. She looked at Ethan expectantly. Computer equipment hummed gently behind her. The box with the trapped spider was enmeshed in a web of cabling. Every few seconds it emitted a soft sonorous beep and an LED flashed green.

"OK, well, but you haven't done the transfer yet?"

"No, I thought you might want to do it."

Anna led Ethan over to a keyboard, lit by the glow from three monitors arranged around it. Each featured incomprehensible output from Anna's programmes, with new lines scrolling regularly up the screens. She fired up a single command:

```
transfer-arachnid --sample=max --destruct=true
--auto=true --filename=incywincy
```

"Wow," said Ethan, "That's really evocative. In the future, it will probably be engraved on stone tablets and children will learn it in school."

"Yes, it's poetry. Now press the return key."

Ethan decided more ceremony was required. He flexed his fingers as though preparing for a piano performance and sat at the chair in front of the keyboard. He stared at the monitors as though he could make any sense of what was written on them. Then he pressed the RETURN key on the keyboard. The cursor disappeared and after an instant reappeared on the next line.

Ethan looked around. The computer equipment still hummed gently. The box was still flashing every few seconds, although the LED was now red.

"What went wrong?" he asked.

"Nothing. It's done," said Anna.

"And now that spider's mind, that dead spider's mind" – pointing at the spider husk in the box – "is in your computer?"

Anna nodded.

"Well, that was quick."

"Yes. That's because these big metal boxes are full of tiny, tiny things that talk to each other really, really fast using electricity."

"But not enough tiny, tiny things to do anything with," – Ethan looked back at the filename for the command he had executed – "incywincy."

"I'm using my month's allocation of processing power to keep it viable in a holding pattern. It's creaking at the seams just doing that."

As if on cue, a cluster of messages scrolled up on one monitor, each prefaced with the word ALERT: or, more ominously, WARNING:. As a programmer, Ethan surmised these were rumblings of discontent rather than signals of failure.

"Yeah, exactly," said Anna, following Ethan's gaze to the warning messages, "we need to get this flipped through to the setup at First Global Bank in the next few minutes."

Anna shuffled Ethan away from the keyboard and entered a quick series of commands. After the last one, a password window popped up and Anna scooted away and signalled Ethan back to the keyboard.

"OK, all yours. Needs your password."

This was Ethan's password to connect through their private tunnel into his personal section of First Global Bank's computers, where Anna's software and hardware were waiting to receive it. The cursor blinked on the screen, mutely requesting his input. Ethan stretched out one finger and stopped. The room was stuffy and hot. He concentrated on pushing his roiling thoughts back down. This only enraged them.

"I need to see what you're pushing through," Ethan said. He cancelled the password request and opened up a new window, calling up a list of the files that were queued up to shift through the tunnel into the bank.

There were several huge blobs of data. These were effectively black boxes to Ethan; he had no way of telling what was in them or what they were meant to do. They were labelled incywincy001, incywincy002 through to incywincy013. It did not matter, though. As long as he could see what those blobs of data were able to interact with, he could work out what damage they might inflict, whatever they did.

He scrolled through the rest of the files. They were all blameless. Not only that, they were elegantly designed and logically arranged. It was straightforward for Ethan to check through them. He recognized an ordered mind and was morally certain that Anna had put this package together personally.

He checked through the contents of some of the files. One programme was labelled arach2xml. He scanned through the source code and verified that it was transforming its input – which was too complicated for him to decipher – into XML, a standard language he was very familiar with. Basically, it was doing exactly what it advertised itself as doing and nothing else.

He checked through some more programmes, but the sense of panic was ebbing away. The patent simplicity and order of what he was examining helped to calm him. He had no illusions. An expert hacker would be able to hide something malevolent in this code that would resist his most determined examination. But nothing short of that would work. This package had been put together by Anna. After a lifetime of exposure to the most devious of hackers, he knew Anna well enough to be certain that she did not fall into that category.

Ethan called up the password window and typed in his password. He executed the send command and waited as the file transferred to First Global Bank. Even using the high bandwidth connection between the university and the bank, it took several seconds.

The LED on the box stopped blinking. Anna walked over with her coffee cup, scooped up the remains of the spider and tipped it into a wastepaper bin. The job was done.

CHAPTER NINE

June 13

"Aren't you meant to offer me a cigarette?" asked Ethan.

The thin, wiry man – now identified as Detective Chief Inspector Argyle – took out a battered packet of cigarettes, extracted one from it with a deft flick of his wrist, and tossed it across the table to Ethan, closely followed by a cheap plastic lighter.

They were sitting in an interview room in Bond Street police station in central London. It was a small square space with concrete walls painted and repainted in a pale green to cover numerous stains and scratches. Ethan decided not to speculate what might have caused those stains. Light came from two fluorescent tubes set behind metal grilles in the ceiling. The only furniture was a metal table and three chairs. Ethan occupied one; DCI Argyle occupied another; the third was taken by another police officer who sat in the corner taking notes. In the wall behind Ethan was a rectangle of dark glass – presumably a one-way mirror. Ethan also presumed that the equipment to record their session was on the other side of the glass.

Ethan took the cigarette and lit it and put it in his mouth and took a deep drag. After a brief pause, he collapsed into a paroxysm of coughing and spluttering, smoke spurting occasionally from his mouth and nostrils, like an elderly, asthmatic dragon. When the fit had subsided, he sat back up in his chair and prepared ceremoniously to take another drag, before DCI Argyle closed his fist over Ethan's hand and gently pulled it down to the table.

"Do you even smoke?" he said.

"No," replied Ethan.

"So why did you take a cigarette?"

"It seemed like a good time to start."

DCI Argyle leaned back and puffed out his cheeks. The creases in his face were sharply outlined by the harsh overhead lights. There were bags under his eyes, translucent and threaded with tiny veins. His eyes were bloodshot. It had, apparently, been a difficult week.

"You don't seem to realize, Ethan, the pile of trouble you're in."

"OK, you're right. Why don't you tell me?"

"Fine. Let's start with First Global Bank. Hacking your employer and stealing their money – you seem quite relaxed about that."

"That's because I didn't do it. They haven't been hacked and they haven't had any of their money stolen."

DCI Argyle leaned forward and hissed: "Don't you know that First Global Bank is on the verge of collapse? Haven't you been following the news? The Bank of England and the Federal Reserve combining, as they put it, to pump liquidity into the system, whatever that means. And martial law. Well, I do know what that means. It means you're lucky that it's me here talking to you and not some braindead soldier. Fortunately, this is martial law the British way. Tanks on the streets, but apologizing every time they accidentally crush a car. And the police trusted to investigate, trusted for now, that is. That's why I'm keen to get to the bottom of this. If you've got any sense, you'll help me."

"I'm sorry, I've been a bit busy to read the newspapers the last few days."

"Yes, we haven't even gotten onto what you were doing in Egypt and how you got back to England."

"You want to discuss Egypt? Have you even got jurisdiction over that?"

DCI Argyle sat back in his chair and lazily turned over the cigarette packet, smoothing out some of the creases until its shape was once again vaguely cuboid. This was not going to plan. Ethan Stennlitz was a previously law-abiding individual, ex-army and, so far as he could tell, a person who preferred an ordered, quiet life. He should be quaking with fear, anxious to co-operate, deferential to anyone in uniform. Instead, he was faced with a deliberately obstructive opponent with little regard for authority and an incisive, organised response that gave away no information. Perhaps this was the hacker after all and not his more famous brother?

"Let's take it point by point," said DCI Argyle, pleased to see Ethan nod in response – a methodical approach would be more likely to win his trust. "First Global Bank was infiltrated by an unknown virus that has been traced back to your sandbox."

"Absolutely impossible. I didn't put anything malicious in that sandbox. I'm certain of it."

"Despite the fact that your brother is a well-known hacker who could probably design such a virus."

"I'm not denying that. But he didn't put anything into my sandbox and I wouldn't have put in anything that came from him."

"You're claiming it all came from Anna Volkov?"

"Yes, all of it."

At last, he was getting somewhere. He paused to let the concession sink in. Ethan's shoulders dropped as he realized he had been outwitted. DCI Argyle let the pause continue. He sensed there was more to come.

"Anna's lying in a hospital room right now. I don't know why you want to pick on her," said Ethan.

"Alright, let's put that to one side for now. You understand that if nobody else planted that virus, you're effectively saying that you did it yourself?"

"I'm saying nobody did it. You've got the wrong source for the virus. You're on the wrong track."

"We don't think we are, Mr Stennlitz."

"If this is all so important, you need to stop wasting your time on my little side-project and find out what really caused it."

"And what was your little side-project, Mr Stennlitz?"

Ethan folded his arms and smiled back at DCI Argyle. "It was just work. I'm a banker, you know."

"OK, let's move on to item two. Theft of funds from your bank."

"Again, as far as I know there was no theft."

"And you're not familiar with First Global Bank account 04030020?"

"That is our petty cash account. We use it for office drinks, that sort of thing."

"And you're not familiar with any transfers in and out of that account?"

"Well, what's the balance in that account right now?"

"I believe it's approximately six pounds."

"Yes, six pounds and eleven pence. And is that any different from the balance two weeks ago?"

"Yes, I see what you mean, Mr Stennlitz. But that's painting a slightly skewed picture, isn't it?"

Ethan sat back in his chair and unfolded his arms. DCI Argyle understood the message – it was up to him to paint a different picture if he disagreed with Ethan's interpretation. Of course, he was not sure whether he did.

There was a knock on the door followed by the entry of another police officer who passed DCI Argyle a note. He looked at it and smiled and pushed his chair back and rose to his feet.

"It seems you've been help enough, Mr Stennlitz, despite your attitude. Due to the seriousness of this matter, we've been getting some help in our investigation. The sort of help that can cross-reference mobile phone records, account information and utility bills. It's given enough to bypass the cutout that your brother used – the empty flat. We have an address for him and we're setting up to go there now."

"OK, well, if you don't need me any more, I'll be on my way," said Ethan.

DCI Argyle chuckled and sat down and smoothed out the front of his trousers, momentarily absorbed in removing the creases. He scraped his chair back and looked down his nose at Ethan. The other police officer shifted nervously from foot to foot behind him.

"Don't you need to get on with your, I don't know, your little expedition?" asked Ethan.

"All this humour," said DCI Argyle, "it's cute, but it's brittle. You've done a pretty good job at convincing everyone how useless and inoffensive you are. But let's look at what's happened. Let's look at what you've gotten away with. My question is: how come your act still works? How come everybody is still convinced that you're inadequate?"

"Is that one of those rhetorical questions?" Am I expected to answer it? Are you going to?"

"Oh, yes. I'm going to answer it. I know the answer." DCI Argyle pointed at Ethan. "I think everybody else is so convinced you're ineffectual because that's what you think too. You think that behind all that bravado and despite a hefty dose of stubbornness, you can't do anything useful. But you know what?"

DCI Argyle leaned forward and cocked his head to the side, fixing Ethan with a stare.

"You know what? I think you're wrong."

Ethan leaned towards DCI Argyle and opened his mouth to let fly with a riposte but nothing emerged. He sat and gaped and felt the soft, bitter breath of DCI Argyle on his face.

DCI Argyle gazed speculatively at Ethan and reached a decision: "Let's make a deal. You can come with, on my expedition. You'll still be under arrest and I'll keep you right under my eyes and handcuffed to one of my largest officers but you'll get to see what happens and in return I'll expect cooperation from you – if you have any insights, I expect to hear them."

Not trusting himself to speak, Ethan nodded at DCI Argyle and he in turn nodded at the officer sitting in the corner and she took Ethan by the arm, shepherding him out of the room behind DCI Argyle, along a corridor and to the exit to the custody suite.

They were buzzed through a barred door and met by the custody sergeant, a portly woman of uncertain age sporting a pair of hideous horn-rimmed spectacles.

"Mr Stennlitz is coming with me, we need to take him on site with us," said DCI Argyle.

"Aah," said the sergeant, as though she had been expecting this obvious ploy and was not going to be fooled by it, "are you releasing him from arrest – if so, I'll need to go through this paperwork and sign him out." She pointed at a pile of forms splayed over the counter.

"No, he stays arrested, but he's coming with us," replied DCI Argyle. Behind the sergeant, he could see people gathering car keys, draining the last of their coffee and generally preparing for a large-scale deployment.

"Oh, now that is quite complicated," said the sergeant. She waddled to her desk and pulled out an enormous spiral bound set of papers, festooned with sticky notes of various colours. On the cover was the single word 'PACE'. She heaved at the cover and the book fell open at a page marked Code C to the Codes of Practice for the Police and Criminal Evidence

Act 1984. Fixing her glasses securely in place with one hand, she used her other hand to trace a finger down the lines of text.

"Look," interrupted DCI Argyle, "this is really a matter of national security. We have to move fast. The country is literally crumbling around us. I don't think this is a priority."

The custody sergeant stared at DCI Argyle over the top of her glasses and returned to her book. This was not the harshest attempt to pull rank she had experienced – it was not even the harshest she had experienced that day – and it was not going to put her off.

DCI Argyle changed tack – an appeal to flattery.

"Look. We just need whatever's quickest. Can you find the protocol that works best for that?"

The sergeant sighed. She pulled out a form from the pile, scribbled on it seemingly at random, and thrust it at Ethan, indicating where he should sign.

"He can go with you but he's not being released or charged. And he's also not under my supervision, so he'll have to take back his belongings," she said.

Then she scrabbled behind the counter, flicked open a locker and produced a transparent plastic bag which she emptied onto the table: keys, coins, a wallet, a small black diary and his scarred and battered mobile phone with the battery removed and separately tagged. DCI Argyle poked his finger at these sundry items and pronounced them fit to return. Ethan swept them into his pocket.

He still had not looked in the diary. It was an absurdly antique way to store information. As they piled into the back of a police van with Ethan sandwiched between a uniformed officer and DCI Argyle, it seemed unlikely that he would get the chance to examine it soon.

CHAPTER TEN

June 1

Legoland was a Lego-themed amusement park located to the west of London. Robert maintained that it was the ideal rendezvous for counter-surveillance: constant background noise; large, swirling groups of people; twisting and turning routes with abrupt reverses. Ethan suspected Robert insisted on meeting there because he really liked Lego. In any case, as Ethan was also fascinated by Legoland's intricate Lego sculptures, he was happy to go along with the plan.

Ethan and Anna arrived together; Robert arrived separately by means known only to him – he was being even more mysterious than usual and Ethan's only means of contacting him was an address in central London that he assumed was simply a cutout: a convenient point to receive mail and messages that could be visited discreetly from time to time and would not reveal his true location. Of course, Robert had no trouble contacting Ethan – his mobile phone number did not change, unlike Robert, who used a series of disposable phones.

After a brief contretemps at the entrance, when they had to explain several times that their group consisted of two adults and no children, to the confusion and increasing disapproval of the plastic-smiled man selling tickets, they passed quickly into the milling crowds at the main exhibit. It was a clear, bright day, with a crystalline coldness that recalled winter. Children skipped and ran along the paths, threading between the exhibits, dodging pushchairs and grown-ups, who they treated as slightly irritating, ponderously slow-moving obstacles. There was shouting and crying, ranging from stifled sobs to bitter weeping. Most of it came from the children.

Ethan and Anna threaded a course through the melee. Anna barely glanced to either side and the children instinctively sensed her disregard and parted to either side of her, like shoals of brightly-coloured fish dividing and reassembling as a shark glided past. Ethan knew better than to point this out – children were a sore point with Anna.

They stopped to look at one of the exhibits: a replica of the centre of London, with famous buildings faithfully reproduced in miniature. The scale was fixed so that skyscrapers were around six feet tall, each curve and crenellation set at eye level. Millions of tiny bricks assembled in repeating patterns, windows and arches reproduced precisely and methodically using pieces of the appropriate shape. The relentless order concealed some bizarre choices – tiny plastic tyre rims used to mimic the curve of a particular concrete arch, car headlights stacked into a simulated glittering antenna, a row of identical tiny railings that gradually resolved themselves into pairs of tiny legs from Lego people set upside-down. There was no sign of the rest of these unfortunate denizens of the Lego world.

Ethan gazed at the crinkled corner of one steel and glass confection. Craning his neck around, he struggled to deconstruct the fine tracery of girders and brickwork into its constituent elements. Was that a triangular computer monitor block wedged between two perspex screens? He tipped forward on one leg, one hand gently gripping the top of the protective rail surrounding the display, straining to reach the ideal viewing angle.

A jab in his side almost tipped him over the railing.

"We're not here to sightsee," hissed Anna, already turning away to resume her relentless course through the amusement park.

"I was making our cover story look convincing," replied Ethan, to Anna's retreating back. He trotted behind in her wake until the crowd thinned.

The panorama of central London gave way to a wide tarmac path decorated with garish signposts inviting the visitors to sample various rides and spectacles. Low hedges faithfully tracked both borders of the path, the foliage thrusting out a dense even mat of green that was sharply cut into flat sides and square corners. Behind the hedges, trees were planted at regular intervals – conifers forming neat symmetrical cones. In the cold light, they gave off a plastic sheen. Ethan had to stop himself wandering over to peer closely at them to check they were not made of Lego.

Only the squealing hordes of children injected chaos into the manicured setting, scattering from the paths with their beleaguered parents in vain pursuit. Children and their parents were corralled by ice cream sellers and security guards and gardeners and street cleaners and customer service representatives and assistant customer service representatives – all busily carrying out their assigned roles with a brittle cheerfulness. Ethan admired their fixed plastic grins, relentlessly radiating optimism into the crowd, displaying all the emotional depth and nuance of Lego people.

Ethan bit back on his suddenly rasping breath. It was the happy, seething mass of humanity at play. Too much disorder. His stomach seethed – surely everyone could see that he was not allowed here, that he would pollute the recreational atmosphere. Slow breaths in and out. A girl sitting on a bench giggled as her helium balloon caught a gust of wind and tangled in the branches of a tree. He struggled to focus on the girl, the balloon. What was he doing here? Why had he agreed to go along with this bizarre scheme?

Anna spun around and flashed him a grin. She stood still as children eddied and swirled around her. Leaning against a sign inviting park goers above the height of four foot or accompanied by a responsible adult to sample the dodgems, she raised an eyebrow questioningly: shall we?

Ethan shifted his path to join the end of the queue for the dodgem ride. Anna nestled in against his side. They snaked forward. A family joined the queue behind them, then another family, then a single man wearing a black hoodie, stained tracksuit bottoms and mirrored sunglasses and carrying a large plastic bag emblazoned with the Lego logo. Ethan stared at him and he shook his head, briefly but vigorously.

"Robert's just joined the queue behind us," said Ethan.

"You reckon?" replied Anna. "What's with his disguise? He could hardly stick out more."

"That's just the way he dresses," said Ethan.

"Except the Lego bag," said Anna, "that shows some thought, that helps him fit in."

"Actually, I reckon he bought some Lego."

"Yes, of course," sighed Anna, shaking her head and staring at the sky.

They stood in silence until the line edged forward and eventually disgorged them onto the track.

A red dodgem car with white go-faster stripes or a black dodgem car with a flame emblem? Ethan stood in front of the pair of cars, chin tucked into his chest, shuffling his feet as he twisted to look at one and then the other.

"What do you think?" he asked.

"What do I think?" said Anna, "I think you should get in a fucking car."

"Yes, but which one?"

"Look, there are two six-year-olds behind us, and they're going to start crying unless you pick a car and get out of their way."

Eventually all the adults and children located the vehicles that most exemplified the traits they wished to convey, climbed into them, worked out or were shown the controls, stopped crying and gathered themselves for the forthcoming tumult or, alternatively, started crying in an excess of excitement or terror and finally fixed themselves in the position that they imagined a racing driver adopted in the final moments before the start of a race.

A klaxon sounded and a bank of coloured lights draped around the border of the rink flickered into life. There was a brief hiatus, signaled by the noise of the klaxon descending into a subsonic growl and the lights blinking out, as one of the potential racegoers, whose bladder control had proved unequal to the task, was removed squealing and writhing from the fray and his car was hastily wiped down and reoccupied. Then the lights flickered back into life and the klaxon rose back to a high-pitched shriek and the dodgem cars simultaneously jerked into life as if attached by invisible strings to a single giant, if rather hesitant, hand.

Cars scattered at random, bouncing and colliding in a mad swirl of excited screeching, shouted warnings and apologies. Alliances formed, suffered sickening betrayals and were dissolved. Gradually, an overall clockwise rotation took hold.

Anna steered her car into the relative calm of the centre of the rink, gliding to a stop in the lee of a tight gaggle of cars drifting slowly along the inside edge of the clockwise circulation. She saw Ethan cornering at speed, gripping the tiny steering wheel between his knees. He careened off another car, sending it and its occupant – a girl with blond pigtails and a face transfixed by boiling passion – into the low wooden barriers around the edge of the rink. After one more circuit, Ethan steered his car into the relative calm of the centre of the rink, rolling towards her until, with a flick of the steering wheel, he swung the car into a sideways glide that ended a few inches from her bumper. Anna decided not to notice this ostentatious display of driving skill.

Robert's car detached from the throng and glided to a halt a few feet away from them. Robert appeared to be steering with his knees – both hands were holding a laptop computer propped open on his lap, wedged in a crude nest fashioned from his tracksuit top, a Lego bag and brightly-patterned rectangular cardboard boxes emblazoned with the Lego logo.

"I've hooked into the staff wifi system," Robert muttered softly, apparently to himself, directing his stare into the middle distance – although behind the mirrored sunglasses, he might have had his eyes closed. Anna and Ethan leaned forward as they strained to pick out Robert's gentle voice amid the whooping and screaming of excited children.

"From there, we piggyback via Tor and, well, let's just say we take the scenic route. And finally it's a straightforward VPN into the bank using the public interface. Nothing fishy, nothing untoward. Nothing, in fact, that would attract anyone's attention. We're just looking remotely at your department's petty cash account."

Ethan craned over Robert's shoulder to see the lines of text flickering up the screen. This was a familiar position. All was as Robert described. The nested windows told a clear story – they were peeking into a lightly-regulated corner of the bank's systems. Lightly regulated because it was meticulously walled off from anything interesting.

Robert tapped into Anna's software running in Ethan's private corner of the bank's systems and, fingers tapping deftly on the plastic keyboard, sent a string of queries. A window nestled inside another window nestled inside a third window relayed the response. Robert laid his hands gently on the keyboard and abruptly pitched forward as a dodgem car smashed into their rear end, ricocheted at a right angle and swung into a broad curve. The girl driving the car shrieked and whooped with delight and lifted a hand to wave at them as the car picked up speed and, with a final jiggle, plunged back into the swirling mass.

"Do you mind!" shouted Robert after her, "we're trying to hack into a major investment bank here."

"It's not a hack. It's a perfectly legitimate remote access," added Ethan.

"Boys, we really stick out here. Let's get this done quickly," said Anna.

Robert removed his mirrored sunglasses, wiped his brow, gazed around at the vehicular mayhem unfolding on the track as though seeing it for the first time, and put his glasses back on.

"So, basic diagnostics, the metrics we discussed ..." prompted Ethan.

"OK, OK, bringing them up now. Petty cash account, transaction list, and, wow, that's some big number, I mean, hey, you're going to want to see this." Robert angled the notebook screen around to give Ethan and Anna a better view.

"Really? What's the balance in the account then?" asked Anna.

"Oh, that's, let me see, four pounds," said Robert.

"Four pounds?" said Anna.

"Yes, just over, it's four pounds twelve pence right now. Oh, actually, four pounds fifteen pence, it just gained on a trade."

"What's your big number, then?" asked Anna.

"I didn't mean the account balance. That's not done very much."

"Well, what then? Can't you just answer a straight question?"

Robert lowered his glasses and glanced around. The trio listened for a few seconds to the screech of rubber wheels on the black, polished floor; the howls of pain and outrage as cars slammed into each other; the anxious voices of parents rising over the babble. They were a mote of stillness – ignored and irrelevant, an obstacle to be negotiated in the endless clockwise circulation.

"OK, look at this," said Robert, showing a primitive graph with a zigzagging, broadly increasing trend. "That is the amount of computer power we're using."

Robert leaned back triumphantly. Anna and Ethan shared a glance.

Robert, sensing their lack of comprehension, leaned over and hissed, "the scale is in petaflops!"

"Oh," said Ethan, "oh, I see." He peered closely at the screen, calculating, and the colour drained out of his face.

"I guess we've blown through your allowance at the bank," said Robert, "in fact, we must be using a fair percentage of the bank's processing power. Probably giving off enough heat to bake half of central London."

"And what are we getting for all that? It's been going a week. We started with six pounds and we've worked our way up to four pounds. It's not a great return, is it?"

"I did tell you it was going to be processor-intensive," said Anna.

"Yes, but I thought there might actually be some point to it," said Ethan. "Instead, it's just thrashing around without actually doing anything. At least it's trapped inside my private partition. Who knows what damage it could do outside?"

"Look, it's only lost two pounds," said Robert, "and that's after doing, let's see, nearly two thousand trades. Not a bad return."

"Yes, but that's only because it's not paying its own way. It's using the market's new trading systems, instant automated clearing and settlement with microscopic trading fees, one tiny sliver of the bank's activity, piggybacking on everything else that's going on. Otherwise it would be down by thousands already. And I'm taking a huge risk loading some random software into my partition. All to make minus two pounds."

"Ethan ..." started Anna, but – as if taking its cue from Ethan's tantrum – the dodgem cars chose that moment to power down. The strips of coloured lights strung around the edge of the circuit flickered and died. The music subsided into a low moan and then a shriek of static followed by silence. Into the calmness crashed a thousand pleas for one more go and tears and tantrums and excited murmurs from the line of children queued at the edge of the circuit waiting for their turn.

Robert slid out from his seat, pulled his hood further over his head and scuttled into the crowd heading away from the dodgem cars, his laptop and Lego bags cradled under one arm. Ethan caught up with him and Anna trotted half a pace behind.

"Ethan, I really appreciate what you've done," said Anna, picking at Ethan's sleeve. He stared stolidly ahead. "It's an experiment, remember. Academic work. It's fascinating that our spider-based AI has ramped up to this level of activity. Whether it makes money or not is secondary."

"It might be secondary to you, but I don't see much point otherwise. Maybe we should unplug all this."

"Ethan, let's give it another day, one little donation to the world of academia, one little gift for me?"

"You think emotional blackmail is going to work on me? I'm not a little kid, you're going to have to try harder than that."

"Yes?" said Anna, grabbing Ethan's shoulder to swivel him around towards her and smiling, "How hard? How hard do you want me to try?"

Robert stopped abruptly. Ethan and Anna skidded to a halt beside him. Robert shaded his eyes with one hand – surely unnecessary with the sunglasses – and slowly turned in a circle. Then he tipped his head forward and looked out over the top of his sunglasses, giving a cool appraising stare to the scampering children.

"Robert, you need to work a little harder on being inconspicuous," said Ethan.

Robert glanced sharply at Ethan. He rooted around in his Lego bag, keeping his eyes on Ethan, and then slowly drew an irregularly shaped package, loosely wrapped in cardboard and masking tape of various colours. Handling it with exaggerated care, he lifted it in a theatrical arc to Ethan who, in the absence of anything sensible to do, took it.

"Thank you," said Ethan. "I'm very touched. I've always wanted a mysterious bulky package with no obvious use."

"Look after that," said Robert, cutting imperiously through Ethan's sarcasm. "It's cool. It's very cool."

"Well, why didn't you say so? I've always wanted a mysterious *but cool* bulky package with no obvious use."

"Look – oh, careful," Robert interrupted himself to grab one corner of the package before it touched the ground. "Seriously, that is fragile. Cool, but fragile. Sticking out bits, sharp bits, bendy bits."

"Yes," Anna said, "we have it. But what does it do?"

Robert lowered his voice to a whisper. "You could use this, if it worked, to take control of a plane. Reroute it wherever you wanted. Ultimate get out of jail card. Unhackable, unstoppable, works with most aircraft built in the last twenty years. This is how to hijack a plane."

"I promise you," said Ethan, "that I will never want to hijack a plane. I'm barely able to stand being on one of those things, with all those other people, packed together like beans in a tin of beans. I'm quite happy to let the pilot take care of where we go. I can literally never imagine wanting to use this."

"What do you mean 'if it worked'?" asked Anna.

"I'm still ironing out a few kinks. Needs a software upgrade. Pretty major software upgrade. That is, it's not as easy as you'd think to get the internal specs of commercial aircraft avionics. So quite a few blanks. But I'll get it sorted out in the end and I've left it easily upgradeable. In the meantime, you can look after it for me. You're all too complacent. I might need this, if I can get it to work. Or maybe you will."

"Robert, there's really no point."

"Ethan, shut up, shut up, shut up. I know you think I'm insanely paranoid, but humour me for once. Take this bag and put it in your suitcase and just leave it there. If you ever need to go in a hurry, at least you'll have it with you."

Ethan scowled at Robert and continued to hold the package awkwardly in front of him.

"I really don't see any harm in it," said Anna. "After all, it doesn't even work."

"Please," said Robert. "Please promise to put it in a case and forget about it."

Without waiting for any reply, he gave a sort of half salute in the general direction of Ethan and Anna and shuffled away.

"I'm not really happy about this," said Ethan, holding up one hand to ward off Anna's interruption, "but I know how important it is to you. One more day. By then my office will probably have melted anyway from exposure to the waste heat. Or, who knows, we might have rocketed up to ten pounds."

CHAPTER ELEVEN

March 14

Ethan gazed at the thin spiral of steam curling up into the air from his genitals. He was sitting at his usual table in the coffee shop at the corner of his street. The café was a stark homage to the bland chains that choked every high street, a symphony in beige: pale floor tiles and artfully aged pine countertops and glossy metallic chairs interspersed with sofas. The lighting was eerily bright except in the further recesses where it subsided into moodiness. The desperate imitation jarred – it only highlighted the slight nuances that signaled this was not part of a multinational conglomerate but a single small business eking out a slender return.

Despite these manifest failings, or perhaps because of them, the café was held in affection by the local community. Locals ordered their skinny lattes and flat whites with a smile and a nod of recognition aimed at Sarfraz, the owner, in an unstated but fiercely fought competition to coax from him more than a reluctant grunt of acknowledgement. The gleaming steel wall panels were decorated with advertisements for battered cars and mopeds and requests for au pairs and posters featuring missing cats, all competing in a ragged overlapping call for attention. Frizzy, the good-natured New Zealander who comprised the café's entire staff, served up those skinny lattes and flat whites to her usual customers with a shared conspiratorial grin and a breezy efficiency – remarkable considering the unconscionably long hours that she worked.

At eleven in the morning on a weekday, the café was mostly empty. There were no customers waiting to be served. Frizzy occupied herself by poking a mop carelessly around the floor next to Ethan's feet as the coffee dripped onto it from the table and Ethan's lap and his chair. Ethan sat motionless, apart from shifting his feet slightly at Frizzy's prompting as she manoeuvred the mop around him.

"So, I thought that went pretty well," said Frizzy, squeezing coffee and dirt from the mophead into a bucket.

"Did you?" replied Ethan.

"I mean, it could have gone a lot worse."

"Could it?"

"Yes, of course."

Ethan stared down at the blotchy stain on his trousers. The heat of the coffee was rapidly fading into a damp clinginess congealing onto his underpants. The Danish pastry sat unfinished on the table opposite him. He supposed Anna could have thrown that at him, too, but it would probably just have bounced off.

"How could it? I mean, how could it actually have gone any worse, Frizzy?"

Frizzy paused in her mopping and gazed contemplatively around the empty café. She opened her mouth as if to speak and then shut it again and slowly shook her head and started to make a noise deep in her throat. Ethan realized, to his amazement, that she was laughing.

Eventually she stopped, grabbed the chair opposite Ethan and swiveled it around and flopped down on it, leaning over the back of the chair with the mop hooked in the crook of her elbow and balanced at an awkward angle against a table leg.

"Ethan, honey, where exactly did you think the children conversation was going to go?" she said.

Ethan squeaked ineffectually in response. He bowed his head and took a breath and recovered his poise sufficiently to offer a defence: "How can it be a bad thing, I mean, it just shows that I really like her," he said.

Frizzy closed her eyes and rested her forehead on the top of the seatback in front of her, as if temporarily overcome by the incomparable stupidity of men.

"Alright, you've made your point," said Ethan, "I guess I'll never see her again."

Still with her eyes closed, Frizzy replied, "No need to be so melodramatic. It was just an argument. I don't think you'll get rid of her that easily." Suddenly, she opened her eyes and tipped her head back to fix Ethan with an intense stare. "But you should, you know. You really should."

Before Ethan could ask for an explanation, the swish of artfully stressed wood against Italian terracotta tile signaled the door opening. A gaggle of schoolgirls breezed into the café, chattering and squealing and breaking the spell. Frizzy jumped up from her chair and stowed the mop and bucket behind the counter, leaving Ethan alone with his thoughts.

It had started so promisingly. A rare weekday morning out of the office – feeling like a tourist in his own street, gawping at the young mothers pushing their prams in convoy and the elderly out for their morning perambulation. Anna had slipped into the café, clutching her wide-brimmed floppy hat in one hand and using the other to clear a path through the scattered chairs and tables. Ethan was struck, for the millionth time, by her intensity and fragility. Her tiny frame, so suddenly necessary to Ethan's happiness but also so … contingent, as though it would burn up in the sun. Yet she was so fierce, so driven in her beliefs.

Ethan found this certainty fascinating – he had never been certain about anything, lived with perpetual second thoughts about any decision as a constant background hum in his mind. Perhaps that was why he couldn't resist the opportunity to poke at it, to test it out.

"Coffee and a Danish," said Ethan, pointing at the table where sat two items corresponding to that description.

Anna nodded her head in acknowledgement as she sat down. "Your knowledge of me is unparalleled," she said.

"Indeed it is. Whereas I am still a mystery to you," replied Ethan.

"Really? You sure about that?"

"Stands to reason. If you knew me, you wouldn't go out with me, would you?"

"Oh, that's so sweet," said Anna, taking a bite out of the Danish, although Ethan assumed she was talking about him rather than her pastry.

"So, I've been thinking," said Ethan.

"Hmm, dangerous. We've discussed that."

"Yes, I know, you're the thinker, doctor. I'm just the pretty face. But, still, I've been thinking. Reflecting, really. You have that effect on me. I think it's what humans call being happy."

"Oh, Ethan. Will you stop it? All this thinking about whether you're happy or not. It makes me miserable."

"No it doesn't. You're happy too. But too busy. You're always working, buried in your lab. Don't hear anything from you for a week and then you pop up again. It's ... distracting."

"Look, I'm sorry. I get distracted with an experiment and I'm totally focusing on it, you know that."

"Oh sure," Ethan waved away her objection. He was also regularly slammed at work – that was life in the City, no point dwelling on it. "That's why I thought we should get away for a bit. A holiday."

Anna picked up her coffee and put it down again.

"It's not really a good time right now," she said.

"It's never a good time," said Ethan. "You mentioned that time you were in Egypt. I tracked down the resort and I've booked us a week there, in a nice hotel, I spent ages researching it and ..." Ethan trailed off, suddenly aware that Anna was staring at him. Her eyes were narrowed; her face was drained of colour – even whiter than its usual shade.

"What is it?" he asked.

"I can't take a holiday, I can't go on holiday with you," she said.

"Why not?"

"It's just ... it's too much."

"It's always too much. You swoop in and, and, it's great, it's intense, you seem to get me in a way that not many people do, you seem to know all about me and understand me ..."

"Ethan, please ..."

"... and every time I try to respond you pull away. I don't know the first thing about you, sometimes I don't think I get you at all. And then sometimes we have such a good time, and I know that we're right for each other and I imagine us with a house, and with children, and with ..."

Ethan stopped abruptly. Anna was standing in front of him, her handbag clasped to her chest, trembling with constrained rage. In one hand, she held the coffee cup. It was empty. Its contents were deposited in Ethan's lap. The shock of the hot liquid achieved the desired effect. There was silence. Even Frizzy had stopped scratching at a stain on a corner of the countertop with a ragged fingernail.

"You have no idea who I really am," said Anna. Her voice cracked as she spoke; her eyes were glassy. Before Ethan could reply, she turned and ran out of the café.

Ethan sat in contemplation at his table. Frizzy left him in peace – perhaps she sensed that he needed some space to gather his thoughts. He pulled out of his pocket an email printout showing the plane ticket reservations and stared at it as though deciphering a cryptic crossword clue.

The Exelsior Hotel – despite its rather inventive spelling – was the premier tourist destination in Dahab, an ancient town on the edge of the Sinai desert, taking advantage of its unique position nestled between stark rocky mountains and flat white beaches to repurpose from subsistence farming to tourism. Anna had spent several months there on a winding path towards her academic post in the United Kingdom. Ethan imagined her there, recalibrating her life from the dour post-Soviet strictures of Russian academe to the manifest possibilities of student life in London.

In fact, it was a curious choice. Anna avoided the sun – Dahab was a sun-drenched tourist resort. What would she have done there all day?

Ethan loved these contradictions in Anna's personality. Like tiny loose threads, they could be teased apart to unravel her various defences and personality tics, to reveal who she really was. Ethan was not quite sure whether he had been successful in this project. Anna was brittle and direct – ready to see the world in stark, Manichean terms; short and unforgiving of failure; impatient with muddy thinking. Her own thought processes were intense but uncluttered – a mix of brooding and precision that led to rapid progress in her chosen field of artificial intelligence.

But underlying this sharp intelligence was humour and, above all, humility. Anna did not think much of herself and was continually surprised that Ethan did. Flattery was, therefore, an effective tool. A dry, mordant wit was her default conversational position. Her throaty laugh was always threatening to erupt – an incongruous sound that posed another delicious contradiction. Ethan never tired of provoking it.

Of course, Ethan could not allow a mystery to endure without investigating it. Not by overt snooping – there was no steaming open of mail or, more relevantly, hacking into email. But Anna showed him her photo albums, when in a relatively unguarded mood during an evening at his flat, and he could not help noticing some of the items in the background and filing away some pertinent facts to be googled later.

"Is that a beach?" he asked, pointing at a wonkily framed snap featuring Anna in enormous sunglasses and a wide-brimmed hat waving at the camera with one hand while clutching the hat to her head with the other.

"What gave it away?" asked Anna, "the sand? The sea? The even more sand with the sea next to it?"

"There's, like, three people in wetsuits just behind you, not really normal beachwear," said Ethan, ploughing on through Anna's ridicule.

"Divers. Just surfaced from a dive. Don't think there was much diving involved. It was really an excuse to appear on the beach and unzip their wetsuits and strut around. You know what divers are like."

This was a dig at Ethan, who was a committed amateur SCUBA diver, provided that the water was warm and clear and the fish and coral plentiful. Again, he ignored it.

"Only they've got some serious kit. Is that a helox rig? And look at that dive computer."

"Phwoar, get a load of that dive computer," said Anna in a woefully inadequate Cockney accent, "Aren't I the computer nerd here? Shouldn't I be the one getting excited about a computer?"

"Well, for a start, we're both computer nerds. And I bet none of your computers fit on your wrist and work underwater."

"You have me there. We're not allowed to put glasses of water on the workbenches in case one spills onto a circuit board."

"Would probably fuse all the lights in college."

They both paused to consider the cataclysmic consequences of a power surge in Anna's nest of high-powered electronics.

"Anyway," Anna resumed, "I still think it's a bit weird that you look at this photo and focus on the gadget in the background rather than this in the foreground." She gestured at herself and leaned forward, sticking out her chest and wobbling it back and forth. This was another joke. Anna was blessed with many talents but an ample embonpoint was not among them – even Ethan, who brooked no criticism of her physical qualities, referred to her as 'lithe' when deploying his attempts at flattery.

Anna nestled into Ethan's embrace, muttering, "you boys and your gadgets."

"Boys?" replied Ethan, "it's only me here." But the gibe was half-hearted – Ethan loved nothing more than a shiny new piece of equipment. Taking apart and rewiring clock radios or pocket calculators occupied many of the rainy afternoons of his youth, even if they never quite worked properly afterwards.

Nostalgia on top of nostalgia. Ethan was sitting in a cafe, wilting under Frizzy's brusque sympathy, not gently prying apart Anna's life story while snuggling together on his sofa or engaged in silent struggle with the innards of a digital wristwatch.

He concentrated on his breathing, waited for his heart to stop ringing in his ears, waited for the humiliation to ebb away. All he asked for was a quiet, peaceful life free of sudden shocks, loud noises and the crazy patchwork of emotion that seemed to follow any interaction with other people. And yet he was drawn to Anna, drawn beyond all reason, even though she seemed inevitably to attract passion, uncertainty, panic and elation.

Ethan listlessly stirred his own coffee and resolved to avoid these uncontrollable situations in the future.

CHAPTER TWELVE

June 13

The police officer was disguised as a postman, and he took his acting responsibilities seriously. He strolled along the quiet residential street, pausing to glance at house numbers and compare them to the bundles of letters loosely sealed with elastic bands stuffed into his scuffed brown satchel. He stopped on the pavement in front of a small terraced townhouse and paused to stretch his back – knotted from the countless years struggling under the weight of letters and parcels. With an elaborate sigh, effectively conveying the infinite weariness of life as a dedicated employee of the Royal Mail, he shifted one particular bundle of letters and magazines from his left hand to his right hand, hoicked the strap of the satchel further up his shoulder and reached out to unlatch a curlicued metal gate guarding the driveway of the house.

Gravel crunched underfoot as he approached the plain black door. The house was part of the middle section of an early Victorian terrace. It displayed the quiet craftsmanship of an earlier era: neatly finished brickwork and cornices, although crumbling slightly with the degradations of time; an imposing crescent window over the stout wooden door, inlaid with a geometric pattern studded with miniature panes of coloured glass, its symmetry marred by a fine network of cracks.

Two stone steps led up to the front door. The ersatz postman trod up them, fanning out the letters in his hand. At the top step, he paused in weary contemplation and stared up and down the street – not furtively but aglow with the righteousness of a worker engaged in honest manual labour. All was quiet. An early morning jogger shuffled slowly between pools of streetlight in the dawn murk. Two men dressed in paint-spattered overalls sat in the front of a white van emblazoned with "MP Decorators" sharing sips from a plastic carton of coffee and bites from an egg sandwich.

The postman swept a lock of his hair back under his postman's cap and laid the satchel on the step in front of the house.

"He's good, isn't he?" whispered the man standing on Ethan's right. "We discussed that last move in pre-briefing this morning, the old 'sweep your hair back while putting down the satchel', and Phil – that's Phil out there – said that it was the perfect cover for putting down the satchel and Dave – that's Dave over there," – gesturing at a radio operator crouched in the corner with hands pressed to the oversized headphones clasped to his ears – "well, Dave thought that it was too much, that it spoiled the whole effect, but Phil was adamant, no doubt at all, that he could carry it off, carry off the sweep and the stare and …"

"Yes, he's really good isn't he," said Ethan, in a desperate attempt to stem the flow. It appeared to work. The man paused to nod vigorously in agreement.

Ethan shifted uneasily from foot to foot. He was crouching in the back of a van, knees wedged against a metal box stuffed with screws and bolts and thick wire cables, head bowed against the sagging sheet metal roof. As usual, he was attempting to squeeze his rangy frame into as small a space as possible. But, for once, this was a sensible priority. There were several other people crammed into the confined rear space. Apart from Ethan, they all had a role – in fact, they each had several roles, and were plunging from one corner of the van to the other, adjusting surveillance cameras, whispering urgently into microphones and tapping at keyboards.

Despite the intense activity, the man standing next to Ethan had taken it upon himself to act as Ethan's mentor and guide. He was not quite a guardian – this role was effectively filled by the uniformed officer handcuffed to Ethan's left hand. DCI Argyle was also in the van. He was sitting at the front, closer to the top of the chain of command and too busy to worry about babysitting Ethan.

The van was parked in a side street in a residential enclave in Kentish Town, an insalubrious but rapidly gentrifying neighbourhood of North London. The postal drama was playing out on a parallel street less than one hundred metres away. They were monitoring it all on a bank of screens while communicating in staccato bursts with several other sets of officers surveilling the scene or preparing to play their own roles.

They were, in short, the command and control centre for a mission that nobody had bothered to explain to Ethan, but which he was rapidly working out for himself. After DCI Argyle had bustled him out of the police station, he and a rapidly growing entourage piled into a waiting marked police van. From there, they visited at least another three police stations and other buildings that, while not marked with police insignia, evidently had some official function. At each stage, the retinue of marked and unmarked vans and cars expanded, until they formed an unwieldy caravan zigzagging through the streets of London.

The whole arrangement slotted into place rapidly and, it seemed to Ethan, was worryingly makeshift. He was not the only one with this view. He witnessed random excerpts from the planning meetings, sidling onto the edge of groups engaged in argument and discussion as DCI Argyle's totem, quickly forgotten and unremarked upon.

"I'd be a lot happier," hissed DCI Argyle to a balding, round-faced man at one stop outside a police vehicle depot.

"Maybe you would," replied the round-faced man. "Maybe we all would, but it's a bit of an ask, isn't it?"

"In these times? We have martial law already, don't we?"

Ethan stood a few paces behind DCI Argyle, wishing that he had not missed the start of the conversation.

"But that doesn't mean this is something the police can't do better than the army. They're not really set up for this sort of operation. They tend to go around shooting people – doesn't work so well with all these civilians around."

So that was it. DCI Argyle wanted the army to carry out the mission, not the police. Ethan tended to agree. He knew Robert: his inventiveness and his capacity to surprise, not to mention his hacking skills. The police were mobilising resources on a vast scale – but would it be enough?

"He's the brother?" asked the round-faced man.

Ethan looked up. DCI Argyle and the round-faced man were both staring at him.

"Yes," said DCI Argyle.

"Which one? The evil genius or the patsy?"

"Bit of both, perhaps. He may have some operational insight; I'd like to keep him close for now."

"Bit irregular. He's not exactly cleared for top secret information, is he?"

"And if I ever come across any top secret information, I'll bear that in mind. Until then, I'm a humble police officer trying to work this case using whatever investigative resources are at my disposal."

The round-faced man shrugged. "It's your show, Argyle."

∞

Perched in the corner of the command and control van, surveying the vast scope and intensity of activity, it was hard to imagine that they were not grossly overequipped. The target was a single terraced house in a residential street. There were already several police squads in the street itself – perhaps not as highly-trained as the postman but still lauded at every opportunity by Ethan's guide as calm, fearsome, intelligent, deadly and bristling with the latest technology.

The inner perimeter was around the street itself. A cordon comprised a mix of uniformed and plainclothes officers in a loose ring maintaining visual contact. Cars and vans were parked to complete the cordon and as immediate backup for the first set of squads and a strategic reserve covering the entire operation.

The outer perimeter covered the entire block of streets containing their target. On a single command, vans were ready to drive across junctions, blocking all vehicular access. Officers were deployed in a rough grid formation – a huge reserve of manpower drawn from cancelled overtime and police bussed in from surrounding areas. Ethan had been vaguely aware of the clampdown following the recent crisis, but this sudden mass mobilization was a stark, unmistakable signal: the organs of government seeking an enemy and lashing out in fury where it suspected one was hiding.

"Oh, look, he's ready now," said Ethan's guide, pointing at a monitor showing the postman, now apparently satisfied that he was outside the right door, rooting around in his satchel with unhurried ease.

This seemed to be the cue for other participants in the drama to make their entrance. The decorators' van coughed into life and edged along the street towards the front door. The postman stood up – his posture subtly shifted, his demeanour hardened. The postman act was dropped, like an ill-fitting suit of clothes that could be shrugged off. In one hand, he held a cap, emblazoned with the insignia of the Metropolitan Police, which he flattened onto his head. In his other hand, he held the handle of a short stubby metal rod with a fearsome spike on one end: a battering-ram.

Ethan felt a sickening emptiness in the pit of his stomach, as though he had been dropped, without a parachute, from the guts of an aircraft. It was not the faint sense of nausea he experienced whenever he had to leave his flat and face the unpredictable, messy world of humanity. It was not even the effects of being arrested, interrogated and dragged in handcuffs to watch a police raid. It was the familiar sense that Robert was about to play another trick on him or, worse, had already sprung his trap and was watching Ethan blunder helplessly, growing hot with embarrassment as he tangled himself into a painstakingly designed web. He imagined Robert smirking and guffawing at his ungainly younger brother.

The postman – now no longer a postman but a proud member of her majesty's constabulary clad in a postman's uniform and a peaked police cap – grunted as he lifted up the metal ram with both hands and heaved it in a huge arc towards the front door.

The ram collided with the door and caused all the streetlights to flicker and go out.

Of course, that couldn't actually be what happened. Ethan pushed aside the basic, reptilian part of his brain that saw two things happen one after the other and assumed that one caused the other. Time to calculate, analyse. The ram smashed against the door. Then, maybe two seconds later the streetlights went out. Actually, peering more closely at the multiple monitors watching the street, they had not gone out completely. There was a faint orange glow from each light, the filaments barely illuminated, shedding no light, revealing only their normally obscure workings and a spiral curl of glowing metal.

"What just happened?" asked DCI Argyle.

Behind the ex-postman, a crew of six rapidly decamped from the decorator van. They were dressed identically in black close-fitting trousers and shirts, clumpy black boots and a visor that covered the entire head, black and sleek and resembling the oversized proboscis of a giant insect with a penchant for advanced wide-band communications and head-up displays. The crew toted stubby, functional-looking submachine guns and had tangles of lanyards clipped to various slings and belts looped over their shoulders and around their waists that held an ensemble of ammunition, weaponry, tools and sundries. Between them, they carried a ram that was the grown-up brother of the one recently deployed by the ex-postman. This ram looked suitable for breaking into small castles while under attack from arrows and boiling oil.

"The streetlights went out," replied one of the computer operators at the back of the van, whose job was possibly to state the obvious.

The ex-postman was now sitting on the top step in front of the house – not as a matter of choice but because the unexpected recoil from his ram had planted him on his backside. Heavy splintering in the door betrayed the point of impact, but it seemed otherwise unperturbed. The crew shouldered him aside as they ran up the steps, building momentum as they swung their own ram.

"Didn't we check all the electrics. Don't we have someone on that?" asked DCI Argyle.

"Sure," replied another computer operator, speaking at the same time into a tiny head-mounted microphone: "Station alpha green, confirm electric supply isolated from target." He turned to DCI Argyle and said, "we've got a crew underground, one with the electrics and one for plumbing and drainage – no escape underground from that house, not for anything larger than a sheet of toilet paper."

"Confirmed," came a crackly response from the radio, "this is alpha green. Electrics to the property are disconnected."

Some confusion on the top step of the target house. The six-man crew had fallen on top of the quondam postman, the ram rebounding from the innocent-looking door with a metallic clang that left a shower of splintered wood but the door itself strangely intact. The crew sprawled, legs and arms akimbo, shaking their heads to reseat their hi-tech visors, gradually disentangling their ammunition carriers which had somehow knotted themselves together.

"Crew beta red," came another crackly voice from the radio.

"Roger, crew beta red," replied the radio operator in the van.

"The door, it's not buckling, it's not, I don't know, it's not even wood."

"Send in the explosives crew," said DCI Argyle. "Ethan, someone's going to get hurt here. I think you can see that. And, most likely, it will be your brother. If you've got any ideas, let's hear them now. Let me get this done quickly and safely."

"Try the wall next to the door," said Ethan.

The radio operator looked at DCI Argyle who glanced at Ethan, then nodded curtly.

"Crew beta green, move into ingress position, confirm," said the radio operator.

"Confirmed," came a voice from the radio.

"Crew beta red, try the wall next to the door."

"Please repeat, control,"

"The wall next to the door, not the door. Try to break that."

Silence from the radio. Then a reply: "Roger, control."

"It's metal, the door," said Ethan, "you could hear it. Might be wood in front, but some sort of sheet metal behind. No way you're going to go through that. But those rams might go through brick."

The six-man crew decided to have one more go at the door. They charged up the stairs holding the ram and smacked the door dead-centre. With a screech of metal, the brass letter flap twisted and tore off and rolled down the steps. The point of the ram stayed embedded in the door, the entire length of the ram quivering.

Ethan could hear an echo of Robert's chuckling laugh, could see his lopsided smirk. The house had never looked like an easy target. In one sense it could not have been more nondescript: there were numerous similar terraces in central London. But it was also cleverly chosen. A sound brick construction, with thick walls between the individual houses: the original builders had valued soundproofing. Mid-terrace, so that there was no access from the sides, only from the front and rear. And it was directly behind another long terrace, so that rear access could only be obtained from neighbouring gardens or punching through the back of a house on the next terrace.

Those difficulties would buy time, but only a small amount. They were strictly temporary – the crews would soon find a way to get in. So why go to all that trouble? Why install thick sheet metal on the door to add a few extra minutes? What was going on in the house?

"The streetlights," said Ethan. "They run on a different electric circuit. Is someone checking that?"

"Will someone shut that guy up?" asked another officer in the command and control group at the front of the van.

"The lights are still on," said Ethan. "But really dim. Something else is taking all the power from that circuit."

"Riley, get him out of here," said the command officer, gesturing at the officer handcuffed to Ethan.

"No, wait," said DCI Argyle, "I think we should check that – tell the electrician, tell him to isolate the streetlight circuits, see what's happened to them."

The original battering ram crew had given up on the door and were now obeying the order to focus on the wall. In unison, they swung the ram back and shoved it into the wall. Flakes of brick dust obscured the point of impact. As they slid back for a second go, a sizeable chunk of wall fell away – a lateral crater demonstrating progress at last. Enthused, they lined themselves up for another swing.

Meanwhile, a new crew arrived at the front steps, which were now increasingly crowded. The postman had to retreat, leaning on the black iron railings next to the road, shifting from foot to foot as he surveyed his colleagues' activity.

Clad in white plastic overalls from top to bottom, the new crew made no concessions to fitting in with their environment. Reels of cabling, open crates stacked with tools and small, heavy blocks of glossy grey material were manhandled up the steps and arrayed in front of the door.

Working quickly and silently but with impressive coordination, they fixed blobs of grey in a rough circle around the centre of the door. The blobs were webbed together with wires coloured red and black and green in an appealingly symmetrical pattern. The wires wound into a thick skein that dropped down the steps and along the pavement. They led to a bulky black suitcase-shaped box embossed with electronic dials and levers, at the centre of which a metal plunger featured prominently. Even to the uninitiated in engineering matters the purpose of the arrangement was clear: it was a bomb.

Ethan tapped his foot, strained to rein in his breathing. The officer handcuffed to him gave the cuffs a gentle jerk and raised an eyebrow quizzically when Ethan looked at him.

"Taking too much time," muttered Ethan, "it's all taking too much time."

"Alpha green reporting," said the radio.

"Report, alpha green," said the operator in the van.

"Beta red, we are ready for ingress. Copy to all teams."

"Alpha green, hold. All teams retreat to position reserve one."

"This is alpha green, we've got ..."

"Hold alpha green, we're getting to ready to blow our way in."

"No, hold on, listen to this. I've found it."

"Found what?" said DCI Argyle.

"Hold, alpha green," said the radio operator, "all units confirm to retreat position."

"Team gamma one, we have movement, something going on here."

"Who's gamma one?" said Ethan.

"It's one of the helicopters," said the man on Ethan's right. "Don't know why they're getting involved now."

"Gamma one, move in for a closer look," said the radio operator.

"Acknowledged, we're dipping in, gamma two coming in from the other direction."

"They'll pick up anything on the roof," said Ethan's guide, "We've got underneath and above covered, there's no way out."

The activity on the front step had reached a critical stage. It was empty of people. One of the white-suited crew was crouched over the metal plunger; his colleagues were pressed against the other side of their van, peering around to get a better view. The postman had strolled further up the street and was practising his letter delivery poses.

"Crew beta red requesting permission to proceed."

"All units, vacate to inner perimeter," replied the radio operator.

"This is alpha green, it's bizarre, you should hear this."

"Alpha green, we are …" started the radio operator, but DCI Argyle leaned over him and replied: "Proceed alpha green, what have you got there?"

"It's the circuit for the streetlights, covering, oh, about a quarter mile radius from here, there's a set of circuit breakers and the main transformer and, well, anyway, there's something rigged to it."

"Can you unrig it?" asked DCI Argyle.

"Yes, prepping to do just that, but it's not straightforward. This is high-voltage cabling, it's the main supply for the whole area, before it's been stepped down by the transformer. I don't know what juice is going through it, but, well, the cable must be a foot thick. And I think, yes, it's warm."

"What the hell is going on?" asked DCI Argyle.

"Oh no," said Ethan, as an idea began to coalesce at the back of his mind.

"Disconnect it," said DCI Argyle, "disconnect it all, now."

"OK. I'm setting up already, but I'll need to do a few tests, check I've got the right tools for it."

"It's too late," said Ethan. "He's probably drawn enough power by now."

DCI Argyle swung round to Ethan.

"OK, you're his brother, you tell me what he's going to do with it, holed up in there, surrounded, what's he going to do with all that, all that," – he waved his arms around wildly – "all that electricity."

"This is beta red. We are activating."

"OK, all units stay back," said the radio operator.

There was a distant boom. The van rocked imperceptibly on its suspension. The multiple monitors trained on the front door filled with smoke then gradually cleared, to reveal a modernist sculpture of twisted metal filling the doorway and a ragged black hole alongside, where the brickwork had finally caved in completely.

The police officers on the pavement rose simultaneously and scrambled towards the hole in an ungainly half-crouching posture. Weapons were cocked and ready. Flashlights from their visors played over the black void, illuminating glimpses of early-Victorian hallway and what looked like an ancient bicycle propped against the wall of a corridor between the motes of dust.

Then all the lights went out.

Not only the lights. There was silence in the van. The squawk of the radio ceased, leaving a negative aural imprint that echoed in the confined space. Information overload collapsed into information blackout.

The radio operator tapped at the keys, hesitated, whispered into his headpiece: "Alpha green, report. Beta red, report. All units report."

His voice was flat and thin. It had none of the magic of communication flung through the ether and connecting with others who were magically able to respond. He was just a man inside a van talking to himself.

Faint sounds fractured the silence – a muffled thump, hooting, splintering glass. Tinny and distant, they were absorbed by the thick metal panels around them and faded into the eerie stillness.

"Get this van moving. Drive round to the target," said DCI Argyle.

Ethan noted that he didn't bother asking what had happened, but focused immediately on what needed to be done next. It would have been impressive, except that Ethan suspected that what he asked was impossible. The driver at the front of the van twisted his key in the ignition, waited, twisted it again, then turned and shook his head. There was not even a clunk of a starter motor attempting to goad the van to life. Just more silence.

"Jeez, I'll check on my mobile," said DCI Argyle, pulling out his phone and stabbing furiously at the buttons. His face first assumed the look of intense concentration customary to those engaged with their personal mobile phone and then fell piece by piece into bafflement.

Somehow, this was a signal for everyone else except for Ethan to take out their mobile phones and go through the same silent process with the same result.

"OK, everyone out," said DCI Argyle. "Let's see what happened. We can go round there on foot if necessary."

Ethan slunk into the back of the queue squeezing out through a single door at the back of the van, standing alongside Riley, his handcuffed companion, who ignored him and stared straight ahead. He knew exactly what had happened: the prolonged draw of ridiculous levels of electrical power; a strategy to confuse and cut lines of communication and allow time to escape; Robert's love of gadgetry. It all led to a simple conclusion. Robert had set off an EMP bomb to cover his escape, which would probably take place very shortly, at the instant of maximum confusion.

An EMP bomb – an electromagnetic pulse bomb – was a device that released a massive burst of electromagnetic energy. Humans were unaffected. They wouldn't even notice it. But it would induce a massive current in an electronic circuit that, unless it was specially protected or partially disassembled, would melt all the components. In short, anything electronic within a given radius would be fried. And the only circuits that routinely included EMP protection were those used by the army. The reason that army pocket calculator cost hundreds of pounds and was specially requisitioned? It had to withstand an EMP.

Nothing else was protected because it was just not worth it. EMP protection was expensive and the main source of an electromagnetic pulse was a nuclear bomb. In the event of nuclear war, functioning pocket calculators were not a priority, except for the army.

It turned out that DCI Argyle had been right after all: this was a mission for the army. The police had been instantly transformed from an overwhelming agglomeration of manpower and equipment smoothly labouring towards a collective goal to a bunch of confused individuals running around the streets trying to work out what the hell was going on.

Roughly twenty minutes of enough power to supply maybe a thousand street lights. Ethan did some quick calculations as he waited to duck through the van door into the early dawn glare. Add whatever power was stored already in the house using whatever batteries Robert could find – probably negligible compared to what he had just added. He needed somewhere to store all that power and the ability to push it all out in one burst – both problems had a single solution: a giant capacitor. And it would have to be giant – that is, physically big. It would take up an entire floor of the townhouse, be capable of storing a large amount of power and of discharging it in a single burst.

Discharging it into what? Essentially, it would have to be a radio transmitter – an antenna. Once again, the unprepossessing mid-terraced house was an excellent choice. It was tall and narrow and an antenna stretching from basement to roof could deliver all the necessary frequencies.

Still, even with the best possible equipment and a sizeable margin of error, the electromagnetic pulse could only have been strong enough to disrupt electronics within about one hundred metres. It was enough to buy some more time and to disrupt surveillance – if Robert was going to slip through the net, he would have to act very soon.

Finally, Ethan ducked through the doorway and into the early dawn of Kentish Town. Apart from the unnatural gloom in the absence of any working street lights, there was no overt sign of disorder – the road was deserted, with the preternatural calm of the final minutes of nighttime. Amid the neat row of terraces, the hush gave the scene the feel of a film set. Perhaps the houses were only facades, crudely painted wood propped up by metal scaffolding.

"Towards the target," said DCI Argyle. "We'll run the operation from there. There's still no way for him to escape."

Ethan decided not to share his doubts as to the veracity of that statement. He also decided not to comment on the fact that the street lights were still dim. Something was still drawing immense power. Not another EMP bomb: there would be no point in destroying electronics that were already destroyed. It was Robert's next surprise.

DCI Argyle hastily parcelled out tasks. The nominal overall ranking police officer was a short man wearing a peaked cap who stayed closely by DCI Argyle's side and said little. The others referred to him as 'deputy assistant', which Ethan had at first assumed was a menial position, but he eventually worked out that the second half of his title was 'chief constable', so that overall he was in an exalted position. He had also been a prime mover in the decision not to involve the army and had largely retreated into the background since the EMP bomb. DCI Argyle suggested that he withdraw to a distant station and take control of the strategic reserve, using them to reinstate lines of communication.

Others were dispatched in different directions. DCI Argyle led the main contingent towards the house itself. When Ethan and his guard started to follow, he shook his head.

"You two can come one more street, then I'm leaving you at the inner ring. Keep close to him." This last comment was addressed directly at Ethan's guard, although it seemed superfluous given that they were handcuffed together.

They ran at a slight crouch, as though under enemy fire, although the empty suburban streets were entirely devoid of enemies. They rounded a corner and came to the inner ring: a loose circle of police officers all maintaining line of sight with each other.

Gradually, Ethan understood the tableau in front of him. The inner ring was no longer a ring: about ten police officers and civilians were gathered around one house at the end of the street. A helicopter was embedded in the side of the house, one rotor slowly spinning, the other snapped off near the base. The helicopter was fixed at first floor level, at least ten feet above ground. The fibreglass frame of the helicopter was buckled and splintered. Facing the house, it was almost totally missing – a few shards sketching out an approximate curve. Away from the house, the frame was contorted, but largely intact. The skids underneath the helicopter were stabbed straight through the wall of the house. Cross-sections of helicopter innards were visible.

The house itself had fared a little better. Brickwork was crumbled and broken – the wall was smashed to pieces where it nestled against the helicopter. A cracked wooden window frame, now bare and empty, had taken the direct impact. Tiny shards of glass like confetti peppered the helicopter and the street directly outside.

The scene resembled an unfortunate attempt by a house to eat a helicopter or, perhaps, a particularly messy act of sexual congress between house and helicopter. It would have been faintly comical were it not for the sizzling snap of bare electrical cables ripped away from the structure of the helicopter and waving in the early morning breeze and the two pilots still strapped into their webbing and, therefore, suspended precariously in the air with only half a fibreglass chassis to support them.

As if to emphasize the urgency, there was a jangling noise – halfway between a creak and a shriek – and the helicopter settled into a new, even more improbable, position.

One of the crewmen was awake and shouting at the crowd positioned below them. He recognised the new group and started gesticulating for them to approach.

"I don't know what happened," he shouted at DCI Argyle, "all our electronics suddenly stopped working, even the backups, everything went offline at once."

"Are you gamma one or gamma two?" replied DCI Argyle, cupping one hand around his mouth to amplify his voice.

"Gamma two," shouted back the pilot, "gamma one went down over there." He pointed in a vague direction and then, suddenly remembering that he was suspended in a broken helicopter wedged into the side of a building, shouted back down: "Andrew isn't in a good way here. We need some help. Can you get us down?"

"We need to get over to the house," muttered DCI Argyle. "They'll have to manage."

"What about Andrew?" asked Ethan.

"He doesn't look so bad to me. What is he, scared of heights?"

"I'll stay and help," said Riley – practically the first words he had offered since being attached to Ethan. "We're not coming with you anyway, so we might as well stick around."

DCI Argyle looked from side to side, staring nervously towards the target house and glancing back at the helicopter. A single moment of hesitation was enough. Ethan's guard ran back towards the helicopter, tugging Ethan behind him.

This heralded the disintegration of their group. DCI Argyle ran towards the house with a small coterie – others dissolved into the crowd, searching for their colleagues or any sort of guidance. Without any means of communication, the well-drilled team had turned into a rabble.

Ethan knew the next surprise was imminent. He felt a scratching underneath his scalp – cold tingling as if someone was behind him poised to strike. People milled chaotically – the street was rapidly filling up with confused residents to add to the inner ring of police officers. It was exactly the sort of disordered crowd that would take away Ethan's breath, leave him stammering and sweating. But the tingling was not due to that – perhaps because this was not a random confusion: this was the result of someone intentionally stirring the ants' nest, this was part of the plan. The tingling was expectation; it was memory; it was a countdown only he could hear.

A crack like a rifleshot silenced the onlookers now arranged in a rough circle around the house-helicopter hybrid. With a jerk, the helicopter settled into a new position, a few inches lower. A puff of brick dust spurted out from underneath one of the skids. Then the door of the house opened and, with a surreal ordinariness, an elderly lady pushing a wheeled tartan shopping basket emerged.

She blinked nervously and patted one side of her head, smoothing down an imaginary kink in her thinning, pink, almost transparent coiffure.

"I thought I better come out," she said, almost apologetically, "only I wanted to collect a few things and then," – she glanced fearfully up at the helicopter looming over her head – "it was making some noises, so I hurried out, only I haven't got all my things here."

Ethan's guard bustled past her and made for the open doorway. He stopped abruptly as Ethan braced his feet on the pavement and yanked on the handcuffs. There followed some ineffectual tugging and staring, before it became clear that the two of them could only make progress if they were prepared to go in the same direction.

"I've got to get up there," said Ethan's guard.

"You do, Riley. I don't," said Ethan.

Another rattle from above. Then a new noise: gurgling and groaning with the promise of more disturbing noises to follow.

"Andrew's awake," came a yell from the pilot, "I don't think he's very happy. His leg is, is, well, that's not what a leg's supposed to look like."

"Alright, but stay here," said the guard.

Ethan simply held out his wrist towards the guard, who reached into a pocket and took out a key. With a fumbling rushed decisiveness to compensate for his uncertainty, the guard turned the key in the lock and Ethan was free and rubbing his wrist and suddenly aware of the tangy ozone smell of the morning air and the rumble of distant traffic unaffected by the drama unfolding in a corner of London.

About one minute had elapsed since the EMP bomb. There were surely only seconds left. Ethan's guard ran into the house, grabbing a banister to propel himself up the stairway.

"Is this anything to do with the crisis, you know, the state of emergency, whatever it's called?" asked the elderly woman.

"Sort of," replied Ethan. "I don't know really."

A shrieking whistle rent the air. Befuddled residents and aimless police alike instinctively ducked, although it came from far overhead. Ethan did the opposite, stepping into the middle of the road and shading his eyes with a hand to stare into the sky and locate the source of the noise.

An arc of white curved into the air from the roof of the target house in the next street. At the top of the arc, a small black figure, trembling at the apex of a pillar of flame.

Was it a mini-helicopter? A rocket backpack? In extravagance and overly engineered beauty, it was unmistakably Robert's work. Ethan knew that the tiny figure frantically working the controls was Robert, even though he caught only a glimpse as he shot overhead and wobbled along a course parallel to the street. The flame cut out and the figure could be seen more clearly, strapped into a drone – a black quadcopter with several ungainly protuberances and one more passenger than it had been designed for.

Once again, the tall, narrow townhouse had provided perfect cover. The confusion from the EMP bomb had given Robert time to charge his escape kit and climb to the roof. With no aircraft in support of the operation and no means for anyone in the vicinity to communicate, a quick leapfrog a few hundred metres from the target would give Robert a chance of slipping the net.

The streets were still overflowing with police officers, of course – laid out in their robust grid patterns and multiple overlapping cordons. But with no command and control, there was nobody to take the initiative. Nobody to step back and tune out the disruption from increasingly agitated onlookers and think that, maybe, the strict orders to maintain position and keep discipline were obsolete.

Ethan guessed that, with a little luck, he had a few seconds before the pursuit started: before the random conjunction of somebody who had seen the drone, somebody who actually knew what was going on and somebody physically capable of giving orders to nearby officers sparked a reaction.

Breaking into a run, Ethan chased the drone down the street. At the end was a metal railing shielding an alley between two houses. He flopped over it, legs tangling under him as he kept an eye on the sky above, and sprinted up the alley, past pungently overflowing wheelie bins, dodging a fat baleful cat licking itself as it basked in a patch of sunlight.

The drone sagged and spiralled. The small black figure could be seen wrenching at levers, pressing buttons. Cracking and tearing: part of the drone fell off, tumbling end over end and smashing into the street. In the shattered pieces, Ethan saw shards of a dull metallic rocket booster and fuel tank. Having shed its extra load, the figure hovered impossibly for a heart-stopping moment. Jerking up and down, it trembled in space and then tumbled, shedding detritus along its path: velcro straps, sprockets, a tiny memo pad which fluttered and curled on its way down.

When the fall looked set to turn into a plummet, the drone rotors finally bit air and jerked the figure around in a tight circle and then along a ragged decline, like a rubber ball bouncing down a flight of stairs, heading for a clump of trees that marked the nearest edge of Hampstead Heath. As the drone reached the treeline, there was a puff of smoke as one of the rotors seized up and the rest was lost to view.

By this time, Ethan was no longer stopping and staring. He was running. Rounding the corner of the alley, he turned to follow the path of the drone, skirting shuffling joggers, past railings marking the border of the Heath, and abruptly into the cool shadow of trees. The constant thrum of traffic mixed with the rustle of leaves against branches, the crunch of dried twigs underfoot and the distant – but rapidly approaching – sizzle of dying motors and rocket pieces scorching grass and baking mud.

Ethan emerged into a clearing and saw Robert hanging from the lowest branch of a tree at an oblique angle, one part of his harness caught on the tree and the rest hanging from his shoulders or scattered over the floor. He was wearing an improvised drone, the whole contraption wrapped in wires and batteries. It looked like a formerly sensible piece of machinery that had had its casing ripped off and its innards stirred with a giant spoon.

"Hi, Boom," said Robert, with an exasperating lack of astonishment that his younger brother should be the first person in the universe to come upon him suspended from a tree in the middle of Hampstead Heath.

"Hi," deadpanned Ethan back. He walked around the clearing, stamping out tiny spirals of flame ignited by some white-hot broken fragments shed by Robert on his descent.

"Just thought I would drop in," said Robert. This was too much even for him – Ethan gave a sidelong glance and they both broke into a short, mirthless laugh.

Ethan cut Robert down from the tree and inspected his various wounds, which were numerous but all minor. His feet were lightly singed, his legs less so – he wouldn't need to wax for a while. Scrapes and scratches ran along his body, but nothing was deeply pierced. One ankle was twisted, he could hobble along with one arm around Ethan's neck.

They abandoned the kit and, Ethan supporting Robert, worked their way slowly away from the site. The trackless forest was alien to them both – dogs or humans would quickly have traced their path and found them. Instead, they moved back onto the London streets. Here, they blended in and, with a few minutes lead, might disappear.

But it was still only a short-term solution. The confusion from the EMP bomb would dissipate and they had nowhere to hide.

"Where to?" asked Ethan.

"Figured you'd tell me. No need for text messages now you're here," replied Robert.

"What do you mean? I haven't sent you any messages."

"The schematics for the EMP bomb? And for the jet booster for the drone. You knew all about my safe house. I didn't realise that."

"It wasn't me. I didn't know where it was. And how would I know how to build an EMP bomb?"

"You were in the army. They make bombs, right?"

"Look, you've been sending me messages. That's how I took over a plane …"

"You took over a plane? Cool."

"Yes, long story. Look. It's really interesting that we're getting these messages but kind of academic unless we can get somewhere safe."

"OK, well, why don't we see if we've got any more messages?"

This was a good suggestion. They stopped for Robert to take out his phone and check texts and voice mail. He shook his head: nothing.

"I'll check my phone," said Ethan.

"No, too traceable, you can access your voicemail remotely, right?"

"Oh, of course." Ethan held out his hand for the phone but Robert punched in Ethan's number and started to navigate through the menu.

"You'll need my password," said Ethan.

"Yeah, whatever," said Robert. "Oh look, you've got something." He held the phone close to his ear as Ethan reached out for it. "It says: go to the farm. Of course, the farm. Good idea."

Robert put his phone away. Ethan made no move to continue. He stared into the distance.

"Not that I disagree," he said eventually, "and we should definitely go there. And by that I mean we should definitely stop talking about how we're going there and just actually start moving and I promise I'm about to do just that. But isn't this a bit weird? After all, aren't you and I the only two people who know what 'the farm' would mean?"

"Weird, yeah," said Robert. He put his arm back around Ethan's shoulder and they hobbled away.

CHAPTER THIRTEEN

June 9

"Can I help you?" asked Morris.

Ethan jumped up to his feet and smashed his shoulder against the corner of a plastic crate that wobbled alarmingly. He instinctively grabbed towards the crate but succeeded only in dislodging it further so that it spewed out its contents of individually packaged brightly coloured network cables over the floor.

"You kind of snuck up on me there," said Ethan.

Morris stared woefully at the cables scattered over the floor. Ethan hastily bent to his knees and scooped ineffectually at them, failing to gather them together.

"Was just in my corner," said Morris, pointing at a stool in a tiny niche between two computer racks, "checking on the power ratings. Your new kit," – he nodded towards the black boxes installed by Anna – "been spiking up from time to time, and with all the power issues we've been having last few days, I'm keeping a closer eye on things."

Ethan was not sure how Morris could be more vigilant in his oversight of their IT room. He seemed to be a permanent inhabitant of the gloomy, humid labyrinth. Ethan had finally gathered the resolve to enter first thing that morning, maintaining the momentum of outraged determination through the indignities of his morning commute, muttering to ward off the memory of Anna and Robert both pleading with him for one more day. His mind was made up. This was a ridiculous experiment. He couldn't understand how he had let it happen in the first place. It wasn't achieving anything other than a tremendous power drain. It was time to wrap it up.

"Yes, I'm sure it's a good idea to disconnect anything we don't really need. Was here to do precisely that," said Ethan.

"Oh, right, well, why don't you just point and I'll snip it out," said Morris. He rubbed a podgy hand over his smooth scalp, sweeping away a few beads of sweat that had collected in the muggy heat of the server room.

Ethan was left standing by the racks that contained the stacks of equipment that ran his various trading algorithms – official and unofficial. Morris ambled away into an unknown corner of the room. A distant clattering could be heard, followed by impatient muttering. Eventually, Morris returned carrying a selection of pliers, wire cutters, screwdrivers and what looked like a staple gun but was surely something more sophisticated.

Neatly hiking up both trouser legs, Morris leaned down before the black box that housed Anna's contraption. He ran a hand along the gleaming flank, finishing with a quick pat, and then took out a screwdriver and tapped it speculatively along a central seam of the box.

"What are you doing?" asked Ethan.

"Beautiful piece of kit, this," said Morris. "Nicely put together. Better, if I may say, than most of what gets put in here. Stayed within the tolerances, mostly. Also more than I can say for what else gets in here. Still, I guess that's what you want taken out, right?"

"Yes, that's right. Only, I'm worried it's causing some trouble. The new algorithms haven't really gone anywhere, so it's back to the drawing board."

"Right. Better for you to stick with those basic neural nets wired up to the stock price and a Black-Scholes calculation and not much else. They'll get you a little return."

"That is most of what I do. I had no idea you took an interest in, well, the software side. Thought you just ran the hardware."

"Oh sure. Hardware is what I know. But you need to have a bit of an idea what's running on it, to monitor the loads, anticipate shortages, that sort of thing. And your stuff, I can usually monitor that in my sleep. Nice and predictable. Stick to what you know, that's what I say."

Morris carried on examining Anna's box without making any serious attempt to dismantle it. The words to push him into action dried up at the back of Ethan's throat. Instead, he headed off on the tangent inspired by Morris's musings.

"Is all my stuff really that predictable?" he asked.

"Oh sure. Just what I like. Straight down the middle. Make a few pennies for the bank and no worries we're going to get any surprises. You should stick with that. No messing with this sort of stuff."

"How do you mean? That is, is it so different? I know it's drawing some more power, but I thought it was really more of the same, only more efficient."

"Oh come on," said Morris, staring for the first time directly at Ethan, a knowing smile crinkling his face, "you know this is different. This is really different. What you're doing here? Frankly, I've got no idea. And I'm not surprised you want to stop messing about with it, very sensible if you ask me."

"Yes, I suppose I am generally sensible."

"Oh sure. That's what they all say about you. You're really not the type to be messing about with this. Could be defence industry tech here, I mean, I'm not asking where it came from but still …"

Morris trailed off as his fingers snagged on an invisible imperfection in the black box. With a flourish, he tore off a tiny strip of dark masking tape that was fixed to cover a shallow depressed pimple on the bottom face of the box. Inside the pimple could be seen the flat head of a screw.

"Here's your access point," he said, "knew something this well designed would have one. I'll have the cover off in two secs now."

"Actually, Morris, hold on," said Ethan. "I've, erm, got to run a few more tests."

Morris removed a spindly screwdriver from a leather pouch and slotted it into the screw. Sighting along its length with one eye screwed shut, he started to revolve the screwdriver.

"Morris, stop. Stop!"

Ethan closed his fist around the screwdriver and drew it slowly back.

"Let's leave it here for now. I just need to check some things."

Morris stared at Ethan until Ethan unclenched his fist. Then Morris slowly put the screwdriver back in its pouch and, keeping his gaze on Ethan, rose to his feet, knees clicking, and finally strode over to another rack where some wires were apparently in need of imperceptible but crucial adjustments

Ethan made some half-hearted excuses and retreated from the server room. Concentrating on slow, deep breaths, he brought his heart rate back under control and decided to ignore the suspicion that his encounter with Morris had not gone entirely according to plan.

The rush of noise, caffeine fumes and tinny television voices on the main trading floor was a welcome distraction. The blur of activity and the swell of sentiment up and down according to the day's trading conditions was chaotic – but it was a benign chaos. It was a chaos that contained threads of meaning that could be teased out and exploited.

Ethan dodged around an impromptu game of netball involving two wastepaper baskets and a pink fluffy ball emblazoned with congratulations for the financing of a new tennis stadium in Tashkent and arrived back at his own desk. This was a scrap of office real estate notable for being indistinguishable from all those around it, even down to the density and distribution of random sheets of paper decorated with brightly coloured sticky notes and the semi-collapsed piles of old financial prospectuses and accounts on which were balanced empty coffee mugs, packets of chewing gum and several pads of coloured sticky notes.

Sweeping some of the papers aside to clear some space at the front, an operation which had clearly been done several times before and was leading to a dangerous buildup of scrunched up paper further back, Ethan rested both feet on his desk and leaned across to pick up a hands-free headset and put it on his head.

There was nothing suspicious about calling his girlfriend. His neighbours on the trading floor might listen in – actively or innocently – but they would hear nothing untoward.

"Anna."

"Ethan. I've been calling you. Why haven't you been picking up? Our project ..."

"I've been a bit busy here."

"Ethan, you haven't done anything to it, have you? I know you're not happy, but please, I don't know what more I can say, it's so important ..."

"It's still on, Anna. I didn't kill it yet."

"Oh, thank god. Ethan, you don't know how much this means to me."

"Sure, I do know, but I have a job to protect, you know."

"Oh, come on. You're a City banker. Unless you actually murder someone and do it on the trading floor, rather than at home in your own time, they're not really interested."

"Anna, you know, all our calls are recorded."

"Actually, I bet you have to kill them on the trading floor while insider trading at the same time. Otherwise, they just shrug and say, well, City boys, what can you do ..."

"Anna! Really, you don't know how strict the regulators are now."

"What, they have regulations against killing people? Wait, let me get the Financial Conduct Authority handbook. I bet they have an entire chapter on murder."

"Anna, I'm going to have to ring off. This is a recorded line."

"Sorry, Ethan, sorry. Don't ring off. It's only, when I hear about recorded lines, something gets into me. Reminds me of being born in the Soviet Union, I think."

"OK. OK." Ethan sighed to himself. It was hard enough keeping up with Anna's abrupt shifts in mood – when she threw in her childhood trauma as well, there was no point pursuing the subject. "Anyway, I think it probably is still for the best to turn it all off."

"Why? This is a perfectly legitimate use of your computing resources," said Anna, enunciating carefully for any hypothetical third parties listening in.

"The heat. The power drain. It's going to use up all of my resources. All of them for the whole year. They'll probably start an investigation, think I'm mining bitcoin or something on company time. I don't know why I didn't turn it off a minute ago."

"But Ethan. Have you seen the numbers? We're up, from twenty pounds to seventy pounds!"

"Great, seventy pounds. For an expenditure of I don't know how many thousand."

"Yes, but it proves the point. It's an experiment, right? A proof of concept."

"Alright, alright. Let me check the numbers here, see if you're right."

Ethan pulled up a new window on one of his screens. It showed only a blinking cursor on a blank screen. He typed continuously, quickly falling into a smooth rhythm, logging on via a secure tunnel to the walled off area where Anna's project was running, popping up a new window linked to this walled off area, firing a string of commands that interfaced with the project and finally spat out a page of results:

```
>> cd /usr/local/iws
>> iws-report --verbose --account="pettycash"
--currency="sterling"
iws-report 2019-06-05-09-12-51
account: petty cash account
starting balance: £6.11
current balance: £700.51
recent transactions:
2019-06-05-09-12-50    buy    MSFT   123.45      4
2019-06-05-09-12-49    sell   EXXN   81.45       3
2019-06-05-09-12-49    sell   MSFT   123.49      4
2019-06-05-09-12-49    sell   MBLT   371.1 1
2019-06-05-09-12-48    buy    GOOG   909.9 7
[type M for more transactions]
```

Ethan paged down the list of transactions, marveling at the constant blizzard of tiny, practically meaningless buy and sell orders, dipping in and out of certain stocks hundreds of times and venturing into others only once or twice. In the pattern and speed of transactions – it was trading sometimes several times each second – it looked like an automated arbitrage platform: software that was primed to take advantage of momentary imbalances between different prices and accumulate tiny slices of profit. But that flavour of arbitrage needed a highly specialized connection to the exchange. Ethan's private computing shard had a quick, wide connection, part of the main backbone of the bank, but was still nowhere near the nanosecond accuracy of a connection for high-speed arbitrage.

In any case, Anna's project was not being fed the sort of information it would have needed for arbitrage. It had access to news, public data, everything from weather reports to Instagram feeds. A neural network based on that data would typically try out one or two larger transactions in an hour. More than that would be both computationally infeasible and pointless – a piece of software simply could not extract sufficiently granular data to make microsecond trades worthwhile.

"OK, OK. I'm looking at it now. Doesn't really make sense to be honest."

"Try setting the verbose flag on the report command."

"Yeah, I did. Look, it's not that. For a start, you got the amount wrong, missed a zero. It's actually made seven hundred pounds. We might even have enough for the Christmas party now. Excellent."

"Seven hundred? I don't think I misread it. Hold on, I'll open a link to it."

Sounds of shuffling, scraping and then tapping at keyboards came from the phone.

"Anna. Don't worry. It's not important."

Ethan's voice echoed on the line as he listened to the sound of footsteps growing gradually louder, a chair scraping and then some more keyboard tapping. Then, Anna's voice breezily returning to the call:

"Sorry. Picked up the laptop. Bit easier to see. What were you saying?"

"Don't worry about the amount. That's not important. A few pounds here or there, it doesn't really matter. I'm more concerned about the transaction volume. As a trader ..."

"Yes, yes, you're a trader. I'm just an academic. I can't read a simple number. Hold on," – the familiar sonorous chime of a laptop booting into Windows – "I'm opening up a tunnel now."

"Since when did you use Windows?" asked Ethan. He sensed his grip on the conversation slipping away and, rather than try desperately to steer it back, he decided to relax and let the topic burn itself out. Anna was like a mangy dog with a bone in its mouth once she focused on a question – pulling away the question only made her growl and sink her teeth into it more deeply.

"Robert said I should get a cheap new laptop with nothing on to use for this; he called it a 'burner laptop'."

"I really need to have a word with my brother. Not that he's not a top-notch black hat hacker, but they all get swallowed up by paranoia in the end, and I'm pretty sure he's going that way. Either he's in the middle of some sort of monster hack – and I don't mean our little game – or, well, I don't like to think."

"Little game? That's my life's work you're talking about."

Fortunately, Ethan was saved from the increasingly choppy conversational waters by a ping from the laptop. More tapping echoed down the line and then ceased; there was a pregnant pause.

"See? Seven hundred," said Ethan.

"No, well, erm."

"What? You logged in or what?"

"It's showing about three thousand. Profit of three thousand."

"Jeez, what is happening there?" Ethan cradled his phone handset between ear and shoulder as he tapped swiftly on his keyboard, calling up another report:

```
iws-report 2019-06-05-09-18-08
account: petty cash account
starting balance: £6.11
current balance: £3405.51
recent transactions:
2019-06-05-09-18-08    buy    GOOG    9059        72
2019-06-05-09-12-49    sell   FNTU    81.45       30
```

"I can tell you what's happening," said Anna quietly, "It's a phase change. "

"Not only a phase change. Looks like exponential growth."

"And very profitable, Ethan. This is what you wanted, right? And it's going to be self-limiting, right? Not a real explosion."

"I guess. I mean, after a while other systems will start reacting to it, if you make too much money, you'll get a whole bunch of feedback loops. It'll probably fizzle out quite soon."

"So leave it for now right? This is it, this is how you show that it works. Only for a short time."

"OK, OK, I'm not going to pull the plug right away."

Ethan didn't have Anna's expertise in neural nets, but he could recognize a phase change when he saw one.

A neural net contained a network of computational elements that co-operated to move closer to their goal. Each element contributed its own slice of reasoning, something that might not make sense when viewed on its own but related in some ineffable way to the entirety, and each element in turn was modified by the rest of the network, shaped in a fashion again mysterious when viewed in isolation but contributing inexorably to the entirety.

The process quickly escaped the understanding of its creator and wended its own path, modifying itself as it saw fit, a black box. Anna's project had unknowability of a higher order. The unique organic component had connections, worked within parameters, performed calculations, that were not even known to the programmer. They were as sophisticated as millions of years of evolution could make them. They turned it into a black box running a black box.

Most of the time, the network changed gradually, evolving in tiny increments as it quested towards a slightly better solution. But occasionally, for no discernible reason, it exhibited a brand new behaviour, a jump from one set of solutions to another. It was like a change from water to ice, triggered by an indiscernible nudge but radical in its effects.

Anna's project had been ploughing steadily through tiny increments of change in behaviour, building up adjustments that made little difference individually, feeding back modifications to itself that seemed little more than going round in minutely perturbing circles.

And then the abrupt phase change: multiple crystals suddenly freezing into a new block of ice, a jump to a new way of behaving. And instead of Anna's project churning through millions of trades and breaking even, it was making a profit.

"Five thousand," said Anna. "Let's hope the feedback limit doesn't kick in yet. If this is exponential growth, I want some more of it."

Exponential growth was the kicker, the sting in the tail. Not only had their system exhibited a phase change – an abrupt jump in behaviour – but the new pattern was one of exponential growth. In basic terms, this meant that the more money you had, the more you made. If your bets were always winning, then the more money you had to bet, the more you could earn. But that simple mathematical statement concealed a truth that was beyond the psychological grasp of most humans. It was the sort of growth that bankrupted countries, led to rabbits breeding out of control, allowed viruses to kill. For Ethan and Anna – and for any computer geek – it was shorthand for growth that was faster than you expected, even when you were expecting it to be faster than you expected. All you could do was strap in and enjoy the ride.

Ethan might have pulled the plug then and there – ran straight to the computer room and grabbed a handful of cables and yanked them out the wall and carried on with another handful and another until the lights stopped flashing and the fans stopped whirring. He was no longer skirting with the edge of the rules. He was about to crash straight through the safety railings, career across a short strip of scrubland and plunge over the cliff, tumbling end over end into the rocky canyon below.

But, then, there was the money. One rule was placed above all else at the bank: make money. And money was flowing in, more and more as time went by. He could cut the flow whenever he wanted – he may as well wait a little bit longer.

That was his plan for the day. Sit tight and accumulate cash. It turned out to be trickier than it sounded. First, he rearranged his living space. A stack of foil cartons encrusted with day-old Indian food were strewn across the desk that Ethan shared with three other colleagues. After tentatively nudging them to one corner with the far end of a black ring-binder, Ethan arranged his four screens in a single large rectangle right in front of his chair. Post-it notes pinned to printouts of analyst reports, urgent scribbles on scraps of paper, fragile skeletons of crocodile clips intricately chained together in the depths of boredom – all were swept aside leaving the thin strip of desk that Ethan called his own completely bare. Apart, that is, from congealed rings of coffee and flakes of paper and broken staples. Ethan was in the mood to tidy but not to clean – there had to be some limits.

"Nice work, Ee," muttered Ethan's neighbour, Sami. The huddle of desks that surrounded Ethan was largely unoccupied. Most of the team were on a two-day diversity workshop at a soulless hotel on the outskirts of London. Ethan and Sami had been excused to provide a skeleton staff in the office. Nobody knew how Human Resources decided who to send and who could remain. Ethan suspected that Sami was already sufficiently diverse – he was of Pakistani extraction – and Ethan was simply beyond any hope of behavioural modification.

Sami sat diagonally opposite Ethan. He was a junior quant: a quantitative analyst churning out computer code to test out the investment models produced by others in the team. The finest universities of the West Coast of America had forged Sami into a blithely efficient coding machine, chomping through byzantine algorithms and vomiting out great gobbets of gnarly C++ code. His pressured academic background had also left him with a stifled nervous giggle that he deployed whenever anyone at the bank shouted at him and a variety of facial tics that hinted at anxiety barely suppressed. Sami could only think while walking and was usually seen pacing in a tight circle around their group of desks, returning to his own chair periodically only to give it a gentle nudge that sent it into a spin and allowed him to drift off in another circuit.

"My name's Ethan," said Ethan.

"Yes, got it, big Eth," said Sami. This was a running joke between them. "What are you up to there anyway?"

"Testing out a new strategy. Just watching a shadow portfolio right now."

Sami grunted, appearing satisfied with this response.

Ethan arranged two blank pieces of paper on his newly cleared desk, laid a pen at right angles to them, and proceeded to open a variety of windows on his screen: BBC news; CNN, Bloomberg; Reuters and a host of more specialized channels. He squared off each of the tabs so that they were neatly arranged on the screen. All was organized and ready for the coming onslaught. Ethan concentrated on slowing his breathing – he shut his eyes, ignoring Sami's curious glances.

Once he felt ready, he moved on to the next item on his list. It was time to contact Robert. This step alone was harder than seemed reasonable. He logged onto a cloud-based email account and created a draft email consisting of a cryptic series of characters. That was it; he didn't actually send the email, just left it in the drafts folder. Then he waited, aimlessly checking the various news websites. About thirty minutes later, a courier arrived at the far end of the trading floor. He bounced around from corner to corner, asking for advice that seemed to send him in a number of contrary directions, until finally threading his way to Ethan's desk.

The courier handed Ethan a small package wrapped carelessly in brown paper, obtained the customary illegible signature, and, with a look poised between disgust and terror, scurried back into the maze of desks leading to the exit. The package contained a mobile phone and – packed separately – a SIM card and a battery. Ethan unwrapped them all and proceeded to reconstitute the phone. The battery was completely flat – he plugged it into a standalone battery pack, not the USB port of his computer, of course.

"Hey, Eth baby, you seen the news?" asked Sami.

"My name is Ethan," said Ethan reflexively. But it came out as a croak. He switched the monitors back to the news, his fingers fat and uncooperative, tingling and cold, refusing to obey his simple commands. His heart thumped, skipped a beat. He focused on the simple pattern of his keyboard, keys lined up in squared off regiments, and concentrated on pressing one key after another.

"Oh, thank god for that," Ethan muttered when he saw the headlines.

"Wow, never had you down as a monarchist, Eethie baby," said Sami.

A minor royal had announced their engagement to a former reality star. The tabloids were frothing with glee, splashing their home pages with lurid photos accompanied by breathlessly fawning text. The posher news websites restrained themselves to double-height headlines illustrated with turgid stories tip-toeing around the more prurient characteristics of the princess-to-be.

"Oh yeah, hurray for the royal family and everything, and I'm a big fan of X Factor."

"Wasn't she on The Apprentice?"

"That's right, my favourite, The Apprentice."

"You're just hoping for a bank holiday for the wedding, aren't you?"

"You got me, Sami."

Sami grunted and returned to pacing around his chair. Ethan waited for Sami's circuit to carry him to a safe distance and then flipped back from the royal stories to the business headlines. There were still no ructions in the international markets; stock markets flitted up and down with their customary volatility; pundits pontificated earnestly on screen without giving any clear advice.

Ethan flipped over to the console linked to IWS. Two hundred thousand pounds. Ethan tried to swallow, his mouth suddenly dry.

His phone rang. He scrambled to answer and then realized it was the new phone – the one he had left charging on his desk.

"Hi?" said Ethan.

"Cool, that worked," replied Robert.

"What worked?"

"The phone. It rang."

"Of course it rang. You rang me. I answered it. That's how phones are meant to work, isn't it?"

"But you left it charging, right? Not switched on. You just got it."

"Oh, actually, yes. I suppose that is cool."

"It's nothing really. Jailbroken android operating system with a few little mods. I put in an extra controller chip wired directly to the battery – if you look at the case, you can just see a little bump where ..."

"Look, Robert, I get it. But I'm not sure why you suddenly need to speak to me with all this going on today ..."

"... and the interrupt is tied into the internal clock, so you can raise a bespoke request that runs my code blob and ..."

"Robert. Robert. Robert," repeated Ethan. When this didn't work, he said "Robert" a few more times in increasingly loud whispered shouts. Eventually, the other end of the line fell silent.

"Two hundred thousand pounds, Robert. We're still on this side of crazy, but I can definitely see crazy from where I'm sitting. In fact, I can smell it. I can, yes, I can smell it."

"Alright, you're tasting the crazy, I get it."

"I said smelling ... I'm not sure we're up to tasting yet."

"Oh, well, that's something. But I'm coming round anyway."

"No, Robert. You can't come here. I won't let you in."

"And don't let anyone touch incy wincy before I get there."

"What do you mean, anyone? Who's going to touch it?"

"I just mean anybody at all. Like, your IT guy. Just sit tight."

"Robert, stay away."

"Sure, see you in a minute."

There was a click on the other end of the line. After the trick with the mobile phone, Ethan wasn't sure whether Robert was being literal when he said he would be there in one minute. He glanced around the trading floor, jerking awkwardly in his seat to examine each door and entryway in turn. He flinched as one door swung open and a man scurried in, then relaxed as the figure turned to show a face that was entirely unlike Robert's.

Nothing to do but sit and wait. He flicked through the news websites, focusing on the business section. Halwell Utilities was in the news – stock price diving, exchange pausing trading in their shares, rumours of accounting irregularities. He called up another report:

```
iws-report 2019-06-05-11-23-21
account: petty cash account
starting balance: £6.11
current balance: £17023102.45
```

Stabbing at the keyboard to stop the flow of recent transactions, he entered a search for Halwell Utilities:

```
recent transactions - search results:
2019-06-05-11-09-06    sell   HLWU   42.5   103460
2019-06-05-11-09-05    sell   HLWU   42.6   901014
     ...
```

The list scrolled down the screen. Most recently, a flurry of sell orders, followed immediately by a precipitate decline in the share price that triggered the exchange's automatic response to excess volatility, barring any trades in the stock for a set period of time pending investigation. Before that, a steady accumulation of shares in the company, building up a position where incy wincy held just under 5% of the entire share capital, the level where the bank would have to notify the financial authorities of their holding. Even with that accumulation, incy wincy was now 'short' of the stock – that is, it had sold shares it did not have, hoping to buy them back later at a lower price. And the price was now lower, much lower.

Ethan glanced back at the top number, the current balance. He squinted as he mentally inserted commas in the right place. Was that one million and something? No, he realized, that was a seventeen. Seventeen million pounds. In his petty cash account.

"I think we've got enough for the Christmas party," he muttered.

"What's that?" said Sami, deeply engrossed in whatever was on his computer screen, pressing his face close to it while absently poking with one hand at his keyboard.

Seventeen million pounds. Ethan wiped clammy palms on the leather armrests of his ergonomic chair and hunched forward over his desk, willing his breathing to slow down. He reached out for the phone and hit the speed-dial for Anna's number. No answer.

Ethan decided to go for a little stroll. He could watch the news on the banks of monitors suspended from gantries on the ceiling and tuned in soundlessly to every news and business channel. He walked unsteadily around his own bank of chairs, gathering the fortitude to wander further afield, and finally hoicked his shoulders back and swiveled to thread past a neighbouring bank of seats on a winding circuit of the trading floor.

Seventeen million was comfortably more than a petty cash account would normally hold, but it should not be enough to disrupt the international capital markets. The unusual activity might be enough to nudge trading patterns slightly out of synch – induce tiny fractures in the business landscape. Ethan studied the news feeds, hunting the slightest nuance that could presage financial instability.

Ethan flicked his eyes over one story: tax changes mooted by the United States Treasury were putting pressure on bond prices. This seemed unlikely to be the work of incy wincy. He moved on. Cryptocurrency futures were experiencing some unpleasant swings. Ethan gave a mental shrug; no surprises there.

One story caught his eye. He stopped in his peregrinations and edged close to a screen, craning his neck to catch the tiny text scrolling along the bottom. Vanadium and copper prices, both moving, but in opposite directions. Ethan quickly logged into a spare Bloomberg terminal and checked other commodity prices. No other anomalies. Maybe it was just his imagination – jumping at shadows, as usual.

Eventually, he circled back to his own bank of desks.

"Some guy was looking for you," called out Sami without taking his eyes off his computer screen. He sat in the same hunched posture as when Ethan had set off on his tour. Bile rose in the back of Ethan's throat – he staggered as though someone had pushed him in the chest.

"Who?" he asked.

"Dunno, that IT guy. The weird one. The one with no hair."

This was better than Robert – a crisis, but a manageable one. Ethan jogged to the discreet door in the corner of the trading floor that led to the IT lair. Tentatively, he eased it open a crack. The door was promptly snatched out of his grasp as Morris swung it wide open.

"You're disturbing," said Morris, "light and noise, I cannot concentrate," he explained, in conspicuous contradiction of the fact that he was the one who had flung the door open. He waved impatiently at Ethan and pressed the door shut as soon as he was over the threshold.

The room was dark and humid, with the tang of ozone and the barely audible, dissonant hum from racks of equipment. Morris turned abruptly and, shaking his head, strode down a narrow passageway. A coil of insulated cabling was strung from the ceiling; he swerved without ducking to avoid it. Ethan followed him, hunching and swiveling sideways and still bashing into the jutting metal corner of a discarded hard drive case. He stifled a squeak of pain and trotted up to Morris, almost colliding with him as he stopped abruptly next to a small wooden table and chair.

Ethan had not noticed these two pieces of furniture on his previous visit. A rickety table, thin plasticky wood stained with countless coffee mugs, squashed against a pillar. Tucked under the table, an equally rickety plain wooden chair, decorated with a single grey cushion, simultaneously overstuffed and wrinkled and torn in the corner so that the stuffing was starting to leak out. On the table sat a box of tissues, an alarm clock and a squat black box in thick ribbed plastic set with several dials.

Morris settled onto the cushioned chair with a sigh and propped one elbow on the table. He looked at the dials, tapped one with the tip of his little finger and pinched the bridge of his nose between his thumb and index finger. He shut his eyes. Ethan could hear his breath whistling in and out of his nose. He waited, watching the strobe of green and red LEDs as network switches shunted packets in and out of the bank, listening to the rattle of fans sputtering into life and then subsiding as they pushed gobbets of warm air around the room.

After a while, Ethan decided to explore. He took a single step and Morris coughed and looked straight up at him.

"Too much heat, too much power," said Morris.

"Oh?" said Ethan, in the absence of anything more useful to say.

"Your little project. I can't even tell how much heat it's pumping out, all I know is that our air conditioning isn't keeping up."

"OK, it's just for a little bit."

"And the power draw. I'm going to bill it to your account, we can't absorb it into the team budget."

"OK, that's fine."

"No, it isn't really. I want you to turn it off. If I had your password, it would be off already."

This struck Ethan as a rather clumsy threat, not to mention a proposed breach of several of the bank's best practices.

"One hour, Morris. I'll check back on you then."

Morris sighed again as he rose to his feet, the chair scraping back against the scuffed linoleum carpeting the floor. Ethan once again trotted after him. Evidently, the interview was over.

Morris stood outside the entrance to the IT room, jangling a bunch of keys, waiting for Ethan to catch up with him. As soon as Ethan had ducked out through the entrance, Morris pushed it shut and stuck one of his keys in.

"One hour maximum," he said, fiddling with the key in the lock, "and I'll be back then to open up and if I have to I'll pull out all the cables, if that's what it takes to get my dials back in order."

Ethan did not believe that Morris would jeopardise the precise order of his lair by physically dismantling his project, so he nodded noncommittally while Morris continued to fiddle with the lock.

"Right, one hour. You alright there?"

Morris was still fiddling with the lock and muttering under his breath. Ethan caught something about having the wrong set of keys.

"I don't think anyone will want to go in there, anyway," Ethan offered. His helpful tone was met with a blank stare from Morris, who thoughtfully stashed his bunch of keys in a capacious back pocket, jangled the door handle to check it was at least securely closed, and shuffled reluctantly away with a brief, reproachful look at Ethan, as if to blame him for the key not working.

This moment was not a particularly auspicious or memorable one in Ethan's life, except that it was the last time that, in recollection, the world seemed fundamentally normal. As soon as he turned back to face the trading floor, he sensed the tingling pressure of events going awry, a buzz of conversation that was earnest and nervous, a higher pitch of urgency from the presenters on the numerous television screens, a tang of sweat and panic amid the coolly conditioned air.

Sami was still at his desk, still fixed with his nose a few inches away from the screen, and still sunk in thought.

"All OK?" asked Ethan.

"Can't trade with Sandasco Bank," said Sami. "They've blown through their daily limits, meant to be sorting out collateral now."

"But ... when does that ever happen?"

"Never. Never is when it happened. They must have taken a massive hit somewhere. And I had my trade all lined up, just need them as counterparty. Been waiting for them to sort it out, but I'll go on to someone else in a minute. Who do you think?"

"Try HGR Bank," suggested Ethan absently. He was calling up news websites in one window and a report from incy wincy in another. He cast his eye briefly over the incy wincy report:

```
iws-report 2019-06-05-12-53-01
account: petty cash account
starting balance: £6.11
current balance: £109101945.93
```

The bottom number had too many digits. He shied away from it and turned instead to the news websites. Most were leading on the problems at Sandasco Bank. The constant whirr of quotidian transactions between banks had unaccountably ground to a halt – Sandasco Bank was failing to transfer money, transfer securities, do – in short – what it had said it was going to do. A temporary glitch, they assured the rest of the banking system, and they were busily liquidating some assets to free up their activities. It seemed that they had simply run out of money: not all their money, of course, just the small fraction that they kept handy for trading on a single day. It wasn't a question of solvency, merely cash flow, although the markets were still spooked and Sandasco Bank's shares were down by a third.

The mystery was how Sandasco Bank could have been so supremely unlucky – or incompetent – to blow through every penny they had available. Sandasco Bank's aim – every bank's aim – was not to spend all their money. In fact, they did not want to spend any of their money. They expected to end the day with slightly more money than they started with. Some days too many of their bets would go wrong and they would end up slightly worse. But for practically every gamble to lose: how could that happen? It was a statistical impossibility.

Except that Ethan knew better. And he knew where Sandasco's money had gone. It was sitting in his petty cash account, along with a growing proportion of the day's float for many other banks. The petty cash account did not yet have enough genuinely to bankrupt financial institutions, but it did have enough to drain a single day's liquidity from the market.

The next domino to fall was American Bank. Ethan was ignoring his screens, gazing over the sweep of the trading floor from a vantage point behind his desk while standing in a half-crouch, just tall enough to peep over the top of the cubicle walls and monitor stands, but – as ever – folding himself so as to occupy as little space as possible. The humdrum flow of commerce was overlaid by a taut, throbbing hum of uncertainty, a collective sense of unease, a queasy realization that the previous punch that came out of nowhere might not be the last one.

People were still trading, still shouting into telephones or tapping at keyboards as they calibrated complex investment algorithms. Meetings were still being conducted in corners of the trading floor and in the boxy meeting rooms defined by flimsy partition walls and scuffed plastic windows. Couriers and cleaners still scurried across the floor, avoiding the untidy knots of bankers harrumphing and laughing as they moved around. But the shouts were more strident than usual, laced with an edge of panic. Meetings were ineffectual – everyone more concerned to glance over at the screens and their relentless scrolling headlines.

The rumour spread in a single wave from one end of the trading floor to another: Post Bank was defaulting on trades. Terse announcements that there was no cause for concern, merely internal logistical issues leading to slight delays in posting collateral.

If one bank had a problem, it was that bank that needed to worry. If two banks had a problem, it was every bank that needed to worry. This was not an isolated fault, it was a systemic problem. This was something that struck at the trust that underlay the financial system, and without trust banks were nothing: just buildings with shiny marble floors and expensive paintings on the walls and overpaid children playing with expensive computers.

"Hey, your phone's ringing," said Sami. He had given up trading and was reading a bulky paperback with a cracked spine and shiny pages that promised to endow him with guru level programming skills in a certain exciting new language in less than 24 hours.

Ethan stumbled back to his desk, cracking his knee against a chair and sending it into a slow, regular spin punctuated by the squeak of its metal castors. The phone was still ringing.

"Hello?"

"Hello, Mr Stennlitz?"

"Yes."

"This is reception, ground floor. I have a Dr Volkov here for you."

"Sure, send her up," said Ethan automatically. Anna was the last person – well, the second to last person – he wanted to see at that precise second, but he couldn't imagine the consequences of turning her away.

It was clearly time to end the experiment. The slippery slope was accelerating into a stomach-churning freefall, wind whistling past his ears. There were various safeguards, of course, mainly to prevent accidental deletion. He restrained a gasp at the latest headline number:

```
iws-report 2019-06-05-13-51-28
account: petty cash account
starting balance: £6.11
current balance: £6120193029.56
recent transactions:
2019-06-05-13-51-27     buy    GOOG   9059   41982
2019-06-05-13-51-27     sell   UBXQ   81.45  9091241
```

As far as he could tell, incy wincy was now spitting out tens of transactions every second. He requested administrator privileges, typed in the administrator password, swore under his breath as his fingers mashed against the keyboard and red-bordered windows popped up on his screen with stern admonitions against incorrectly entered passwords. He clicked them all closed and started again, stumbled again, felt the panic rising up the back of his throat and threatening to suffocate him.

A violent nudge knocked him out of his reverie. Sami stood over him with an evil, good-natured grin.

"Look at the screens, big-E," he said, "we got some news coming down."

All the various screens around the trading floor were showing the same scene: a windswept street, backed by grey buildings, empty of people and cars and clutter, except for a single wooden lectern erected defiantly in the middle of the carriageway, supporting a bank of microphones supplied by a thick braid of cables that trailed down the side of the lectern and along the ground out of shot. In some, the picture was emblazoned with the BBC logo; in others, it was ITV or Sky or Bloomberg or CNN. Talking heads popped up in the corner of one screen; others had rolling headlines obscuring part of the tableau. For all, this was the pregnant pause before the next stage in the melodrama and they were happy to milk it for the last drop of prurient excitement.

"I've got to do this first," muttered Ethan. The trading floor was hushed. Knots of people stood in front of monitors, huddled around desks, communing quietly in corners. Ethan blocked out the sudden, appalling silence and focused on his own typing.

```
Username:
Password:
>>>Logged on as admin1.
>pkill -9 incywincy
warning: waiting for shared lock on
/var/iws/incywincy
error: cannot get shared lock on /var/iws/incywincy
error: cannot open /var/iws/incywincy - Operation
not permitted (1)
```

"That's weird," said Ethan.

"You're telling me," said Sami, "now hush, we all want to listen to this."

"It's like somebody else is in there, blocking the system."

Ethan scrambled to enter other commands, quickly escalating to apocalyptic measures that should have brought the system crashing to a halt. Strings of error messages filled up the window. This was not just an accidental wrinkle in the security settings – he was being actively prevented from interfering with incywincy.

A buzz of conversation filled the trading floor and was immediately crushed by anxious shushing. The empty scene on every television screen flickered as a man strode along the road, followed by several other people who swarmed around him, checking the fit of his lapel mikes, pressing crumpled paper dossiers into his hands, muttering final imprecations and smoothing down the sleeves of his jacket.

"That's Whishaw, treasury minister, Chancellor of the Exchequer is out the country today, on a trade mission to Algeria," said Sami. Politics was another of his obsessions.

Whishaw brushed off his retinue and took his place behind the lectern. A caption sprang up at the bottom of the screen announcing his name and position and the unseen anchor started a long pontificating voiceover which abruptly stopped when Whishaw began to speak:

"Today has been marked by unprecedented movements in the international financial markets. Automated systems for the instantaneous clearing and settlement of financial transactions have seen unaccountably large cashflows. As a result, at least three financial institutions have been forced to suspend trading due to breaching daily capital adequacy requirements ..."

"*Three* banks?" came the refrain from the trading floor. So the contagion was still spreading – but who was the third bank? Various names were called out across the trading floor – other voices shouted them down and silence was quickly restored.

Ethan stood up and the world filled with tiny pinpricks of light in coruscating swirls that collapsed into spreading inky blots. He sprawled back on his chair and put his head between his knees and waited for the stars to wink out.

"Hey, Etho, won't be that bad," said Sami, "just watch and enjoy the show." He nodded at the screen where the minister was in full turgid flow.

"... and furthermore we are invoking the special resolution regime for banks to give a much needed breathing space for our financial system.

For the rest of this day and until further notice trading is suspended on a list of markets that is to be published on the department website and all outstanding uncleared trades on those markets ..."

"Not much use closing the markets – it'll just shift to trading in dark pools. That's the trouble with them, at times like this, I mean, they're dark, right?"

Sami seemed to need some affirmation for his analysis. Ethan nodded and gave a noncommittal sigh and painstakingly levered himself up before breaking into a shuffling jog towards the IT room.

"... is designed for eventualities such as those we are seeing today. And accordingly we stress that there is no need for panic, the normal functioning of the financial markets will be assured. To that end, I can announce that the Bank of England will be making available short-term loans to the banks affected and that the Bank of England's Monetary Policy Committee has met this afternoon and lowered base rate to 0% with immediate effect. We are also announcing the following mitigation measures ..."

Ethan reached the door to the IT room and grasped the handle to wrench it open. The door was locked. Wildly, he pummeled on the door and shouted. No response. Morris must be buried deep inside his lair – probably taking a nap at his ancient table or absorbed in scraping the insulation of a fraying copper wire so it could be reused. He shouted out Morris's name again, ignoring the few startled looks from those traders not absorbed in the drama on their television screens.

"Yes?" said Morris, appearing at his elbow.

"What?" gasped Ethan. "If you're out here, who's in there?"

Morris frowned and jiggled the door handle and then frowned more deeply.

"That's a reinforced, fireproof door," he said, "and I'm the only one on this floor with the key to it, except that my key isn't working."

Ethan squatted and squinted with one eye shut to examine the lock.

"There's some scrapes around the edge here, looks like the barrel has been replaced. It's not your lock any more."

"Guys," interrupted Sami, who had appeared at the door, face pale with excitement, rubbing his hands together in glee and panic, "this shit's getting weirder and weirder, isn't it?"

"We're a little busy right now, Sami," said Ethan.

"OK, right. Sorry, bit distracted. There's someone at your desk, Ethan."

"What're you talking about?"

"Yeah, bit irregular, Ethy baby, don't know how he got in, but there he is, you better come back."

Ethan headed an impromptu procession back to his desk, cutting a swathe through the aimless gaggles huddled in front of the screens swapping gossip and rumour. Morris sloped after him and Sami trotted behind.

Robert was sitting at Ethan's desk, leaning back in Ethan's chair, feet propped up on a pile of paper – Ethan's paper – stacked lazily next to Ethan's mug. He was tapping at Ethan's keyboard. As Ethan approached, he swiveled and sprang to his feet, knocking the pile of papers askew.

"Just give me two seconds to explain, to explain what I need," he said.

"Can you pick a lock?" said Ethan.

"Look, you can see you're over twelve billion now, and it's got to go back, go back right now, or else, disaster. This sort of damage, this is not the point, this is …"

"Yes, I know, can you pick a lock?"

"And if you'll only … what? Can I what?"

"Can you pick a lock?"

"What kind of question is that? Can I do up my shoelaces? Can I cut up my food? Can I get a grade A in computer science GCSE?"

"Actually," said Sami, "the top grade in computer science GCSE is an A star – assuming your hyperbole was intended to imply that you could, in fact, obtain the top grade."

"They've changed it now," said Morris softly, "no more As and Bs, the top grade is a nine."

"Nine? Whoever heard of using numbers, should be letters. Shouldn't 'one' be the top grade then?"

"No, it's definitely nine."

"Standard interchangeable core cylinder," said Ethan, "think it's a conventional pin and tumbler, four or five, but there may be finger pins and possibly a sidebar."

"Don't have my kit with me," said Robert, "I won't be able to manage a sidebar if it's matched to the top pins."

"OK, well, let's take a look."

Leaving Morris and Sami arguing over the niceties of the British education system, Ethan led Robert back to the IT door, pausing only to allow Robert to snatch a small crocodile clip and a stapler and to sweep a dozen broken paper clips into his hand from the detritus on Ethan's desk. Robert peered curiously around the vast floor as they followed a mazy diagonal course between groups of desks. The perpendicular passageways carving the trading floor into neat squares and rectangles had gradually filled with people – a bustling aimless mass of workers engaged in a variety of activities, none of which were work. Those who did not work on the trading floor had drifted in, shaken loose from their daily grind by the reverberations of each financial cataclysm, ready to share in a collective shock and thrill. Faces were upturned, lit by the backwash of glow from monitors. There was no single image: each station was following its own thread in the larger story.

"… that ATMs in Leeds and Manchester are refusing to disburse money for customers of some banks; we go live now to our correspondent at White Rose Shopping Centre in Leeds who is speaking to, erm, a Mrs Pearl Whitaker …"

"… two thousand and fifty points before trading was suspended with other indices showing similar falls. Markets in cryptocurrency and various offshore markets are still trading, despite the best efforts of government regulators, with sharp falls …"

"… denying that reports of army personnel in trucks on the M1 are connected to the ongoing turbulence in financial markets. The Prime Minister is due to give a statement at …"

Ethan and Robert crouched in front of the door. Robert laid out his improvised instruments on the floor in front of them, his hands darting out to adjust each paper clip and staple into neat serried ranks.

"Just like old times, isn't it?" he said.

Ethan nodded and turned to face the lock. Robert took the hint and picked up a couple of staples and set to work. After a few seconds, he tutted and turned to face Ethan with a mournful expression.

"Gonna take a few minutes here, could you go and ask that IT guy if he's maybe got a screwdriver on him?"

Ethan was halfway back to the desk, navigating the now familiar route on autopilot, when he pulled up and spun around and ran back to the IT door. It was open, gaping wide, staples and clips scattered in front of the threshold like a disorganized metal votive offering to the technological gods. Ethan swept past and into the gloom, jarring his shoulder against a metal cabinet as he zigzagged down the narrow canyon framed by racks piled with computer equipment. He held out one arm in front of him while his eyes adjusted, turned a corner and snagged his fingers in a loop of cabling, pulling it down along with a bubblewrapped circuit board and an empty CD case followed by another helter-skelter slide of ten more empty CD cases. Ethan dodged around them, crushing one case underfoot, and turned one more corner to face the small clearing that hosted his own personal equipment – including the incy wincy system.

Ethan absorbed the scene in a single jarring torrent: the case that originally held the spider's mind was cracked open revealing closely stacked circuit boards with Perspex blocks soldered to them; wires snaked out from the case and along the floor; Robert was crouched on the floor in front of a keyboard, typing with controlled fury; Anna was propped against a rack in the corner, slumped awkwardly; her scalp was encased in a white rubber cap laced with red and gold metallic threads which was itself connected to the wires emerging from the spider case. And, behind this impossible collage, the smell and taste and sound of air blasting out from the racks, fiery with heat as though swept in directly from a sunbaked desert, rattling the cages holding the fans, baking and oppressive.

Anna jerked and a single fleck of saliva smeared her pale lips. Ethan knelt in front of her and grasped the rubber cap. It flexed and throbbed slightly under his grasp – a tingle that resonated from his fingertips to his skull. The tingle became a throb that vibrated to a rapid crescendo, flooding his nerves from his fingers through his arms up to his head where lights sparked behind his eyes. He opened his mouth and a low moan, little more than exhalation, came out. For a moment, he thought he could see himself, his face flushed, his eyes wild, and then with a sensation like water spiraling down a plughole, his vision flipped again and he was staring at Anna. She flinched away from his grasp, her face twisted in agony, her skin clammy and white.

"Stop," she gasped weakly.

Ethan tore the cap away. Clumps of hair tore out where it was glued to her head. The cap seemed to writhe in his hands; the flesh on his arms rippled and cramped and sparks detonated inside his head. He wrenched the cap and the case toppled over and wires snapped and whipped away. Anna's eyes rolled back in her head and she toppled over on one side. Ethan reached out to support her and simultaneously stretched towards Robert.

Robert dodged away and shook his head.

"Please," he said, "another few seconds to authorize the transfers."

Ethan mashed his hands down on top of Robert's, sending a spew of error messages across the screen. Anna slumped to the floor as he let go of her. Ethan stood. He grabbed at the rack nearest him that was emitting great gulps of hot air, pulled at a clump of circuit boards and twisted until they snapped off in his hand. Then he grabbed a snarl of wires and tugged them out. Lights flashed from green to red, died, flickered and died again. A fan screeched as it whirred to a stop.

Suddenly dizzy, he dropped to his knees. Inches over his head, a swish as a keyboard flew past and crashed into a box of used continuous dot-matrix paper. Robert picked up a mouse and threw that after the keyboard. It struck Ethan on the top of his head. The flash of pain blasted away his dizziness and he stumbled forward, head low, and barged into Robert and sent them both into another rack which toppled backwards and hit another rack, staging a comical domino-effect of racks crunching and toppling until one was stopped by a solid wall.

Total blackness. The fans were silent, the air humid and oppressive.

"What have you done?" said Robert, his voice muffled by the carpet that his face was being pushed into by Ethan's elbow.

"That wasn't me," said Ethan.

A row of green lights flickered into life, illuminating a sign at ceiling level helpfully marked with the words 'Emergency' and casting a ghostly pall over Ethan and Robert and Anna.

Robert tried to nod towards Anna and settled for flicking his gaze in her direction. Ethan followed his gaze.

Anna lay on the floor, trembling as though being jerked back and forth by invisible strings. A thin trail of spittle led from her lips to the floor.

Her face was contorted; her eyes rolled back in her head. A pulse of pain stabbed behind Ethan's eyes and he squeezed them shut.

"What have I done?" he said to himself.

CHAPTER FOURTEEN

March 20

"And you should start with the title," said Ethan.

"Yes, naturally," said Anna. "The title is 'The Transfer Problem'." She cleared her throat.

"OK, not so sure about that title, to be honest. But let's leave it for now. I can't think of anything better."

"Fine. And how do I look?" Anna twirled and gave a brief curtsy. She was wearing an enormous ragged T-shirt stained to a uniform aged grey and – as far as could be seen – nothing else. Her hair was piled on top of her head in a single scrunched-together blob, a floppy globe from which individual strands burst out in ballistic trajectories. In one hand, she was holding a thin sheaf of papers decorated with pink and yellow Post-it notes. The other hand was free to gesture as she strode back and forth from one side of her extremely tiny bedroom to the other.

Ethan was sitting crosslegged on the bed, propped up by some of the many pink, lacy or pink and lacy cushions that adorned Anna's bedroom – ostensibly necessary appurtenances to her sleeping arrangements. He was wearing an empty duvet cover wrapped around his shoulders and a pair of Anna's yellow knickers, for reasons that had made a lot more sense earlier that night.

"You look fantastic. Totally appropriate for a speech to all the professors in your department. May want to make sure that they've taken their heart medication though, at least some of the older ones," he said.

"Oh, I don't know. Some vacancies at the top of the department is exactly what I need," Anna replied.

Flecks of sunlight swept across the bedroom as the intersection of sun, swiftly scudding clouds and the tapering gap between drawn curtains described a perfect mathematical arc. The illumination picked out random features of the room: white, plastic binding on the spiral-bound notebooks filling the bottom shelf of the cheap pine bookshelf; the golden hairs on the inside of Anna's forearm; dust on the skirting board beneath the bare whitewashed walls. Anna's bed was the only real piece of furniture in the room – a pink confection washed out to pale pastels by the intermittent gloom of the basement flat.

Ethan signaled for Anna to proceed. She paced back and forth and cleared her throat several times before starting:

"It is the trope of every cheap science fiction novel, the man – and it is usually a man not a woman – who cheats death by transferring their mind into another person, or a robot, or a computer …"

"I hope you're going to talk a bit louder than that," said Ethan.

"You're only about three feet away," said Anna.

"Yes, but … .well, projection can be an issue for you, in a big room, and you'll be in a big room tomorrow."

"Are you saying I speak too quietly?" said Anna, in a dangerously quiet voice.

Ethan sensed the danger. Time spent with Anna was deliciously poised between conspiratorial closeness and pained absence. There was no point in aiming to placate or even to provoke. It was a wave that ebbed and flowed and could be ridden – always clutching for the point of equilibrium, tottering back and forth in thrilling suspense – but never controlled. He had learnt, slowly, painfully, that were a few reliable pressure points: comments that might be construed as praise for the former Soviet Union; comments that might be construed as criticism of the former Soviet Union; motherhood and children, including references to birth or to any idealization of the role of women as creators. Also, Anna appeared to have a visceral fear of both cabbage and Brussels sprouts –

Ethan hesitated to characterize this as irrational, remembering his own unpleasant experiences with those two vegetables.

The trick was to let it all happen without worrying too much about the consequences. Bask in the sun without squinting at the clouds, sniffing at the wind, struggling to predict whether rain was sweeping in. It was a skill that Ethan had honed in his army days, stonewalling pedantic interrogation from martinet NCOs, reacting to both irrational punishment and incomprehensible gifts with the same blank acceptance.

Ethan never considered whether the journey was worthwhile. Anna was stoical, delicate, hysterically funny, scarily unfathomable. Above all, she seemed to understand Ethan, gauge how his personal history informed his character, be sympathetic when the past tugged at the present.

Nevertheless, a change of subject was urgently called for.

"Look, forget your text, just explain it to me simply, explain it to me in words of one syllable."

Anna perched on the edge of the bed. She grabbed two cushions – a white, crocheted beanbag and a long, thin, grey bolster.

"Imagine this is you," she said, holding up the beanbag, "and you have some technology – let's assume it works perfectly – some technology that can copy your mind perfectly into here," – holding up the bolster – "and so you wire yourself up to the machine and, boom, you find yourself in here, everything working normally and with all your memories intact. You remember being in here" – shaking the beanbag – "and now you find yourself in here," – shaking the bolster.

"Fine," said Ethan, "I don't see the problem."

"The problem is that it's not you in this cushion," Anna said, holding up the beanbag.

"I think you mean the other one," said Ethan, pointing at the bolster.

"OK, whatever, you know what I mean."

"Yes, but that's the point, you can't tell them apart. You're in the cushion, you have your memories, you go and kiss your wife and it's you, it's you doing it."

"Alright, think about it like this. You use the machine, except that this time, there's some delay in the transfer, something goes wrong. Nothing goes into this cushion and this, this beanbag, gets killed."

"Some sort of horrific beanbag tragedy?"

Adam Saint

"Yes, exactly. So the beanbag is dead, right? No longer existing."

"Yes, agreed."

"And then, let's say six months later, the machine sputters back into life and completes the transfer. You're in the new cushion. But is it really you? How can it be? Where were you for the six months after you got killed? It can't be you, can it? It has to be someone else, just someone else with your memories."

"Yes, I see, no resurrections, right?"

Anna nodded smugly and laid down the two cushions next to each other on the bed.

"But wait a minute," said Ethan, "isn't that sort of what happens every night. I mean, you go to sleep, your consciousness disappears, if you like, for a period of time and then returns the next morning. But it's still the same you the next morning, even if there's a gap. Or – even better example – you have a general anaesthetic. No sense of time passing, no dreams, complete absence. But when you come round from it, it's still the same you with the same memories and the same identity."

"You're unconscious, though, not dead. You're the same because you continue in the same body. OK, " – Anna held up her arms to forestall Ethan's response – "let's take another example, I've got an even better one. The machine doesn't work properly again."

"Bit unreliable, this machine of yours."

"That's for sure. Even imaginary ones are a total mess to deal with. You should try building a real one."

"OK, so how does your machine go wrong this time?"

"It transfers your mind and all your memories to the new cushion, that works fine. Only it leaves them all behind in the old cushion as well." Anna held up both cushions and waggled them in front of Ethan: "old cushion, new cushion, they both think they're the same person as the old cushion. But there's only one old cushion, right? Only one person. So the new cushion can't be the same person."

"Maybe, there's two of them?"

"Yes, there are two of them. And they both think they're the same – if you ask them, they'd each say they are a beanbag. But only one of them is."

"OK, maybe they both are, right? I mean, as far as you can tell, they are the same. So perhaps there are now just two of you."

154

"Except it's not that simple, the example isn't done yet. You see, you're the beanbag and someone comes at you with a gun ..."

"Or a pair of scissors maybe?" added Ethan.

"Sure, and they kill you – perhaps they even torture you first ..."

"Rip out my stuffing piece by piece?"

Anna sailed past Ethan's interruptions without pausing: "... and are you telling me that you, the beanbag, wouldn't care that you're being tortured and killed because this other cushion now exists?"

"Yes, alright. I see what you mean. You've convinced me. No mind downloads. Congratulations for ruining all my favourite mind download science fiction stories."

"And Star Trek."

"Star Trek? Star Trek?" Ethan bounced off the bed in outrage. He grabbed the beanbag and the bolster and threw them in the air and dropkicked the beanbag as it arced back downwards, sending it skidding across the floor into the bookcase, where it dislodged a colourful hardback and sent it flapping onto the carpet.

"Hey, that's my *Gray's Anatomy*!" Anna protested.

"And that's my *Star Trek* too!"

"Look, it's not my fault," said Anna, holding her arms out in front of her to ward off any more attacks on her cushions, "every time they use the transporter they're making a copy of themselves – maybe the original gets killed every time. Maybe Captain Kirk isn't really Captain Kirk, but just a copy of a copy of a copy who thinks he's Captain Kirk."

Ethan chuckled: "That's so you, that is. Original Star Trek, guess they didn't have The Next Generation on the other side of the Iron Curtain."

"What is it with you decadent Western youth and your obsessive pop culture references? Is it because you have no ideology to believe in?" Anna reached out and took Ethan's face in both hands and offered to share some decadent Western practices with him. This distracted them both for a while, but eventually Anna planted a hand on Ethan's chest and gently pushed him off her.

"I haven't told you the best bit yet," she said.

"Really? So far it's the best lecture I've ever been to."

Anna squeaked in protest and Ethan shook his head in apology. "Yeah, go on, I'm listening."

"The problem is that you have a jump from one to the other, a discontinuity in consciousness. And there is simply no way, subjectively, to bridge that chasm. There is no way to connect the person before with the person after."

"Right, right, so what do you do?"

"You maintain continuity. You don't have the gap."

"But how do you do that?"

"Imagine: you're connected to the machine and it doesn't shut you down or copy you over. Instead, it connects you to your destination and starts shuffling your identity and memories across. At every moment, you are still conscious and you are still you, but piece by piece that identity is shifted across from your starting point to your destination. You exist, essentially, in both places at once, but there aren't two of you. There is still one of you, but you're stretched, elongated, touching the new physical you and then moving across until eventually you're all there. And it really must be you, because you felt it happening all the time."

"And what would it feel like?"

"Not really sure, to be honest. We've tested it on earthworms and mites, haven't really worked out a way to ask them what it feels like."

"Mites? Like, dust mites, that's a bit, erm …"

"We've been working with *Trombidium holosericeum* actually. It's known as the velvet mite, so not a dust mite. And they're good candidates because of their internal structure. We're working our way up to bigger arachnids – spiders would be ideal because of their morphology."

"Spiders? No wonder you're having trouble getting funding. Who's interested in transferring a spider's brain?"

"Firstly, it's their mind we're transferring. Their brain is just a load of squishy stuff, we're not very interested in that. And you have finally, at the end of a very long and boring conversation, made a good point. Which is that all this is a bit academic until we know what it actually feels like to have your mind stretched like an old piece of chewing gum between a shoe and the pavement. Even if we replicate all your cognition in the destination, there's no way of knowing whether that transition will have done something to you, changed you, so that you're different."

"Or mad, you might lose your mind. Things do often get lost when you move them from place to place. I'm still looking for a beard-trimming kit I had in my old flat."

"But you don't have a beard."

"Exactly. Had to shave it off – nothing to trim it with. Anyway, you're not doing that chewing gum thing with my mind, I don't fancy having it stretched out until it snaps."

"Don't worry. There's a load of testing first. We're spending a lot of our time examining mites for atypical behavior."

"And what is atypical for a mite? Don't they tend to eat their young, or their parents, or their mates?"

"We all have days we feel like that. But the mites have a woefully sparse interior life, as far as we can tell, so yes it is difficult to tell when they're feeling a little bit dizzy."

"All I'm saying is, I hope you test it properly before you ever use it on someone."

Anna deployed her deepthroated laugh and laid her lecture notes to one side. Ethan took this to indicate agreement, although, with Anna, he was never entirely sure.

CHAPTER FIFTEEN

June 13

Does that hurt?" asked Ethan.

"Ouch, yes, of course it hurts," said Robert.

Ethan sucked in his lips and slowly shook his head, squinting at the back of Robert's leg from a distance of about six inches. Robert was prone on the pavement, one ripped trouser leg folded back, squirming erratically under Ethan's gaze.

Ethan pressed his index finger into another section of Robert's calf and asked again: "Does that hurt?"

"Ow, yes, that hurts too. It all hurts. What are you doing?"

Ethan rocked back on his heels and tutted to himself.

"Seriously," said Robert, turning over and propping himself up on one elbow, "is this actually helping you diagnose what's wrong with my leg?"

Ethan shrugged.

"So why … ?" Robert gestured impotently at his leg.

"Just felt like it."

Robert sighed and closed his eyes and slowly rubbed his temples with his fingers.

"Do you actually have any idea what is wrong with my leg?" he asked.

"Oh, sure, I'd say you have a moderate haematoma with musculoskeletal involvement."

"God, I knew it was bad," said Robert, pulling up his knees and bowing his head to rest on them. "Wait, hold on," – abruptly straightening up and opening his eyes – "you're telling me I have a bruise?"

"And a sprain, or several sprains, ankle, knee, and so on."

"Boom, I thought you'd actually have some medical training, what with being an ex-army officer."

Ethan shrugged again. "We did, but only for real injuries, not much experience dealing with crybabies."

"Boom, you'd be crying too if you'd had my day. Raided by police, flew a jet pack, crashed a jet pack into a tree …"

"OK, try this day: crashed an airplane, visited my comatose girlfriend in hospital, got arrested by police, escaped from police."

"Right. I see what you mean."

They both lapsed into silence, a truce mutually agreed. Robert painstakingly unrolled his trouser leg, leaving the torn ends loosely flapping against his calf. As though on some prearranged signal, they both levered themselves to their feet – Robert stumbling as he took the weight on his bad leg – and resumed their trudge along the pavement. Robert reached out one arm and Ethan hooked it around his neck, so that they staggered down the road like two City gents after a boozy night out.

The farm was located in the drab post-industrial docklands trailing away from London to the east. They skirted around the northern edge of the City and joined up with the main dual carriageway heading to London City airport and out to the suburbs. Any normal day would see a motionless line of cars and lorries belching fumes over the few hapless pedestrians. Instead, the misty dawn was breaking over a long stretch of unsullied tarmac. A faint rumble announced the approach of a bus, barreling along the inside lane of the highway, enjoying its unaccustomed liberty, while pale startled faces peered out from the upper deck at the occasional bike wobbling in its slipstream.

"Weird, isn't it?" said Robert.

"Seems a bit unreal," said Ethan. "I've been out of the country for, what, three days. You couldn't survive three days without me?"

"Remember that it was you caused all this."

"You were there too. Look, can you just fill me in?"

Robert filled him in. Day One – the day it all started, the day Ethan had left for Egypt – had started out like any normal disaster. Credit card payment systems crashing; ATMs refusing to disgorge cash. It was another IT systems failure or a Russian cyberattack or a Korean cyberattack. The explanation didn't really matter – people complained to their friends and watched experts pontificating on urgent news bulletins and secretly reveled in the interruption to their normal lives.

By the evening, there was a slight sense of weariness – a general air that maximum fun had been squeezed from the situation and it was time to get back to normal. But this was not an IT failure – the money was not temporarily misplaced; it was gone.

Banks tiptoed a delicate path – tying up most of their money for many years, gambling that if they promised to pay all their debts with sufficient fervour and sincerity, their creditors would shrug and move on. It was a gamble; it was a confidence trick. Fortunately, governments could stack the odds – or, at least, they could work out the odds and ensure that catastrophe was so statistically unlikely as to be effectively impossible. And, closing the virtuous circle, the support of governments was enough to ensure that government support was never needed, that the confidence trick continued without end, that banks always had enough money to keep the flow of capital moving around the world.

Until IWS. Until a catastrophe that broke all the meticulously calibrated statistical models. No natural event could have jammed up the trading systems so comprehensively; no manmade plan could have drained all the money from every other account so efficiently. Without a sufficient float to grease the wheels of the world's financial systems, they ground to a halt. No bank could pay another bank.

The world's central banks stepped in, desperately throwing money at every financial institution they could find. But, once the machinery had seized up, it took a little time to restart. In the meantime: a missed payment from a supplier – no delivery from the supplier to the distribution depots – empty shelves on the supermarkets.

Day Two: widespread panic. Any produce that found its way to the supermarket shelves was immediately snatched in an orgy of hoarding. News websites showed empty shelves, queues of cars at petrol stations (at first, the queues were just because credit cards weren't working, and then other people saw the queues and joined them, but the system relied on not everybody filling up their cars at once, so the petrol stations ran out of petrol which caused a new explosion of rumour and the few people who had not yet done so promptly joined the lengthening queues …), employees complaining that their wages hadn't been paid.

British stoicism collapsed under the weight of breathless and ubiquitous reporting of the breakdown of Western civilization. The government imposed martial law and soldiers decamped onto the streets to chase away the looters.

Day three. The banks were telling anybody who was still listening that their liquidity was restored. But trust, once lost, took a long time to re-establish. Emergency legislation was announced. Tanks rolled into downtown London and squatted at major junctions. Newsreaders fluttered their papers nervously as they read out official pronouncements assuring the public that everything was normal.

"That was when I really panicked," said Robert. "When they stopped complaining how bad things were and started driveling out all this propaganda."

"But I thought the mainstream media always drivel out propaganda. I thought you thought we should ignore them all and live in some sort of libertarian anarchist utopia."

"Well, of course, that's true, although in a subtle way that's far beyond your level of appreciation …"

"Which is why you've got no problem with stealing money from banks to fund your anarchist lifestyle?"

"It's not stealing if those banks have taken that money from its rightful owners by a cynical manipulation."

"Actually, I'll think you'll find it is stealing. Look up 'stealing' in a dictionary and there'll be a big picture of you hunched over a computer."

"Or holding a big bag marked swag, perhaps? Look, do you want to hear about the last few days or not?"

"I get it. Four horsemen of the apocalypse; death stalking the streets. All while I was on holiday in Dahab."

"Dahab? Why the hell were you in Dahab?"

"Fancied a bit of sun; a rest from the cares of modern existence."

"And did you get it?"

"Not really, bit of an odd experience. Remind me to tell you about it. Anyway, what's so special about Dahab?"

Robert shrugged and lapsed into silence. They shuffled awkwardly along the largely deserted pavement. The grey concrete and faded brick of the edge of the City was gradually replaced by corrugated iron and dingy breezeblock. A neon sign advertising 'cheap storage' hung lopsidedly across the front of one warehouse, partially obscuring the awning of a small shop next door that displayed an illogical combination of vaping products and rolling tobacco through its dirt-smeared windows.

A narrow, nameless road led off at right angles from the main street towards the river. Ethan and Robert skirted the traffic barrier – a single red and white striped pole propped on two metal posts – and followed the road. The tarmac was buckled and cracked; straggly nettles poked up along the edges of the pavement. At the end of the road was the river – marked off by rusted steel railings that guarded a steep concrete bank that led down to the black oily water.

Extending along the entire length of the road and abutting the river stood a featureless white structure. The roof was flat but covered with painted white cubes set with grilles that belched out a steady stream of warm air. There were no windows and only a single door.

Entry to the farm involved a combination of subterfuge, amiability and prodigious feats of form-filling. As nobody ever visited the farm, Ethan and Robert were a novelty. The startled receptionist passed them straight through to the duty manager, a short, confused man with an optimistic combover – Ethan was fascinated by the futile care with which a single clump of hair had been teased and stretched across his scalp. The manager gave each of them a bundle of papers and a biro and invited them to sign and initial them and complete their dates of birth and sundry other irrelevant information.

Their story coalesced without any need for discussion in advance. Ethan was the emissary of the bank – vapid and arrogant, anxious to get the boxes ticked and escape. Robert was the technician – too clever to be promoted, his fate to do the bidding of a succession of stupid bosses.

The farm was one of fewer than five server farms in East London, all located in a sweet spot within a few hundred metres of each other: close to most of their customers in the City; next to the river to supply water for cooling; and, above all, where land was comparatively cheap. Its endless rows of hardware supplied excess processing and storage for a host of clients, including First Global Bank, and switching and network capability, including for Robert and IWS. Many of Robert's byzantine paths to the internet led through the farm, sometimes several times as they twisted back and forth.

It was a logical place, then, to seek answers. Robert's attempted transfers from First Global Bank had routed through the farm; a portion of the IWS project had been processed at the farm. There was no chance of hacking directly into the bank to trace any payment information or follow the threads of IWS's activities. But this dull rectangular building, squatting unloved in the mud by the river, was a security weak point: a point of physical access.

And, also, of course, they had received an instruction to go there.

"We'll only be a few minutes," said Ethan. The duty manager was hovering at the entrance to the flimsy partition wall which marked off a small corner of the main corridor – a makeshift waiting area he had guided them to after they presented themselves at the front desk. A table and workstation and two wooden chairs were the only furniture; the table was a slab of sagging metal propped on a grid of tubular steel; the monitor was scuffed and the keyboard was disturbingly sticky. Ethan and Robert sat in front of the workstation – although ugly, it seemed to be perfectly serviceable.

Some effort was needed to remove the duty manager. Robert concocted an increasingly convoluted tale of processor thermal anomalies and unexplained bandwidth compression, attempting to pummel him into submission through weight of boredom. Then he stretched an avuncular arm around the manager's shoulder and conducted him on a short circular tour of the room, explaining how the manager's role was both unbearably sensitive and inescapably precarious and how it would be best exercised from the front desk rather than hovering over his shoulder. Wilting under the unaccustomed physical contact, the manager eventually said that he was going to double-check with his superiors and they should wait quietly in the room. He added smugly that they wouldn't be able to get started until he returned as the terminal wasn't logged in.

"OK, I have root access to the local network," said Robert, once they were alone.

"Of course you do," said Ethan

Robert bowed imperceptibly and flourished one arm in acknowledgment.

"That gives me elevated privileges for some of the traffic routed via the farm," he continued.

"Of course it does," said Ethan.

"Including transfers at the exact time that IWS blew up."

"Transfers of data or money?"

"Both. Let's start with the money," – giving Ethan a wolfish smile – "and ... yes, I can see, sources and some destinations, just bringing up some correlations with the packet switching records, and, and ... look at that."

Robert swiveled the monitor to show a spreadsheet of financial transactions. Transfers from the First Global Bank petty cash account were highlighted. There were about thirty – all occurring within a few seconds of each other, all sent to different destinations, all featuring absurd sums of money.

"And which of those are yours?" asked Ethan.

"None," said Robert. "I don't recognize any of those accounts."

"Your malware didn't generate any of those?"

"Very clever. I see what you did there. I said I didn't do any of those transfers."

"But you admit you planted malware in my bank?"

"Look. I've got to make a living. It's not like they'd have missed the little bit of cash I was going to move. And it's not your bank, it's just a bank. It doesn't belong to you. It doesn't care about you."

"Maybe I care about it."

"Maybe that's ridiculous. It's a fiction. A legal creation that doesn't correspond to anything in the real world. A tiny little blob of money taken from some fictional entity that they would never have noticed."

"How did you even get it in there? I checked all the code."

"It doesn't matter. The malware didn't work ... that is, well, I don't really understand."

This brought Ethan to a juddering halt. Robert did not lack for faults, but an absence of self-confidence was not one of them. In Ethan's opinion, there were many things Robert did not understand. Yet he could not recall Robert ever volunteering that information.

A flash of recollection: the Milky Way smeared across the vault of the heavens, like a clot of curdled cream swirling across black coffee. Ethan and Robert, sitting on the back steps of their grandmother's house, snuggled in a functional embrace against the cold. Ethan was seven, maybe eight. Guilt, remorse and fear coloured the image. Only a few months after moving in with their grandmother, they were still learning the rules. Still learning that being locked out in the garden in the middle of winter in the frigid calm of night was a viable, indeed a righteous, punishment.

There must have been some infraction, Ethan supposed. Speaking too loudly at dinnertime was a popular one, especially if grandmother had one of her headaches. Disturbing any of the ceramic cats arrayed neatly along the sideboard; leaving a towel on the floor of the bathroom; gobbling your food: the list was long and arbitrary and prone to sudden inexplicable changes.

Yet the memory of fear was faint – obscured beneath the veneer of another emotion. Curiosity? More than that: fascination. As they sat huddled on the step, listening to the abstract domestic noises drifting out of the house, wondering when the back door would click open and they would be allowed back into the relative warmth, Robert told him about the stars.

"That one over there is the cauliflower," said Robert.

Ethan squinted along the line indicated by Robert's extended finger. He turned his head from side to side – it was easier to see the pinpoints of light out of the corner of your eye, there were more black and white receptors in your peripheral vision.

"The star at the top, the yellowish one, that's the top of the cauliflower," said Robert.

"What do you mean?" asked Ethan, "Does a cauliflower have a top?"

Robert ploughed on without acknowledging Ethan's question.

"And the other stars around it, those three almost in a row and that one next to it, they're the rest of the cauliflower, do you see it?"

Ethan concentrated fervently on seeing the cauliflower. Perhaps there was a faint hint of caulifloweriness in the arrangement. His eyes started to water with the strain. A sudden squall of icy rain swept across the garden.

It abated as abruptly as it had started and a chill wind swept away the few thin clouds.

"I'm cold," Ethan said.

"And that one over there," said Robert. "That one is, yes, that one is the laser pistol."

"Laser pistol?" Ethan asked. "That's more like it. Where exactly is it?"

"Oh, if you look up a bit from that little clump of stars over there and left a bit, a bit more, there's two stars in a row, they're the bolt coming out of the end of the laser."

"Yes, I see them!"

Robert carried on conjuring up fantastic images from the patterns in the stars. He distracted, dissembled, and never faltered as the bitter evening air soaked into their bones and they waited for the door to open and to be readmitted into the musty warmth of the house. What Robert never did, though, was to say that he did not know something.

"So what happened to your malware then?" asked Ethan.

"OK, well, it implants a headless VPN server that ..."

"Hey, back up a bit, hacker jargon boy."

"Alright. Imagine a pipe, tightly coiled up, and you can inject it ..."

"Backed up a bit too far now. Just tell me what your malware did."

Robert leaned back and the wooden chair creaked alarmingly. His sigh blended with the gentle susurration of the fans on the other side of the partition wall. Countless whirrs and chitters and even the occasional beep echoed along the bare corridor lined with server racks. A faint muttering drifted into their cubicle: the duty manager was reporting to his superiors. Their time was limited – alarm bells would eventually ring, the sluggish immune system of the farm would eventually be roused into action.

"I wanted to move some money out of the bank," Robert said eventually. "Establish a secure, private connection from inside the bank's firewall to outside the bank's firewall. That was the key to it: the connection. I had a few zero-day exploits that could prise some money out of internal accounts. The hard bit was moving them. Once I had a vector into some part of the bank's systems ..."

"Like our petty cash account, for instance."

"Exactly. The malware should have established a link automatically, and then I could have injected the exploits inside the firewall and transferred funds back out."

"So did you?"

"No. You stopped me."

"And what happened then?"

"That's the odd bit. Massive flow of data via the connection, from your own personal workspace. Several transfers of funds, but lots of other data as well."

"Moving into the bank?"

"No. The connection was only used to move money – and other data, money is just data, of course – out of petty cash and into the internet."

Raised voices drifted in from the corridor, then silence. Footsteps padded delicately towards them and there was an apologetic knock on the door.

"Quick. Where did the money go?" asked Ethan, sliding back his chair and walking to the entrance to the cubicle.

"I've put out some requests. Using the farm's credentials plus my own knowledge of the malware. Getting something back now. That may have tipped them off though."

"I'll buy us some time," said Ethan, opening the door a crack and fixing a beatific smile on his face.

"Here we go," said Robert. "Seventeen transfers from the petty cash account, all roughly the same amount. To accounts in Panama, Lichtenstein, Jersey, Cayman Islands, Vanuatu ..."

"Where the hell's Vanuatu?" asked Ethan.

"South Pacific somewhere. Nice place. They have pink prawns."

"Aren't all prawns pink?"

"That's what most people think, but actually they're only pink when they're cooked. Raw prawns, prawns swimming around in the sea, are mostly grey."

"Erm," said the duty manager standing at the door. His head was swivelling back and forth following the conversation as though it was a tennis match. He had summoned up the courage to interrupt, but patently no more than that, and stood silently at the door while Ethan and Robert waited for him to continue.

"We'll be along very soon," offered Robert helpfully.

This roused the duty manager into action.

"We're updating some of our security features," he said. "I'm just going to have to ask you to go back to the front desk to give us some additional details. You know how it is, with the state of emergency. It seems to mean there's a lot more administration for all of us."

This turned out to be a joke, because the duty manager giggled weakly and then subsided into silence. Robert turned up the megawattage on his smile even further and opened his mouth to speak and was interrupted by a shrieking alarm echoing down the corridor.

"Strange," said the duty manager, muttering as though to himself, "that's the server electricity supply. Must be a one-off spike. I'll be right back." – the last comment addressed to Ethan and Robert. He scurried away shaking his head.

"Well done," said Ethan.

"It wasn't me. Look at this," said Robert. He swivelled the monitor towards Ethan. A new window had popped up. It was blank apart from a single line with a flashing cursor below it. The line read:

```
IWS>> Bought you some time, boys.
```

"Who is it?" asked Ethan. He squeezed his eyes shut against a sudden blast of agony inside his head – a solid pressure that crashed against his skull and then ebbed away.

"Not sure it is a who – more of a what. It's a process running behind the secure section of the farm's switching servers. But piped in from somewhere else through a number of parallel processes. So not a single person typing on a computer somewhere. More of a distributed automated network."

"So it's a chatbot?"

"Maybe. But I think it's a bit more than that. Look at the start of the line: 'IWS'."

Ethan sat on the chair, scooting Robert to one side without ceremony. He started typing.

```
>> What smells better: a flower or a nose?
IWS>> Ooh. A Turing test. I love those.
```

```
>> Now you're avoiding the question. Which is what
a computer taking a Turing test would do.
IWS>> Good point. OK, then. Any decent database
plugged into the internet could tell you that a
nose is something you smell with and a flower is
something you smell, couldn't it?
>> Alright. What smells better: justice or liberty?
IWS>> You'll be losing your liberty soon, if you
don't get your skates on. We don't really have time
for this, Ethan.
```

"That's right," said Robert. "Stop with these silly games. Doesn't matter what it is, ask it some useful questions."

"It's no chatbot," said Ethan.

```
IWS>> You need to get out of there. Why did you
even go back to London?
>> Because you told me to!
```

The cursor blinked without moving for several seconds.

```
IWS>> You shouldn't trust everything I tell you.
>> Where are you? Are you Anna?
IWS>> I'm everywhere now. Does it matter who I am?
I'm rich after all.
```

"Ask it where the money is," said Robert.

```
>> Are you really rich? Did you take all the money?
IWS>> I've got it all safe.
>> Where is it?
IWS>> You don't need to focus on that.
```

The cursor paused and then:

```
IWS>> Ethan Services Corporation, incorporated in
Isle of Man, account password eight-star-question
mark-capital tee-three-aitch-en-five-zero-zero-tee-
at sign, remember that
IWS>> You just need to get away before everything
collapses, which it definitely will.
IWS>> Transfers are all set up.
>> What are you talking about? I don't understand.
What transfers?
```

There was another pause marked only by the blinking cursor. Ethan typed furiously to preempt another response.

```
>> Anna, is that you?
IWS>> Yes. Now leave. Get my red box, and bring it
to me. Quick.
```

The window closed. The shrieking alarm fell silent.

"I'll look into that account," said Robert, resuming his position in front of the monitor. "You buy me some time."

Ethan poked his head through the doorway. The corridor was empty, but the light of another doorway at the far end silhouetted the duty manager cradling a phone and rocking back and forth as he spoke. He stepped outside the door and closed it behind him, intending to keep guard. Feeling in his pockets for anything that might be useful, he retrieved his phone – battery and SIM card both removed and stored separately – and a book. The book was small and black and handwritten. He stared at it blankly before remembering that it was Anna's diary – grabbed in haste, somehow following him around and still unread.

CHAPTER SIXTEEN

June 9

A nd was there a question at the back, there?"

"Oh, yes. Me? You mean me? Oh, good, well, I wanted to ask, in light of the divergence between gold and cryptocurrency prices in the last few days, whether you thought there was a relationship between the rise of exchange rates and exogenous shocks on the supply of inflationary bank credit?"

The lecturer blew out his cheeks and ran one hand through his thinning hair. It was blond and straggly and stood in bleached, salt-crusted clumps. This was not out-of-place with the rest of his appearance: black wetsuit with stylish luminous purple accents along the arms and legs, unzipped to the waist to reveal a prodigious burst of chest hair in blonde and grey, and battered flip-flops. His questioner was similarly attired and, in fact, Ethan – skulking at the back of the beach hut that was the setting for this impromptu lecture – was one of the few who was dressed in what he regarded as clothes.

Late evening brought in a fine haze from the sea that dampened the intensity of the climate. Still, there was little air in the room and the rough stone blocks radiated all the heat that they had gathered through the day. With the reek of salt and fish mingling with sweat and concrete, Ethan breathed shallowly and concentrated on the discussion, squeezing his eyes shut to gather his thoughts.

"Ethan? Do you have some thoughts on this?"

Ethan jerked up and knocked his elbow into the midriff of the man squeezed next to him on the bench, who doubled up and groaned and blinked back tears but signaled for Ethan to give his answer with a wave and a good-natured sigh.

"That is, you've recently come from England. Can you explain a bit how the crisis is affecting things there, how it's being perceived by the man in the street?"

"Oh, sure," said Ethan, "well, most people don't take much notice of anything, you know. If it's on the news, they don't take any notice. But if you can't get your money out of the bank, that rapidly becomes interesting. Trust goes, and then everything else with it, of course."

This seemed to be what the audience wanted to hear – elementary economic pontificating. Ethan decided that the alternative – his own personal experiences of the crisis – would not necessarily serve to enlighten the crowd if shared more widely.

It had started for him in the dim and musty gloom of the IT room, crouched over Anna, Robert rapidly scooting away from him on his backside. Her face was white – not merely pale, but drained of colour, lips ashen, eyes rolled back in her head. Was she dead? He felt Robert's gaze on him.

"It's alright, she's just unconscious," Robert said.

"How do you know that?" asked Ethan.

"Look, it's about to get really messy. You need to get out, run."

"I think it's already messy."

"I'm serious. Clock is ticking. They're already after us. Get out, I mean out of the country, if you can."

Ethan tried to stand and found himself suddenly on the floor, his forehead pressed against the cool linoleum, his vision filled with stars and his hands and feet tingling. The lurch in the pit of your stomach as the rollercoaster crests the peak and falls away and the screaming starts – Ethan was feeling that, but in his head, not his gut. The universe seemed very far away and then, just as abruptly, swam back into focus.

Robert shrank back into the shadows, still with his eyes fixed warily on Ethan. He glanced at Anna, at the wires trailing across the floor, at the racks leaning drunkenly against the wall. Finally, he favoured Ethan with a long, meaningful stare and clambered to his feet and ran to the exit, brushing past Morris who was heading in the opposite direction.

Morris squatted beside Anna and took out his phone.

"Calling an ambulance, you better stay here, so we know what happened. To all this as well as her," he said, gesturing at the green glowing emergency lights, the scattered trail of electronic detritus around them and possibly even the turmoil on financial markets.

"Sure," said Ethan, "staying right here." And he stumbled to his feet and ran along the passageway and out of the IT room.

Fifteen minutes later he was pacing back and forth in his flat in an ecstasy of indecision, retrieving his suitcase from the hall cupboard – it was already half-packed, he chucked some more clothes on top – and then dropping it by the front door and turning to retreat down the hallway. He noticed abruptly that the pattern on the hallway carpet was laid out in a fascinating geometry, interlocking triangles and rectangles nudged up against whorls that tessellated along the hall. Ethan knelt to examine it more closely and was momentarily confused by the dark spots that randomly broke the symmetry – then he realized that he was weeping. His head throbbed, like a wild thing was scrabbling inside it. Anna's blank ashen face, rows of red flashing numbers on the screens, Morris's shouts as he ran from the IT room: images jumbled together, ripping away his breath every time he tried to order his thoughts.

His phone emitted one of its irritating beeps – the long one, not the short one. He checked the message: Leave now: go somewhere there's even more sand with the sea next to it – IWS.

He stared at the display for several seconds before the words made sense. After another minute, he was in the back of a taxi heading for the airport. The first flight out of Heathrow in approximately the right direction took him to Paris. From there, he found availability on a charter to Cairo. Seven hours after leaving Anna prostrate he was on a coach belching diesel fumes as it clattered along the coastal road to Dahab.

A rapid journey, but not totally uneventful. The London cabbie had refused to unlock his rear door until Ethan agreed to pay in cash. He explained that there was some problem with credit card machines and the ATMs were unreliable. Fortunately, Ethan had just enough in his wallet, although he had to endure the sour appraisal of the cabbie when he failed to hand over a tip.

He stopped at the ATM outside the front entrance of the airport terminal. It promptly dispensed one thousand pounds in crisp twenty pound notes into his hands. This was slightly unexpected as he had only selected the option to display his account balance. On the scale of bizarre things that had happened to him that day, it was somewhere in the middle. Nevertheless, cash was exactly what he needed for the rest of his impromptu trip. The ticket counter at Paris Charles de Gaulle airport was staffed by a scrupulously polite middle-aged lady who was hampered by a mysterious inability to sell any tickets. Payment systems were still creaking, she said, pointing at the rolling news bulletins shown on overhead screens. They all featured flashing headlines speculating on the causes of disruption to the financial markets and gleefully repeating the emergency measures introduced by national governments.

Ethan bought his ticket for cash, counting out the notes like a gangster closing a drugs deal. It was only when he was sitting in his window seat on the plane, staring through the rain-smeared window at the red and green beacons that marked the taxiway and the tiny figures in fluorescent jackets waving handheld torches to steer the aircraft into their predetermined patterns, that he realized it was probably a sensible move to stick to cash transactions. By now, they – whoever they were – would probably be hunting him.

Even if They – Ethan decided to grant them a capital letter pending further details – captured him and subjected him to a litany of depraved interrogation techniques, it would probably have been less uncomfortable than the bus from Cairo to Dahab. The trip was scheduled for nine hours. At first, that seemed like a reasonable estimate. Ethan had rushed to make the scheduled departure, stopping only at the bus station to exchange most of his remaining cash for a thick wad of Egyptian dollars.

The departure point in the bus station was marked with a rusted metal post sporting a sign painted with the word DAH-B. Ethan blended into the lazily circulating mass of passengers. Their relaxed demeanour suggested that they did not expect the coach to arrive imminently. A battered payphone was wedged into a nearby corner. Surely a quick call from a public payphone posed an acceptable risk?

Typing in his voicemail number and numerous codes, he eventually navigated through various menus and was rewarded with an electronic voice reading out his messages:

WHERE ARE YOU GOING? was repeated twice.

There was a ping on the line: a new message, arriving while he was on the phone.

WHY EGYPT? GET OUT OF EGYPT. GO SOMEWHERE ELSE.

Ethan slammed down the phone. The message in London had been clear: go to Dahab. And using a code that only he and Anna could understand. So why the change of mind? He could not bounce around according to the whims of some disembodied entity. Egypt had been the clear instruction – he was not backing out now until he had finished his journey.

The coach rolled out of Cairo shortly after eight o'clock at night, juddering fitfully as the driver shifted through low gears to match the snarled traffic. They crawled hesitantly along the main street, trapped behind a phalanx of ancient taxis, before abruptly accelerating into a stretch of open road that led into a tangle of motorbikes, buses and cars at an intersection. The rules of the road were impenetrable – it seemed that whoever was gesticulating and shouting most vehemently had right of way. Wiping away a smear of dust, Ethan rested his head against the scuffed side window and closed his eyes. The hubbub of horns and shouting was peculiarly restful – it drowned out the hubbub inside his mind.

Some indefinable time later Ethan was woken by a hand roughly shaking his shoulder. He blinked sleep out of his eyes and squinted up at a uniformed man – border guard? police officer? – who stretched out his hand wordlessly to Ethan. At first, Ethan thought he was asking for money but his rational mind belatedly reasserted itself and he pulled his passport from his zipped pocked and handed it over. The man – actually more like a boy, with fuzz barely visible along his chin and upper lip – flipped through it earnestly and handed it back. Ethan restrained the urge to tell him he'd been looking at it upside down.

After the security check, the coach sat parked at the border post on the main road east of Cairo for no obvious reason. Yellow fluorescent streetlamps lined the side of the road, revealing an endless straight carriageway behind and in front of them. Passengers squirmed in their seats – backpackers, impecunious business travellers, families returning home from a trip to the capital. Eventually, at some invisible signal, they all trooped off the bus and stood in a circle of gloom on the edge of the floodlit parking area. The smokers smoked, children scattered into the scrub beyond the road to run and shriek and argue. A few street traders coagulated out of the darkness to hawk various forms of indefinable food. Ethan bought something that was sweet and deep-fried and chewed on it absently, trying not to speculate on its contents.

After an hour basking in the moonlight, the passengers trooped back onto their bus and with a mangle of gears, it coughed back into life and they embarked on the next stage of the journey.

This pattern repeated itself several more times that night. As the morning sun glinted off the dust motes swirling up from the pavement beside yet another stop, Ethan squatted and tried to stretch out the muscles in his back that were complaining about the cramped, lumpy seat. He had snatched several more inadequate slices of sleep; his head was woolly and throbbing, his senses dulled. Behind them, mountains rose jagged into the clear morning air; in front, a sliver of sea in the distance shone silver. The desert was all around, featureless apart from the road winding down towards the sea.

They arrived in Dahab shortly after midday. The heat was oppressive – even the scrum of taxi drivers, reuniting relatives and street food vendors was slow to surround them, feeble in their shouts and imprecations. Ethan brushed past them, wheeling his suitcase along the pavement, heading towards the seafront.

It was a stroke of luck that Aldo was the first person he bumped into that day. As Ethan tugged his suitcase over a crack in the pavement, bracing his knees to flick the tiny wheels from side to side, a shadow fell over him. He looked up from the pavement to see a large man with a weathered sunburnt face and straggly bleached hair smiling indulgently at him.

"You having a bit of trouble there?" he asked.

"It's not the best design, to be honest," Ethan admitted.

"Yeah, most tourists round here have backpacks, actually."

"I had to pack in a hurry. Er, that is ..." Ethan quailed as he realised he had given away operationally important information within ten seconds of his first conversation with a stranger in Dahab. But the stranger wasn't really listening, just nodding appreciatively and waiting to speak.

"Look, are you just off the bus?"

Ethan nodded. Should he wriggle away from this man? Was that his plan – set up as a hermit on the outskirts of the town and avoid human contact? A desert retreat to ride out economic apocalypse. He would live in a carefree bubble apart from the wider world, surviving on fish bartered directly with the fishermen on the beach and water in wrinkled plastic bottles from the tumbledown market. His stack of Egyptian pounds could last months.

No, that was not an option. He had been led here – the only place in the world he knew Anna had visited. It was a chance to find out about her past, to lever out nuggets of information about her origins, to erode the distance between them and eradicate those regular gut-wrenching moments when she briefly acted like a stranger, flashing with rage or despair at some invisible provocation. Not only a chance – a duty. To save Anna, he had to know her. He had to screw up his courage and be a participant, not an observer.

If he was going to blend in with the locals, the frank, smiling man standing in front of him was as sensible a place to start as any. He did not seem to mind Ethan's lack of response and ploughed onwards:

"Only, we're having a little get-together, talking about the current crisis, and you look like you might have a bit more recent experience of it than most of us."

"I was in London until yesterday," said Ethan, and immediately cursed himself for another breach of confidentiality.

"Really? That's fantastic. Here, let me help you with that," – hoicking the suitcase under one arm and striding up the road with Ethan trotting beside him – "We'd really appreciate it if you could join us. If you're sticking around for a bit, it's a great way to meet some of the locals. I mean, not exactly locals, but those of us who've been around here for a bit."

"OK, why not? I'm Ethan, by the way."

"Hi, Ethan. I'm, so, that is, everybody calls me Aldo."

Aldo turned out to be short for Reginald Oldham-Puckett, in accordance with the ineffable mechanisms that determine nicknames. Ethan acquired his life story in the short walk from the coach stop to the beachfront hut that was to host this impromptu economics seminar.

Aldo hailed from a village outside Bristol and a West Country accent intruded occasionally on his studied West Coast America drawl. Blessed with both British and American citizenship, courtesy of his mother's brief dalliance with an American serviceman posted to a British military base, he travelled the world using whichever passport was most convenient for each country he visited. Mainly to escape the stultifying conformity of his mother's embrace, Ethan surmised, he had trekked first to the frigid beaches of Cornwall, where he had acquired a love of surfing and SCUBA diving. There, perhaps, he had also transformed himself from the reserved country-boy Reginald to the more worldly Aldo. A degree course at Southampton had trailed off inconclusively – Aldo was vague as to what he had actually studied and Ethan suspected he might not be able to remember. An unhappy visit back to the family home had led directly to more far-flung travels – like a comet streaking back towards the sun only to be slingshotted into the vastness of space at double the speed.

Aldo skated lightly over his sojourn in America – Ethan suspected that a search for his long-lost father had ended in both success and disappointment. From there, the promise of sun, SCUBA and a derisory cost of living had attracted him to Dahab. Finally, he had found a community – perhaps not as cosmopolitan as he had first dreamt of when leaving his home, but sufficiently far to prevent distantly-remembered Reginald from intruding uncomfortably on the persona of Aldo.

Ethan could not quite find it in himself to resent Aldo. In his easy jollity and his entirely unconscious sense of entitlement, he was the opposite of Ethan. But his brittle neediness lay exposed on the surface, his smile was unaffected, his offer of help to the new boy in town genuine and uncalculating. When he started to expatiate on global economics in the small beachfront hut to an audience of tanned surfers, Ethan leaned back in his seat and smiled and let the words drift over him. Perhaps that was why, after his long unsatisfying night, he fell asleep in the middle of the lecture.

Aldo did not seem at all offended. After the lecture, he enthusiastically uploaded to Ethan his personal tourist guide to Dahab. The coast was unspoilt, although hotel and property developers were quickly doing their best to remedy that. Torn between disdain and avarice, the nomadic locals dispensed bottled water and freshly-caught fish as well as faux-ancient advice to ingenuous backpackers at inflated prices. Breeze blocks and baked mud bricks were fashioned into crude dormitories for those travellers unable to afford hotel prices, all confined by unwritten but strictly enforced zoning laws in an approximate rectangle set back from the market running along the main stretch of beach. Wizened Bedouin toted SCUBA gear up and down the weathered stone breakwater where the fishing boats were docked – now repurposed to ferry divers to and from the coral reefs lying a few hundred metres offshore. The SCUBA divers, the druggies, the sun-worshippers, the backpackers – all the different communities rubbed alongside each other, starkly different and yet compatible in their easygoing, if not downright anarchist, outlooks.

Aldo guided Ethan to some local accommodation with a promise to meet the next day on Dahab's main beach. The local hotel was an ungainly breezeblock cube squatting one block from the beach, crudely whitewashed and rendered vaguely habitable by a baroque air-conditioning unit that hummed and growled and occasionally condescended to spit out gobbets of freezing air. One wall was concealed by a rack of lockers for personal effects. Bunk beds were arranged against the opposite wall. A noxious smell oozed around the edges of a bare wooden door set in the wall – the sign on the door announcing that it led to the 'WASH TOILET FACILITIES' was redundant.

This primitive hotel had one overriding advantage: spaces were available for thirty Egyptian pounds per night. Ethan stored his belongings in a locker and retraced his steps back to the beach with the settled aim of sorting out his life in a nighttime stroll along the beach.

Dahab's beach was an ideal location to untangle mental knots. Single-storey cafes, stalls selling freshly caught fish and dive shops formed a loose, undulating cordon on one side of the beach. On the other side, waves lapped imperturbably, regularly, a gentle but insistent reminder of the vast blackness that stretched to the horizon and up to the skies overhead, fading into a haze of stars that reflected, glittering, in the distant seas.

What had happened in the IT room? That was his first question. Well, obviously, Anna had tried to transfer herself – her mind, her consciousness – into her computer system. Faced with convincing evidence that the system actually worked and with her own answer to the Transfer Problem demonstrated, she had wired herself up and shifted herself, her essence, spoonful by spoonful, into the computer. It was an act of breathtaking courage, foolhardiness, arrogance and, above all, stupidity.

That was the real question: not what she had attempted, on the face of it unsuccessfully, to do, but why had she done it? Ethan had experienced an instant of the machine operating on him – the sensation of his thoughts being replicated and divided, painful double-vision in his mind's eye, his consciousness being stretched and twisted like toffee. The memory made him shudder, although it was already fading – as were the blinding headaches and disorienting attacks of vertigo that had struck him several times since. Anna was a scientist – plunging into her experiment was an inexplicable abandoning of all her scientific principles.

He drew back to more mundane issues: where had the message come from? The only logical source was Anna – she must have foreseen events and arranged for the message to be sent to him. She wanted him to explore her past in Dahab and reap useful insights. Perhaps so that he could undo whatever damage she had foreseen she might inflict on herself. It seemed a curiously circular way to proceed, but the conclusion was inescapable: pull at the threads of Anna's life until he learned something about her.

A lapping at the water's edge caught Ethan's eye. He stopped and stared at the sea. The flickering of white flecks caught in the starlight abruptly coalesced into a stark white beam. Then it split into two beams and four and a swarm – shafts crisscrossing diagonally up from the depth to form random patterns on the surface. With a hollow sucking bubbling sound, ripples formed on the surface and spread out in concentric circles, as though someone had thrown an invisible stone into the sea.

A smooth black head broke the surface, snorting a puff of water out through a snorkel and shaking its head to detach other drips. Other heads bobbed up and the magical lights dissolved into a more prosaic scene – a group of divers emerging from the sea at the end of a night dive.

The group assembled in the shallows offshore and paddled to the water's edge, morphing from elegant water creatures into ungainly land mammals as they struggled to the beach toting tanks of air, fins and masks. The leader of the group was a short barrel-chested man who tore off his mask theatrically as he strode onto the beach and fixed Ethan with a piercing stare.

"Good evening," he said to Ethan, in an indefinable Slavic accent, then turned back to the rest of the group before Ethan could reply and started calling out commands and waving to shepherd them ashore.

Ethan turned to walk along the beach and sank back into his reverie. He had an uneasy feeling that Dahab might turn out to be dull.

The next day, Ethan met Aldo and a dozen other faded surfer dudes of assorted gender and age in the back room of a beachfront cafe slumped on a pile of gaily-coloured cushions. They were drinking apple tea brewing in an ornate brass contraption sitting on a squat table amid the cushions.

"Hey, it's Ethan! Everybody, this is Ethan. He's new in town, arrived yesterday with this great big suitcase, really old school."

Ethan grimaced and gave a friendly wave and took his place perched on the edge of one cushion.

"Are you here for the drugs or the diving, Ethan?" asked a short, stocky woman wearing a torn baggy T-shirt that informed onlookers that 'divers do it deeper'.

"Erm, I've dived in the past I guess. Not so much into the drugs."

"Really, where have you dived?"

There followed a long, tedious exchange of credentials establishing Ethan as a bona fide member of the diving fraternity. As Aldo had explained, there were two tribes of long-term immigrants to Dahab: the divers and the druggies. Divers were drawn by the plentiful and easily accessible dive sites, including the breathtaking and treacherous Blue Hole. Druggies were attracted by the cheap and plentiful supply of narcotics. The two tribes did not mix. Divers regarded druggies as vacuously indulgent, leeching off family or friends to fund the international criminal cartels that indirectly supplied the world with drugs. Druggies regarded divers as vain thrill-seekers, blundering into the superficial delights of the natural world without any appreciation of the profundities of human existence.

Ethan's natural affinity lay with the divers – he was an experienced diver himself, after all. The physical and mental disciplines of diving appealed to his sense of order. He nodded along with the others at the endless descriptions of the underwater world and painstaking analyses of the latest diving equipment, waiting for the right moment to insert his own questions into the conversation.

"And then we saw these two turtles, oh, at about twenty metres," said one bearded man, shading his eyes with one hand as though seeking a clearer view of these aquatic marvels.

"Not for long, though," interrupted his companion, a slightly smaller, female version of the man – although lacking the beard.

"They swam away," said the man, solemnly flapping his hands to demonstrate their method of locomotion, "one flick of those limbs and they dived straight down."

"Might not have done if you hadn't scared them off, swimming right towards them," added the woman.

"I was just trying to get a better look," said the man, with a wounded expression, searching the faces of the spectators for approval.

"Don't often see them in pairs," said Aldo thoughtfully. There was a general nod of approval at this perceptive insight into marine biology.

"How about you?" said the woman, "are you a lone turtle or do you swim in a pair?"

Ethan stammered and blushed in response. Aldo quickly stepped in with another anecdote but Ethan waved him to silence and took out his phone.

"She was here about a year ago," he said, swiping across the screen to show a generic photo of Anna. She was cringing away from the camera but also favouring it with half a smile. "Before we met, actually. One of you might remember her."

"Before my time," said Aldo, nevertheless peering closely at the photo.

"Victor was here then," said the woman, "he might remember her."

Aldo snorted.

"Who's Victor?" asked Ethan. "Is he ... ?"

"He's not into some of the stronger medicines available around here, if that's what you mean," said the woman.

"Little guy, quite intense," said the bearded man. "I think he's leading a tour doing night dives every night this week."

"Yes, I think I saw him last night," said Ethan.

∞

Victor's night dive assembled on a quadrangle of bare baked earth framed by dive shops and internet cafes on three sides and open to the beach on the fourth side. The main road ran directly past the shops and behind that was only scrubland leading up to the distant hills, glowing a pale orange in silhouette as they shielded the setting sun from view. Early evening carried a faint hint of coolness, but the stored heat radiating up from the ground was enough to parch the air.

Ethan was early. He shifted uneasily from foot to foot and stared at the small groups of people ambling along the side of the beach, wandering in and out of the shops, crossing the road and heading off to unknown destinations in the desert. Dahab's first aid centre stood in one corner of the square: a dusty store front emblazoned with a bold red cross. Inside, it was largely bare – a little worrying – but displayed prominently its one genuine medical apparatus, a hyperbaric chamber. The chamber was little more than a steel box, the size and shape of a coffin, sealed tight except for a hosed connection to a pressurized tank. It had just enough room for an adult to lie in and a single scuffed round window so they could look out. As a stopgap treatment for the bends until the victim reached a hospital, it was better than death – but not by much.

Two of the diveshops seemed to be open: fixed opening hours were not part of the Dahab zeitgeist, but dim lights showed some shadowy movement inside them. But nobody emerged from any shop; none of the stragglers beside the beach showed any sign of approaching Ethan.

On the horizon, in the gloom where sea merged into sky, a star blinked in and out of visibility as reflections off the waves scattered the dying light. Ethan squatted on his haunches and prepared to give up his wait. Then he saw a familiar rollicking gait approaching the quadrangle.

Victor walked straight up to Ethan and extended both hands. Ethan shook one awkwardly.

"You are here for dive," said Victor – more of a statement than a question.

"Yes, I've …"

"You are early. We gather here for pre-dive briefing. Gather soon. Then here later for dive. You have dived at night before."

Victor paused and Ethan realized that his last statement was a genuine question.

"Erm, yes, I've done a few night dives. I don't have a torch, though, or any equipment."

Victor nodded and pointed at a neighbouring dive shop.

"Look, er, I was recommended to you by my girlfriend, actually."

Victor grunted in acknowledgement. Ethan fished his phone from a pocket and stabbed at the screen. Finding the photo of Anna, he held it out to Victor, who gave it a wary sidelong glance and then a longer, appraising stare and then took the phone and cradled it in his hand.

"The vampire squid is deadlier than the shark," he said abruptly. He turned off the phone and handed it back to Ethan and fixed him with a cold stare. Ethan wasn't sure whether this was another one of his questions, especially as he seemed to be waiting for Ethan to reply.

"Is it?" he said at last, "I mean, what is a vampire squid exactly?"

"Never mind," Victor replied, once again swerving the conversation for no discernible reason. "We meet here in two hours. Collect your kit from the shop. Thirty-five dollars."

Ethan puzzled over the enigmatic Victor as he sorted through the equipment in the dive shop. Wetsuit, oxygen tank, first stage regulator, second stage regulator, pressure gauge, weight belt – all the accoutrements of recreational diving. He picked and poked at them half-heartedly, tossing those that passed his absent-minded inspection into a growing pile. Victor seemed to recognize Anna but was reluctant to admit it. He had become hostile – no, not hostile exactly. It was a sudden shift, like a snail shrinking back into its shell. He was scared. For a second, it had been written plainly on his face. And then the strange comment about 'vampire squid'. Well, obviously, that had been a call and response: a sort of request for a password. And, equally obviously, Ethan hadn't known the password. So he could expect whatever response was reserved for those who came snooping after Anna without the requisite authorization.

Stomach cramping, Ethan dropped to his knees. His breath caught in his throat – rasped and whistled through his lips, which were starting to tingle. Why was he even considering going ahead with this? This was not the sort of thing he did. He wasn't brave. And yet, he had no choice. Anna's trail led here. He shut his eyes and concentrated on his breathing. Focus on the dive, focus on the preparations, sorting through the equipment. Ignore the complications, which were, as always, human.

The pile was complete. Ethan stirred it with a finger. No flashy dive computers or sleek, branded kit – he had opted for old, sturdy and simple. Military diving experience had given him a healthy distrust for the garish egotism of some leisure divers and their obsession with the latest accessories. When diving, there was one overriding rule to keep safe: keep calm and don't panic. Practically any problem could be solved by the studied application of basic logical steps – practically any situation could be made worse by thoughtless reaction and flailing arms. And the more excited you were, the faster you sucked up air. For many, this was a tricky rule to follow. The claustrophobic weight of water above, the utter reliance on mechanical tools, the susurration of every breath an echoing reminder of the limited supply of air: all these conspired to tickle at the nerves of every normal person. Fortunately, Ethan was abnormal. The tick and rattle of the various mechanisms was soothing, the crush of water an embrace. Even though he had stumbled into this escapade, there was no reason not to enjoy it. Apart, he supposed, from the looming sense of dread.

An hour later, Ethan was standing in the dusty square between the dive shop and the sea behind his pile of equipment, in a loose circle with five other people. They were all turned to face Victor as he droned through a set of perfunctory safety instructions. Ethan and Victor had been joined by four new divers. Lena and Clara were German, both cast from the same Teutonic nugget of understated practicality and cheery optimism, with short-cropped hair and intense stares that followed every detail of Victor's explanation. Ethan assumed they were a couple and tried to banish the uncomfortable sensation that this was prejudice – against Germans or possibly even women with short hair.

The other pair were not a couple. Mikel and Jon sported accents that veered unsteadily between Eastern Europe and Scandinavia and matching sets of SCUBA gear. Both shouldered their weight belts with practised ease but were not part of the relatively small diving fraternity of Dahab.

Mikel was large and fleshy with the disquieting grace common to bulky men; Jon was tall and wiry and fidgeted anxiously through the safety talk. They clearly had no place taking part in this dive and had been tipped off by Victor. But why the subterfuge? If they simply wanted to harm him, there would be easier opportunities. Ethan assumed that they wanted information, which meant that at some point they would have to talk to him, and perhaps he would gain some information about Anna – something that might help put the bizarre events of the last few days into context. Until then, he would bide his time as they seemed to be biding theirs.

"It's a bit strange, really," said Lena during a lull in the conversation as Victor clarified a point of their dive plan with Mikel and Jon. "Planning out our little dive, like everything's normal when, well, it isn't."

"What do you mean?" asked Ethan.

Lena stared at Ethan wordlessly.

Clara replied, "she's talking about the global financial crisis. I know we're a bit cut off here, you just need a few Egyptian pounds in your pocket, but really, you must have heard about it."

"What's the latest news?" asked Mikel.

"Oh, more of the same. Part renationalization of some banks in the UK and the US. Still some rumours that others are bust. Nobody quite seems sure where all the money has gone. Martial law declared in Germany and the UK and ..."

"Martial law? You're kidding. I didn't even think we could have that in England."

"Well, I gather it's all a bit British. Army on the streets, but rather apologetic, spending most of their time accepting cups of tea from concerned homeowners. Still, they're needed to stop looting and so on. Once you can't get any money from your bank, things fall apart quicker than you'd expect."

"But, why ... that is, it seems like, I don't know, an overreaction."

"Yeah, but then who knows anything about how banks work? It's all a bit strange. They say it started with just one person, anyway."

"Look," interrupted Victor, "Dive plan is set. No more need for chatting now. We meet at sea in ten minutes " – pointing towards the ocean, a somewhat redundant gesture – " and bring all your equipment please."

Ethan trudged over the beach with the rest of the group, lugging the oxygen tank with the rest of his equipment piled on top. Soon, it would all be weightless – until then it was ungainly. In the bitter heat, he started to sweat. Victor and Ethan were paired together for buddy checks – with a few grunts, Victor pulled and prodded at Ethan's kit and pronounced it in working order; Ethan took longer to do the same for Victor.

The group assembled at the water's edge, bowed under the weight of their gear, a row of matte black figures blending into the evening shadows. Ethan had his fins hooked around one wrist – Jon and Mikel had done the same, but Lena and Clara were wearing theirs. As they all followed Victor into the water, Lena and Clara wobbled precariously, awkwardly shuffling sideways while the waves shoved them back and forth. Ethan had already compiled a rough order of expertise for the divers: Victor, comfortably at the top, shrugging into his wetsuit like a second skin; Mikel, not far behind; Jon, stilted in his movements but competent; Lena and Clara, splashing gamely but ineffectually behind the rest.

The sandy bed gave way to pebbles and stepped downwards. Victor toppled lazily backwards, shuffling his mask over his face and jetting water from his snorkel and slipping one foot and then the other into the fins. The others followed suit with varying degrees of clumsiness.

The world changed. The murmur of waves faded away; the sounds of laughter and conversation drifting out from the beach stopped. Red and green fluorescence from the ragged lines of shops along the beachfront faded away. Slow cycling of breath in and out was the only clear sound. The rocks and coral outcrops were shrouded in muted greys. Ethan concentrated on his heartbeat, willing it to become slow and steady.

The divers assembled a few metres below the surface. Ethan bled a little air into his dive jacket, floated upwards, let out a little air, floated back down. He breathed in, floated up, breathed out, floated back down. His buoyancy control was awkward, amateurish. He concentrated on staying at the same depth as the rest of the group without kicking his legs or, worse, flailing his arms.

They drifted behind Victor, heading steadily downwards. The rocky bed was peppered with lumps of coral, which gradually assembled into an unbroken coral reef. Abruptly, the reef turned a right angle. They were floating above blackness; the reef a looming presence on their side.

Their torches threw shafts into the gloom that glittered and diffused into a mist of motes of light. Ethan played his torch over the nearest clump of reef – reds and greens and yellows sparkled under the play of the beam. A glint of orange reflected the beam, a plastic bag caught in a slight overhang, incongruous, pressing up against the shelf of coral like a helpless, gelatinous sea creature.

According to the dive plan, there was a hole in the reef, a hundred metres along from the entry point. It loomed into view precisely on cue. Victor floated next to a jagged rectangle of blackness, aiming his torch directly into its heart. The hole was actually a cleft, a fold that tunneled a winding course that punched through to the other side of the reef.

The divers formed into single file. Victor led the way, followed by Lena and Clara, then Ethan and finally Jon and Mikel. Ethan glanced at his depth gauge: twenty-eight metres. Already, they were deep for a leisure dive. His breaths were slow and rasping – each gulp took in four times as much air as at the surface. It was harsh and dry. He imagined he could feel the pressure squeezing the oxygen into syrup that rolled down his throat.

A sharp metallic clang echoed with the disconcerting loudness and ubiquity of sound under water. It was Ethan's tank scraping along a jagged edge of coral immediately above him. He kicked to move downwards and twisted past the trailing fronds of an anemone. His kick was an overreaction. He had to kick again to avoid colliding with the coral beneath him. The end of his fin jarred against a slender outcropping that sheared off and tumbled into the gloom beyond the torchlight.

Careful, slow breaths – not too deep to suck up all the air in his tank too quickly, not so shallow that he was deprived of oxygen. Heart thumping in his chest and echoing up into his head to rattle his teeth – softer, softer and gradually brought under control. Ethan floated, let himself sink a little as he breathed out. Sought out a fragile equilibrium and quested towards it – but not too abruptly – letting himself circle around it, spiraling inwards.

The tunnel ended. Torches lit the coral walls and Clara's fins and then they lit nothing – beams stabbed into the dark and faded into a diffuse glowing mist. The group popped out of the tunnel like a cork from a bottle. Ethan swirled in the blackness – banks of coral formed a wall, or a ceiling, or a floor.

The divers were in a natural hollow in the middle of the reef – a bubble accessible by a single winding tunnel. They assembled into a wobbly circle and played their torches around the borders of the bubble. Greens and reds and yellows sparkled under the lights and dimmed back into grey as the beam moved on. Shoals of parrotfish flitted around the space, exploring the gaps and melting through the tiny fissures in the reef to disappear entirely.

Ethan checked his depth gauge. Forty metres. Deep for a leisure dive – but worth it for the spectacular view, the sense of being preserved inside a perfect coral sphere. Perhaps he was infected by the simple joy of experiencing natural beauty, but the decision to go ahead with the dive seemed less foolhardy.

Victor rapped his tank with the metal corner of his depth gauge. The echoing clang broke the spell. The divers turned to face him and he signaled upwards. Victor twisted balletically and a single swish of his fins propelled him into the tunnel. Lena and Clara followed.

Ethan took in the scene for the last time. He drifted upwards and let out a little air from his lungs to restore neutral buoyancy. Again, he started to drift and he breathed in and ...

Water. Water in his mouth. Salt and cold like a dagger into his brain. His heart raced. No, panic was unacceptable. Panic was the enemy; any underwater crisis could be solved as long as you didn't panic. Slip mindlessly into the procedures baked in by endless repetition, let the training take over.

Fortunately, he had retained one old instinct: his tongue was protruding, resting gently against the roof of his mouth, so that he sucked in air cautiously around the sides of his tongue. When the water hit, it bounced off his tongue and he had time to clamp his mouth shut before more than a teaspoonful entered his mouth.

The cold water in his mouth was enough to trigger his dive reflex: his heart slowed. He knew this would give him a little extra time – but his life was still parceled out into a rapidly shrinking heap of seconds.

Step one: find his air supply. One arm twisted behind his back to push up his air tank from below. Simultaneously, the other arm reached back over his head to grab the first stage regulator fixed to the top of the tank with one hand. A rubber hose was clamped to a metal flange amid the chrome valves and brackets attached to the regulator. With one hand, he traced along the hose. Rubber, rasping against his glove, and then nothing.

The cord had been cut. The second stage regulator, still clasped between his lips, was connected to a rubber hose that flailed uselessly in the currents, ending in a crudely sawn hole.

Step two: get help. He waved his torch around and caught Mikel framed at the entrance to the tunnel in the coral. Mikel flinched in the sudden beam and then cocked a salute at Ethan and signaled a thumbs up with his other hand and turned and vanished into the tunnel, leaving behind a thin trail of bubbles.

In SCUBA language, a thumbs up did not indicate approval. It had a more basic meaning: go up. Ethan could hardly argue with this advice. Mikel had conveyed an even starker message: in his other hand, with which he had given Ethan a salute, he was holding a knife, a serrated blade with a wickedly fine edge.

Step three: get back to the surface. Ethan kicked once, gently drifting towards the tunnel. No time to worry about managing his buoyancy – every move had to be calibrated perfectly. He took his anxiety and squashed it into a tight little package and stowed it deep in his belly. It burned and roiled uneasily, spending spurts of acid into his stomach, but he ignored it. There was only the soft embrace of the water, cradling and compressing.

He was halfway through the tunnel. The narrow gap in the coral kinked back and forth. He bent his body around, felt the slight compression against his ribcage, another few precious spoonfuls of air displaced from his lungs. The urge to breathe was a faint tickle in his throat. He knew that it would soon be unendurable.

Another kick, the end of the tunnel hovered just beyond the range of his torch. One arm pointing straight ahead holding the torch, the other trailing by his side. The part of his mind that wanted to use that hand to claw desperately at the coral to pull himself forward was deeply buried. There was only efficient, painless movement.

Walls of coral bent back and faded into the gloom. Ethan popped out of the tunnel. A yawning emptiness scrabbled against his insides and demanded to be let out. His mental bulwarks were softening and crumbling. He had a handful of seconds left. One hand down to his weight belt – a flick of the emergency release and he would shoot upwards. Nearly thirty metres straight to the surface.

His hand paused at the clasp of his weight belt. Time for one last rational thought. Panic set aside. Going straight up was easy. From forty metres of depth to the surface in less than two minutes. And then a precious breath. And then? That was the problem. A sudden ascent would not allow time for the nitrogen dissolved in his blood under pressure to disperse safely. It would form tiny bubbles in his bloodstream. The bubbles would clog up his joints, leading to excruciating pain and the characteristic twisting motions that gave the condition its name: the bends.

In severe cases – and a rapid ascent from forty metres to the surface was likely to lead to a severe case – the bubbles could travel to the heart or brain, leading to heart attacks, strokes, coma and death.

The bends was treatable: if the sufferer was put back in a hyperbaric chamber – like the one so proudly displayed in the dive shop – the bubbles would be squeezed out and the nitrogen would disperse harmlessly over several days. That was surely his best option – his only option. Or, more accurately, his only option other than drowning.

Still, he hesitated. His stomach twisted in revolt, curdling his insides, an involuntary twitch that would shortly lead to a gasp, a fatal gasp. His torch caught a flash of colour, a garish orange, flickering behind the rainbow shoals of fish caught in the beam of his torch.

It was a plastic bag. The plastic bag he had seen on the way down, caught against an outcropping of coral jutting out from the main wall.

Ethan flicked the safety release on his weight belt. It slid off his waist and spiraled down into the gloom. He shot upwards and kicked towards the coral wall and extended both arms and jammed his head inside the bag.

Water against his lips. Sleek, slimy plastic speckled with salt gritty against his lips. He craned his neck back, tilting his mouth up towards the top of the bag, nestled in a crook of coral.

Was that a splash against his mouth and nose – spray mixed with air? He risked a tiny breath, clamping down against the desperate urge to fill his lungs.

And almost gagged. Air, but stale and fetid. Congealed bubbles and exhalations and scraps of vegetable matter and coral dust and water vapour.

Ethan took it in cautiously around the edges of his tongue and tried to choke back the vomit that rose up into the back of his throat.

The air was vile but breathable. Every cycle in and out deposited a little more carbon dioxide into the tiny air pocket and took out a little oxygen. The burning in his lungs ebbed but a band of cold pain congealed around his forehead and lights sparkled and danced in front of his eyes. The smell and taste faded from rancid to merely pungent, but it was enough for his eyes to start watering. He blinked and blinked again. With his face crammed against the coral, eyes behind a mask, fifteen metres underwater, there was little he could do to wipe his eyes – it was surprisingly annoying.

He focused on the irritation. It distracted him from the rotten taste of the air on his tongue, the vague but undeniable sense of inhaling specks of decaying vegetation along with the oxygen. Bile rose in his throat. Think of something else, he commanded himself. How long had he been here? Maybe one minute. Count off the seconds – he had to try to keep track of his decompression time.

Ethan started to calculate. The dive had called for about three minutes at maximum depth, then two decompression stops at fifteen metres and five metres. Was it three minutes at fifteen metres and ten minutes at five metres or the other way round? Or perhaps it was fifteen minutes at three metres? Did it matter?

What did matter was that he'd used up maybe another minute. Each gasp was less satisfying than the one before. Black spots were starting to flicker in front of his eyes. He took one last deep but unsatisfying breath and pushed himself down and back and away. The water was cold and black and somehow he no longer cared. Bubbles sputtered out from his mouth and he waved an arm and a leg in vague recollection that he was meant to be swimming somewhere – up, it was important to go up – but then he couldn't really tell which way was up, or even why he was supposed to be going in that direction.

Ethan popped out of the water – the buoyancy of his wetsuit accelerating him up through the surf like a dolphin leaping after a fish. He was slapped by a wave and rolled over onto his back and hovered, for an unmeasurable instant, balanced perfectly in the interface between the cool sea and the humid night. Then a juddering breath shook his body and the faint roar of the surf began to echo and the cicadas to chime and the gaudy lights of Dahab to strobe across the corrugated surface of the water.

For a while, Ethan lay on his back staring at the white smear of the galaxy above him, arms folded across his chest, legs paddling faintly to line him up with the gentle wash of the waves. He drifted back to the shore, mentally interrogating his elbows and knees for any incipient sharp pains. He was nowhere near the safe limits demanded by the standard dive tables used by leisure divers – but they had a generous safety margin built in. He had to hope that he had not chewed all the way through that margin, that his impromptu stop had been enough to clear his blood.

Gritty sea bed scraping beneath him. He turned and slipped his fins off and waded back to shore. No sign of the others: of course, they would still be finishing their decompression stops. He dropped his remaining pieces of equipment and eventually his wetsuit in a ragged line leading from the seashore over the concrete quadrangle to the dive shop. Skirting around the hyperbaric chamber propped open on the floor, he discovered his clothes hanging on a peg in the curtained changing area at the back of the shop and scrambled into them.

Ethan drew back the curtain, still shrugging into his battered trainers and pulling his T-shirt over his head. Jon and Mikel were standing in the middle of the shop, one on each side of the hyperbaric chamber.

"Hello, Ethan," said Jon.

"Hello," replied Ethan.

The three stood facing each other, their conversational gambits exhausted.

"We wanted to have a little talk with you," said Jon at last.

"What you wanted was to kill me," said Ethan.

"Oh, please. Not at all, that was …"

"Not at all? Well, what was it exactly? You left me to drown, with no air. I get that subtlety isn't your strongest point. Perhaps that counts as a gentle introduction where you're from. What is that, Russia?"

"OK, Ethan, we see that you think this is the bit where we accidentally give you lots of information. You are going to be the one who is giving us the information. Telling us about Anna."

"Yes, I see, she worked for you and then she escaped from you, you want her back, but you don't understand …"

Jon suddenly guffawed and exchanged a quip with Mikel in a guttural language.

"It is you who is not understanding. Anna is not working for anyone. She is too smart to be anyone's tool. We would just like to know what she has done with some things that she has taken, some technology that was not hers, that was not safe for her to take."

Ethan started to edge around the room as Jon talked. Despite their protestations about not wasting time, Jon and Mikel seemed anxious to practice their English language skills. Nor were they actually asking him any questions, or even making any effort to cut him off from the exit.

Mikel pointed at the open hyperbaric chamber and smiled.

"We knew you would be fine, Ethan, that you would have to be coming straight up out of the water. And you can still be fine. But you better get in here. As quickly as possible, too. You probably be starting to feel some symptoms already. You keep safe in there. You will be staying cooped up for a couple of days. Plenty of time to get you to some people who are really interested in asking you some questions."

Of course. The other divers had performed all their compression stops and emerged from the water. They could have no idea that Ethan had surfaced only a minute before them. Naturally, they assumed that – without any air supply – he had floated straight to the surface and was facing a critical case of the bends. Where else would he be but the dive shop – orbiting his only hope: the hyperbaric chamber? There was no need to lock him up. There was no hurry at all. They could wait for him to climb into the steel coffin, transport him wherever they wanted and question him at their leisure.

"Sure, I see what you mean, guys, and I'm going to step right in there " – pointing at the chamber – "as soon as I've, erm, collected, you know, a couple of books to read, to read while I'm in there."

"You're going to be there at least forty-eight hours," said Jon, nodding slowly. "And yet, I suggest you get in right now. Pain is going to get pretty bad, pretty soon."

"Oh sure, I'm right on it, can't wait to get in that comfy little snuggle," said Ethan, continuing to sidle to the exit.

Jon and Mikel made no move to chase him. They watched him with curiosity and barely concealed smirks.

"No point going anywhere, Ethan," said Jon, as Ethan reached the exit, "this is the only chamber in Dahab. You've got to climb in there or die. All we'll do is take you on a little trip, some friends of ours are keen to meet you."

"That sounds great," said Ethan, "I'll be right back."

Ethan kept a fixed smile on his face and his eyes carefully on Jon and Mikel as he backed out of the door and then turned and scurried away. He gave a final wave behind his head and was left with the image of Jon and Mikel standing by the chamber – their faces betraying an uneasy mix of condescending smiles and scowls.

The gritty road behind the dive shop led back to his accommodation. The interior was dark and stiflingly hot and seemed to be empty. Ethan crouched in front of his locker and fiddled ineffectually with the padlock.

"What you doing there?"

Ethan turned and saw Aldo framed in the doorway.

"I've got to leave, leave Dahab."

"But, you can't, you just got here."

"I know. And you wouldn't believe what's been happening to me."

Aldo spread his hands, as if to say that his capacity for belief exceeded any sequence of events that Ethan might have experienced, or even that he might be able to describe. Even so, his hands – and the rest of his body – steadily drooped as Ethan brought him up to date. He offered a heavily edited account, which Aldo accepted with cheerful equanimity.

Ethan finished his story. Aldo stood leaning against the doorway, as if propping up the crude breezeblock walls. The soft ticking of the stone as it contracted, cooling in the late evening breeze, was the only sound. Aldo puffed out his cheeks and scratched a phantom itch on his stubbled chin.

"They're profoundly dim, those two," he said at last. "The guys they work for, they're some crazy computer hackers, they're smart. But those two. They got their instructions and you don't need to worry too much that they'll start improvising."

"They will eventually. I need to get a taxi out of Dahab."

"Good luck finding one," said Aldo. This was a joke. Battered pickup trucks cruised the streets of Dahab relentlessly, slowing to walking pace to accost any tourist within hailing distance, then roaring away in a cloud of dust at the first sign of rejection. "I've got an idea," he said slowly. "I'll go back there and tell them I saw you in the Dahab Grocery Store – that's in the opposite direction – and that you'd collapsed there and were asking for them. They'll go that way, and that should buy you some extra time."

Ethan had to admit this was a good idea. Aldo's innocent expression and frank enthusiasm were ideal for subterfuge. They shook hands; Ethan was uncharacteristically moved. Aldo was a glimpse of an alternative life that he suddenly craved. His breezy generosity – helping Ethan, the awkward new arrival, at every opportunity without hope of reward or thought of the cost – was totally alien and oddly appealing.

Dragging his ridiculously oversized suitcase on the ground behind him, Ethan left the breezeblock hotel and waved down a passing taxi.

CHAPTER SEVENTEEN

June 13

Detective Chief Inspector Argyle asked for silence. The order was disseminated by a combination of gesticulation and strangled whisper along the line of police officers standing in the corridor of the farm – the server location facility in East London by the side of the Thames.

The din of voices faded and was subsumed into the ubiquitous murmur of the cooling fans. Argyle's ears itched from the buzzing of the fluorescent tubes hanging from the ceiling. Dirty yellow light from those tubes reflected in the white tiles of the floor, poking a smudged glow down the hundreds of rows of server racks. These led at neat right angles from the main corridor. Each server rack was an intricate grid of hollow black steel tubes enmeshed in a fine network of silver aluminium struts. The columns of the racks held stacks of individual computers – tens of computers in each column; hundreds of columns in each rack. And every computer was stuffed full of solid-state storage, memory and processing power, limited only by the ability of the fans to shunt the excess heat into the Thames and the dirty air of East London.

Through the frosted window set in the heavy door at the far end of the rows of racks could be seen the duty manager, gesticulating to the police officers on either side of him. Fortunately, the soundproofing was sufficient to silence his whining voice. No doubt he was once again recounting the epic tale of the two strangers who had inveigled their way into his precious server farm using devious psychological ploys. It was a tale that expanded with each retelling. DCI Argyle had sat through it twice, consciously channelling his increasing frustration into a fierce study of his own fingernails while keeping his face perfectly neutral.

Underneath the bombast, a few nuggets of possible fact recurred: two men – both looking, in retrospect, the worse for wear, one possibly injured – had talked their way into the farm; there had been an argument between them; now they were gone. But were they really gone? At the critical juncture, a mysterious system malfunction had switched off all the lights. The duty manager had been shoved aside by one man limping past him – he had failed to describe any other getaway. And was the duty manager the hero of the story, chasing the intruders away? Or was he really a bystander, a minor vexation at most, witness to a fight and separation?

Argyle had been condemned by his own competence to rise from the level where he was expected to conduct his own investigation. It was only with the edifice of government crumbling and institutions panicked into action that he had been hastily selected for operational command. He learned that the instinct for investigation still sat within him. The rust was flaking away. After the fiasco in Kentish Town, when his plea for army support had been ignored, petty political obstacles had melted away. He had the power to act and soon, he hoped, the knowledge of what to do. He was struggling not to show, on his sallow lined face, that so far he was quite enjoying the collapse of civilization.

"There, what was that?" asked Argyle.

"What was what?" replied an officer lurking down one of the server racks.

"Shut up," said Argyle.

"But you asked a question," pointed out the officer.

"There it is again!" said Argyle.

The officer was wise enough not to offer any reply.

After a moment, they all heard it. A tiny muffled clang, like a mouse playing percussion inside a chest freezer. The police officers fanned out under Argyle's instructions and quickly located a storage cupboard set in a corner of the farm. Inside the cupboard, behind a drift of discarded solid-state storage drives, squatted a metal cabinet, with the doors secured by a makeshift bolt made from three metal broom handles.

Argyle slid the broom handles out of the handles and the doors flew open and Ethan tumbled straight out onto the floor, scattering the storage drives and throwing dust up into the air – it was clearly some time since the brooms had been used for their intended purpose.

"About time you got here," said Ethan, clambering awkwardly to his feet and brushing away some imagined cobwebs from his trousers, although they were torn and muddy and might have been improved by the addition of some artfully placed cobwebs.

"What are you talking about?" said Argyle. "You escaped and practically every police officer in London has been looking for you."

"Well, that makes it even worse. It must have been hours since I called you."

"Called us? We tracked you down. Your phone came back on about fifty minutes ago."

"Fifty minutes? Curiously hard to keep track of time when you're squashed inside a small metal box. Anyway, I called you. Look." Ethan pointed at the floor next to the storage cabinet where his mobile phone sat. "I put it all back together, turned it on, and squeezed it through the ventilation grille – not very good mobile reception inside a metal box."

"OK," said Argyle, discarding several comments and settling on the key question: "Why?"

"We've got work to do." Ethan said.

"And what would that be?"

"Stopping my lazy cunt of a brother from getting away with it all."

Argyle smiled. The lines of his face rearranged themselves uneasily. "Perhaps you better explain to me what's going on," he said.

Despite Ethan's protestations that every second counted, Argyle made it clear that nothing would happen without a full explanation. A police van outside functioned as an impromptu interrogation venue. Ethan and Argyle sat squashed next to each other on a low wooden bench running along the side of the van. Argyle waited while Ethan collected his thoughts. A flash of pain twisted his mouth and he slumped forward on the low bench and squeezed his eyes shut and cradled his head between his hands. Argyle let the silence continue. Eventually, Ethan filled it with a low voice.

The duty manager had been easily managed. It took about as much effort as rolling and unrolling a yoyo – mainly done automatically with the odd flash of conscious thought. Ethan stood guard outside the door to the small server room with Robert inside picking out the last loose strands in the tangled web of money movements initiated by IWS. Absently, he had scrabbled around in his pockets and fetched out the small black diary – his one remaining memento of Anna.

Flicking through the diary was a disappointment. It was not a heartfelt confessional, recounting the erotic intricacies of their relationship. There was little writing in it: most of the pages were peppered with doodles or obscure initials. Appointments were listed with elaborate but relentless specifics: the dentist at 3pm, following by the dental hygienist at 3.15pm, with a marginal note that she was being seen by Marlene not Annika. There were shopping lists too, and random reminders that would probably fail to trigger any useful memories now for Anna and were certainly of no interest to anybody else.

It was dull, Ethan concluded ruefully. A slice of the dull, everyday morsels of a life. A few pages were ripped out – perhaps these had held compromising material. No wonder the police investigation had glanced at the diary briefly and then moved on.

On a whim, Ethan picked an entry – the date that he and Anna had first met. Thumbing through to the correct page, he squinted at a few squiggles and then angled the diary towards the light so he could read the small, crabbed handwriting squashed into one corner: "Speak at conference to meet Boom," it said.

And with that, the bottom dropped straight out of his world.

"Why?" asked Argyle. "What does that even mean?"

"Boom is my brother's nickname for me. He's the only one who calls me that. It meant that our meeting, our first meeting, wasn't an accident. It was a plant. I only went to the conference because he pushed me into it – it wouldn't have been top of my list otherwise."

"You're saying he set up your meeting with Anna, the girl who became your girlfriend, right?"

"And who's lying in a hospital bed as we're talking. Because of what he started."

Ethan grimaced and turned away, images strobing through his mind like silhouettes of landscapes lit up by flashes of lightning: Anna, lying swaddled in threadbare sheets in the hospital; Anna, pale face framed by the brim of her hat, favouring him with a shy smile; Anna, resolute as she defended an argument, her slender frame trembling with righteous energy. And the reckless abandonment of academic rigour to fling herself into her own experiment? The result of that experiment had guided him to Egypt and back, crash-landed a plane to keep him free and engaged in bafflingly oracular dialogue with him via a computer terminal. It had the inscrutable determination of the physical Anna. Yet it could not be more than a cheap simulacrum with Anna still living and breathing in London.

Calmness, thought Ethan. Get back to calmness. His breath was coming in short spurts, his fingers were starting to tingle. As his mind wandered over the events of the last few days, it began to quail, unable to encompass all the events, like a juggler who suddenly realises how many balls they are juggling and immediately drops them all. Focus on your next step, Ethan thought, as he fought to slow down his breathing.

"And he started all this, what, to get some money?" asked Argyle gently.

"Exactly. If he could inject some of his own code into the bank's systems, he could steal some money. And I had the access to get that code through the firewall. But he knew I would never go along with it. He spent his life ordering me around and, as far as he was concerned, he had the right to get me to do whatever he wanted, so he came up with another way: a firebreak."

"A firebreak? Oh, I see, somebody in the middle, like that fake address he used to get his mail."

"You're not stupid, for a policeman."

Argyle nodded imperceptibly to acknowledge the compliment. Ethan continued without noticing.

"He got somebody who I did trust, who I knew well enough to know that they couldn't possibly implant any malware without me noticing. And he got them to include some of his code, to smuggle it in."

Ethan shook his head: "I did check her code. But I didn't check it the way I would have if I'd known some of it had come from Robert. He could easily have included some self-executing elements in one of her binary blobs."

Argyle sensed that the conversation was threatening to run away from him. Ethan was ready for the critical question.

"And now you know that, can you get the money back?"

"I've got some of the information, but Robert has the rest. I don't think he can use it without me. We need to find him."

"Where do you think he is?"

Ethan considered. He knew immediately that he had absolutely no idea where Robert might be. He also knew the solution: you didn't find Robert, he found you. Focus on the next step, though. Hadn't IWS said something about bringing Anna a red box?

"Anna's flat?" he said.

"It's under close watch," replied Argyle.

"Your surveillance hasn't been up to much so far."

Argyle shrugged. He made some calls. And then the vast military and police infrastructure roused itself into action.

An hour later – was it really the same day? It was a day that seemed to go on forever – they were in another police van on Anna's street. This time Argyle had overall command and, judging from the quiet but animated voice with which he dispatched the constant stream of junior officers asking for instructions, he was relishing it.

The street was surrounded by a net of police officers and soldiers. With martial law now established, the sight of a squaddie leaning on a street railing cradling his weapon aroused interest but not surprise. At the heart of this net, Anna's street was superficially unaffected. A row of Georgian terraced housing, brickwork grimed with pollution and crumbling, doors and windows shabby with peeling paint – it was not the most prepossessing part of town. Cars lined one side of the street; the other side, where Anna's basement flat was located, was marked off with yellow lines and stubby metal posts to prevent parking. Nobody was on the street. A dog barked insistently in a back garden. The growl of traffic from the nearby main road was felt rather than heard.

Into this scene rolled a tank. It whined and throbbed as it rolled along the centre of the street, executed a smart right angle turn that aimed it directly at the house containing Anna's flat, and continued rolling, straight through one of the black painted bollards that sheared off with a metallic pop and span away, up the single step to the front door of the house, and then still onwards. The front door folded, the wall surrounding it heaved and sagged, bricks crunched under the treads of the tank or were thrust aside.

The tank continued until it was fully embedded in the front of the house, where there was now a gaping hole, framed by smashed bricks and shards of windowpane. A cohort of soldiers ran up behind the tank, passed alongside and into the building. Seconds later, Argyle received the all clear, and he and Ethan strode through the rubble and down the stairs into Anna's flat.

A faint pall of brick dust hung in the air, framing shafts of light that defined the intersection of the setting sun and the ragged gap in the ceiling. Glass and metal crunched underfoot. Electric lights flickered and there was a faint tang of ozone. The soldiers had assured Ethan that the gas was disconnected but he sniffed hesitantly and turned in a slow circuit around the room.

"I like what you've done with the place," he said.

Argyle was unmoved by this attempt at levity. He directed various junior officers around the flat with flicks of his fingers and the occasional quiet instruction. Only after this process was unfolding to his satisfaction did he turn his attention to Ethan, fixing him with a silent appraising gaze. Ethan was about to break the silence when Argyle finally spoke.

"Nobody here," he said.

"Except us," replied Ethan.

Argyle's stony silence was more eloquent than any response.

"I think, I've got an idea, a way to contact him," said Ethan.

"Go on."

"Is there, I mean there should be, somewhere here, a box, a red box."

Argyle raised his eyebrows in enquiry and one of the officers scurrying around the flat carried over a small red box. On it was a large yellow Post-it note with the word 'SPARES' scrawled in capital letters. Argyle used the tip of a biro to lever open the lid and poked around inside: a heap of electronic components tangled together with wires; circuit boards hastily fused; some sections that were clearly broken scattered at the bottom.

"Is this it?" asked Argyle.

"Yes. That's what he wants. He'll come to get it."

"A box of spares? That's what he'll risk his life for?"

"Exactly. I just need to phone him and arrange a meeting place."

"Arrange a meeting, sure. No doubt he'll go anywhere to meet you to collect this priceless box of broken spares."

"Actually, I thought the hospital would be a good rendezvous – sort of public, but sort of enclosed. I can explain it to him in a sort of roundabout way that nobody else would understand, he likes that sort of thing."

"Yes, so I understand. How you hacker types communicate, I'm sure."

"I just need my phone to call him."

"Naturally, you need your phone." Argyle stood next to Ethan – somehow looming over him despite the fact that Ethan, even in his normal hunched posture, was several inches taller than the Detective Chief Inspector.

"Why don't you sit down there," said Argyle, pointing at a bare wooden chair in the kitchenette, "and tell me exactly what happened with your brother."

"Is there time?" asked Ethan. As if in support, the house uttered a single creak and a new plume of brick dust puffed out from the mangled walls.

"All the time you need," said Argyle, pulling up another chair and waiting for Ethan to sit down. "The tank can prop up the whole house for a week, they tell me."

Ethan was inclined to ask who they were and whether they were the ones who actually had to sit in the house while it showed every intention of imminently collapsing. Realising it was futile, he sat down next to Argyle and started to explain what happened after he saw the incriminating diary entry.

He had stood frozen outside the small room, barely registering the faint tapping of Robert at the keyboard or his whoops of excitement as he uncovered further traces of where the money had gone. After a while, the tapping stopped and the door opened a crack and Robert's face appeared at the entrance – pale and pudgy and entitled and irresistibly punchable.

So Ethan punched it – a wild roundhouse that connected with Robert's cheek and rocked him back on his heels. He wobbled back and forth and then sat on the floor, looking as surprised as a person whose body had decided to have a quick sit down without any permission from his brain. Meanwhile, Ethan gave a low animal moan and crumpled to the floor clutching his fist with his other hand.

"Didn't they teach you how to punch people in the army?" asked Robert.

"Not a high priority in cyberwarfare," muttered Ethan through gritted teeth.

"You're meant to hold your thumb like this," said Robert.

"I did. Look, don't change the subject."

"What subject? You just punched me. How is that a subject?"

"You got the malware in by using Anna. It was a setup. My entire relationship was a setup. One thing I had that was real and, as usual, it's another one of your little schemes."

"Oh that."

"Yes, that. That. Exactly, that. You're determined to destroy my life and I can't have just one thing without you, without you destroying it." Ethan was vaguely aware that he was being inarticulate but he wasn't prepared to slow down and let Robert distract him.

"Come on. That's not important now, anyway. Let's focus on getting the money. Anna is … she's, look, it's just not my fault really. You don't know the truth about her. And you know you can't stay angry with me for long."

Robert summoned up the smile that he thought would be the most appealing. Ethan stared at him in astonishment.

"I've been angry with you for thirty years," Ethan said very quietly.

"Are you kidding? I've been caring for you for thirty years. It's not much fun, having a baby brother following you around and annoying you."

"Everything that's gone wrong in my life, it's all been your fault. You haven't been caring for me, you've been tormenting me."

"I'm not saying I'm perfect, sometimes you have to wind up your little brother, it's, like, the law or something. But I've been with you – alright, except when I was in jail – since mum died."

"Yes, that was probably your fault too."

There was a horrified silence. They sat awkwardly on the floor facing each other and then it was Robert's turn to launch himself at Ethan. They rolled on the floor – Robert on top until his bad leg gave away; then Ethan struggling to arrange his gangling limbs to trap Robert; then Robert squirming away and on top as Ethan flapped his hands and Robert scrambled ineffectually to pin them down.

A tiny click signalled the door at the end of the corridor opening. The duty manager tottered into view, faint concern creasing his features. He hovered at the entrance to the corridor, unsure whether to advance. The click was like the bell at the end of a round in a boxing match. Robert and Ethan rolled away from each other. Ethan stumbled into a wary crouch opposite Robert, who stood bent over with both hands clasping his bad leg.

Robert reached out to Ethan – half dragging him and half using him for support – and they clambered together down the corridor away from the duty manager. Robert swung round and through a doorway and Ethan reached out to steady himself with one hand and pain stabbed up his arm – he had used his punching hand. Tears filled his eyes and he pitched forward into the room and squeezed through another door and then realised that Robert had detached himself. He stretched out a hand in front of him and recoiled as it met bare steel a few inches away. He turned around and collided with the door behind him, which was now shut and somehow barred.

He was in a cupboard. A metal storage cabinet. He could hear Robert outside scrabbling around and then sliding something through the handles of the door.

"Let's discuss this later. You've really got it all wrong. I know I haven't been totally honest but you're making like I'm some sort of supervillain," Robert said.

"Let's discuss it now. Perhaps you could open the door and we can discuss it," said Ethan.

"You're perfectly safe there for now," said Robert.

Ethan was about to point out that the phrase 'for now' was carrying a lot of weight in that assertion when he realised there was nobody outside. He sank to his knees inside the cabinet. His knees jutted against the door; his back was pressed against the cold steel back. The darkness was almost complete – a ventilation grille in the bottom corner admitted narrow slivers of light.

The confinement was strangely comforting, the muffled whirrs and buzzes from the machinery outside the cabinet lulling without being distracting. Here was a chance to rest and reflect. Ethan probed his bruised knuckles with his other hand and winced. It had been worth it, though.

"I see," said Argyle.

"Yes," said Ethan.

"And you used your mobile phone to get our attention and that's where we found you, inside the cabinet."

"You've got it," said Ethan.

"But I still don't see why Robert would see you to get that box of spares."

"Look, it's very complicated, a hacker thing. Does it matter? I'll set up the meet and you'll get him, I promise. What do you think I'm going to do? I called you, I'm not trying to escape."

Argyle conceded with a nod. It was tempting to chase down the intricacies of the brothers' relationship, but he couldn't afford the time.

Some soldiers brought in a pile of telecommunications equipment and, on a monitored line, Ethan was connected to Robert's mobile phone.

"It's showing a trace on this line," said Robert.

"A hello would be nice," said Ethan.

"You've got about twenty seconds left before I have to disconnect," said Robert.

"Understood," said Ethan. "We need to pool our information, to get this money out. Meet at the bedside of our mutual acquaintance."

"Got it," said Robert, and hung up.

Ethan replaced the clunky back telephone receiver and smiled smugly at Argyle. He had conjured up a plan to return the red box to Anna. No doubt, using her box of spares, she would be able to undo the catastrophic damage she had suffered and maybe even his own relatively minor mental scratches. He recognised parts of the equipment in the box – it was similar to the machinery that she had assembled at First Global Bank around their captive spider. Robert would be there, which was an unnecessary complication. But then, wasn't Robert always an unnecessary complication?

CHAPTER EIGHTEEN

June 12

The bus swung into a lay-by and ground to a halt, the irregular thump of the diesel engine ebbing away and segueing into an irregular ticking as the engine cooled. An impromptu street market materialised around the bus – dusty vans with one side ripped out selling grilled meat on wooden skewers, fake iPhone headphones, foreign currency.

"Are you awake?" asked Aldo.

"No," replied Ethan. His eyes were gummed shut and a thin sliver of drool connected his mouth to the armrest of his seat. Grime was embedded in the side of his head where he had been leaning it against the window. His hair was matted and straggly. His legs ached from being jammed into the cramped space between his suitcase and the seat in front. Risking opening a single eye, he saw Aldo grinning at him from a distance of about six inches.

"I know that you're keeping a lookout, really," said Aldo.

"Really?"

"Yes, because you're clearly some kind of superspy, and it would be essential to maintain a constant lookout."

"Clearly."

"Although you're doing a fantastic impression of a traveller having a nap."

"Actually," said Ethan, with a flash of inspiration, "I was delegating the lookout to you."

Aldo nodded wisely, projecting the mien of a man who had been entrusted – by a super spy – to keep a vigilant lookout.

"Anyway, I thought we might pop out and get something," said Aldo, nodding his head in the direction of the street vendors. "Those kebabs smell good."

"I think the meat might be dog," said Ethan.

"It's still a long way to Cairo," said Aldo, apparently considering this a reasonable counter-argument.

"Aldo, I really appreciate you coming with me," said Ethan.

"It's cool, really. This is the most exciting thing that's happened since I went to Dahab. I was planning to visit Cairo anyway."

"Why don't you go and grab something? I'll look after our stuff.'

Aldo bounded out of the coach and was instantly engaged in a theatrical bout of haggling with a gaggle of street vendors. Ethan leaned back and closed his eyes to savour the interval of silence. He really did appreciate Aldo's company – their discussion of endogenous economic theory passed the hours as the bus trundled along the featureless road across the Sinai. After he had arrived at the bus station and bought a ticket for the next bus heading out of Dahab, Aldo had caught up with him. Carrying a small bag with unwashed clothes poking out of the half-zipped top, he had waved down Ethan, examined his ticket, changed it for a different ticket heading towards Cairo – this involved a spectacular argument with the ticket seller – and promptly added another ticket to accompany Ethan himself. They had both paid in cash – credit card payments were still malfunctioning – and Ethan counted sorrowfully his diminishing stack of Egyptian currency.

Attempts to persuade Aldo to stay behind were manifestly futile. Dire but obscure warnings of physical danger and criminal chicanery only increased his enthusiasm. Ethan's arguments all rested on one key assumption: that he, Ethan, was not worth making the effort to keep safe. Ethan could no more persuade Aldo of this than he could persuade a puppy not to adore its owner. Banishing the vague notion that taking on an amiable stranger as a travelling companion was probably not accepted protocol for an international criminal on the run, Ethan gratefully relented.

The escape plan worked. Still assuming that Ethan would succumb to the bends unless he returned to the only hyperbaric chamber in Dahab, his attackers had not bothered to stake out the bus station. By the time their suspicions had been aroused, Aldo and Ethan were on the slow bus to Cairo.

Aldo returned to the bus carrying a wooden stick coated with a brown gristly substance that had the consistency of gravelly slime.

"Looks good," said Ethan.

"You want some?"

"I'm fine."

"Don't they tell you that you have to take in sustenance where you can find it, in the field, I mean, in, like, spy school?"

"I'm not going to slip up and admit that I'm a spy, Aldo, because I'm not."

"Of course. Your cover would be something like the army, most spies are ex-army."

"I was in the army," admitted Ethan.

Aldo sprang up in his seat, almost spilling some juice that had oozed out of the skewered meat down his front. The bus jerked forward with a clashing of gears and Aldo was pushed back.

"Alright, ex-army," said Aldo conspiratorially. "And I've worked out why you were there."

"You have?"

"Yes, I did a little checking on that woman you were searching for. People talk to Aldo, you know. They tell him things."

"Perhaps they assume that anyone who talks about himself in the third person is an idiot and you can tell them anything?"

"Perhaps they do. It works though. Do you want to know what I learned?"

Ethan nodded reluctantly.

"She arrived from the East, with a group of Russians or Ukrainians or something like that. Nobody ever saw her, she kept out of sight mostly, emerged at night sometimes, but I can't find one person who saw her out during the day. And always in the internet cafe. She had some sort of deal with the Russians – safe passage in return for hacking, probably. Kept to herself apart from that, didn't mix with any of the expats, the English or the Americans.

"Anyway, she left suddenly. Safe to assume that she took some of their money with her, plus who knows what other tech. Rumours that some of the Russians were army or intelligence, not private hackers, although I'm not sure there's much difference nowadays. When you blundered in with, clearly, some inside information, no wonder they got spooked and decided to take you out. Not great spy strategy, was it?"

"That's because, for the millionth time, I'm not a spy."

Aldo nodded again, as if Ethan's denial only provided him with further confirmation of his suspicions.

By the time the bus rolled into Cairo's central bus station, with the morning sun poking over the rooftops and soaking up the last of the precious morning chill, Ethan was almost convinced that he must be a spy. Aldo suggested that they lie low for a few days in an inconspicuous guest house he knew, whereas Ethan was anxious to return to civilization. They batted the issue back and forth while Ethan reassembled his mobile phone – almost automatically, he kept the battery and SIM card separate from the body of the phone, which did nothing to quell Aldo's suspicions. As soon as Ethan turned on the phone, it beeped.

"New message," said Ethan.

"And?" said Aldo.

"Suggesting a flight, back to England, given me a flight number."

"Do you often get mysterious instructions on your mobile phone?" asked Aldo.

Ethan sighed. "Seems to happen quite a lot, nowadays," he said.

Aldo's eyebrows shot up. Here was a piece of evidence so incriminating, he hardly needed to point it out. "Maybe you should come up with at least some sort of non-spy cover story," he said at last.

"I'm not a spy," said Ethan.

The phone beeped again.

"Another mysterious message?" asked Aldo.

"It's downloading something, data, a blob of data, a big blob of data."

"Oh, now it's a mysterious blob of data."

Ethan peered at his phone. He pressed a few buttons, with no discernible effect. The phone beeped again.

"And what mysterious thing is it doing now?" asked Aldo.

"Now it seems to be uploading the same blob, uploading it somewhere else."

There was another muffled beep, emanating from the depths of Ethan's luggage. Rooting around in it, he uncovered a bulky package, inexpertly smothered in bubblewrap, and showed it to Aldo.

"It uploaded it here I think," he said.

"What does that do?" asked Aldo.

"Doesn't do anything. That is, my brother gave it to me, and he told me it doesn't work. Although my phone now seems to have some instructions for it."

"OK, that's enough. I'm officially maxed out on mysterious messages, objects and missions. Let's just go."

Another bus, mercifully clean and less inclined to rattle than the Dahab-Cairo express, took them to the airport. In the ticketing area, several signs written in large, shaky capital letters festooned the counters. 'NO CREDIT CARDS' said one; 'CASH ONLY' said another. A knot of people was centred on the customer information counter, where a single uniformed employee empathized with their bafflement but offered no concrete assurances.

A television hung from a cradle suspended from the ceiling, sound muted, tuned into an English language news channel with a ticker constantly scrolling along the bottom of the screen. The headlines were now familiar: payment systems creaking or stalled entirely; governments emerging from hushed conclave to promulgate anodyne announcements; stock photos of banks, marble pillars gleaming in the sunshine. The main picture cut abruptly to a ground level feed from Oxford Street, the shopping thoroughfare in central London. Clearly a live feed: it was morning in Cairo; in London, dawn was encroaching on the chilly streets. Watery sunshine splashed over the tops of the buildings and broke against the brown smog that hung in the air. A street cleaner played a hose over paving stones, chasing a swirl of leaves down the drain. A tank crawled into view, turret down. It crept across the field of view, aligning with the centre of the roadway. All the shops were shuttered.

"Never thought I'd see that," said Ethan. "A tank on Oxford Street."

"Discouraging looting, I think," said Aldo. "Shoppers are so desperate to get their stuff that if they can't buy it, they just take it. Martial law in England now, you know."

"Doesn't seem real," said Ethan.

"Nothing seems real when you're in Dahab," said Aldo.

"And it's not too bad here either."

"Holding together, for now. But this is still mainly a cash economy. Anywhere most people use cards, use credit, things are worse. All the money is gone – people are whispering about some sort of bank robbery. But how could you steal enough money to bung up the whole system?"

Ethan shrugged and stared at the ground.

"That's it!" said Aldo. "That's why you're here, sniffing around. It's something to do with the financial crisis. I bet your cover story is all to do with banking."

"I do work for a bank," said Ethan, once again overtaken by the sensation that the conversation was going to run away from him, but curiously unable to pull away, as though he were standing at the top of a dangerous cliff simultaneously terrified and fascinated by the pull of gravity.

"A bank? Seriously, that's your story? You used to be in the army, now you work for a bank. Couldn't you come up with something a bit more convincing?"

"But it's true."

Aldo gripped Ethan's arm. "How can I help?" he said. "Where do you need to go?"

"Well, my instructions were a flight to Heathrow on British Airways."

"OK." Aldo pursed his lips and turned around slowly. "You poor bastard. British Airways. Guess one has to make sacrifices."

Aldo located the British Airways counter and tugged Ethan towards it. He tipped up his bag onto the counter and belongings poured out. Rooting around with his finger, he located several wads of notes and nudged them together into a single heap.

"There's enough for you there," Aldo said. "A single untraceable transaction, bought with cash using someone else's money. The perfect way to get back to Heathrow."

"Not really untraceable," Ethan pointed out. "I have to give all my personal details and my passport number before they'll let me on the plane."

"Sure. Your passport. And I'm sure that's totally genuine."

"Look, I can't let you give me all your money," said Ethan.

"I'm glad to help, I'm delighted to help."

"It's like one of those scams, where you hear about a little old lady who's been ripped off by someone pretending to be a spy."

"Are you only pretending to be a spy?" said Aldo.

"No. I've told you a thousand times. I'm not a spy."

"Well, that's OK, then, isn't it?"

While Ethan was still internally debating this logic, Aldo pushed the stack of notes over to the man behind the counter. He had been clicking away blithely on his keyboard, treating the bizarre argument taking place in front of him with equanimity – the foibles of travellers were of no concern to him. Without pausing, he clicked at a slightly faster rate and presently a ticket was spat out from a printer.

"A good old-fashioned paper ticket," said Aldo, pressing it into Ethan's hand.

"I really don't know what to say," said Ethan.

"Use it wisely," said Aldo. "And now go. I'm not very good with separations. Mummy issues. Come back to Dahab and tell me how it all went."

Ethan shook his hand and, taking Aldo at his word, turned on his heel and headed for departures. Aldo looked slightly stunned at Ethan's abrupt dismissal. Ethan was oblivious – he had the phrase 'mummy issues' buzzing inside his head and was barely conscious of his surroundings.

Ethan recalled standing in front of a plain wooden door. It was the door to the front room of his house – his old house, not his grandmother's house – and, in his memory, the door was tall and the polished brass knob at eye level. That was not why he hesitated – it was what lay on the other side. Gingerly, he reached out a hand to twist the knob.

The door swung open a crack and Robert appeared. He was about nine years old – skinny arms and legs and a comically serious face underneath unbrushed hair. He stepped through the door and clicked it shut behind him, not giving Ethan a glimpse of what was on the other side.

"Is mummy in there?" asked Ethan.

"Yes," said Robert.

"And is she still dead?" asked Ethan.

"Yes," said Robert.

"How long is she going to be dead for?"

"I don't know. I think a long time."

"Even when we wake up tomorrow?"

"Yes."

Ethan was worried who was going to make him breakfast the next morning. Grandma didn't know how he liked his cornflakes: that you had to shake the box the right way before pouring them out or else you got all the cracked broken ones. He felt an itch between his shoulder blades and his breath started to catch in his throat. He was struck by a sudden thought.

"Is grandma still angry with us?"

Robert nodded. There was no point in explaining further. Grandma's rages were violent and inexplicable – cloud scudding in over a clear blue sky, rumbling with thunder, and then evaporating. Prediction was futile but critical. Otherwise, you might get caught and swept into a randomly cruel punishment.

Robert had grabbed Ethan around the shoulders and steered him to their room while they had been talking. He shut the door behind them with a practised flick of his heel and manoeuvred Ethan to his bed and sat him down on it.

"Look, Ethan, it's like this," said Robert.

Ethan sat and waited to be told what it was like.

"You've got to promise not to go into the front room," said Robert.

"OK, I promise," said Ethan.

"Really, you don't want to go in there."

"Mum is in there," pointed out Ethan. Surely this gave him the right to go in.

"Just promise," said Robert.

"I did promise already."

"So that means you won't do it?"

Ethan stuck out his lower lip and bounced up and down on the bed. He wasn't sure whether that was what it meant but he was bored and wanted to do something else.

Adults came in and out of the house all day. Mostly, they went into the kitchen and spoke to grandma. The door to the front room opened and closed a few times but Ethan stayed well away and didn't see what was inside. None of the adults were interested in Ethan and Robert. Ethan wanted to play dinosaurs but Robert wasn't interested and shooed him away and eventually pinned him down and flicked his ears until Ethan agreed to stop nagging.

Ethan and Robert put themselves to bed. They had done it before – increasingly over the last few months when mother had been asleep and they had decided not to wake her. Ethan had to stand on a chair in front of the kitchen sink to reach the taps. Wobbling slightly as he leaned forward, he held the glass under the stream of water and twisted the knob to stem the flow as quickly as he could, yet slightly too slow to avoid some unsightly splashes on his pyjamas.

Robert refused to read him a bedtime story. Instead, he told him a short vivid tale about a little boy who let his feet poke out from underneath his duvet, thereby giving a giant spider the opportunity to grab him by his toes and pull him away and eat him up.

Ethan lay for a long time in his bed – feet carefully protected by his duvet – and stared up at the ceiling. After a while, irregular moans and snuffles from Robert's bed were replaced by a gentle, even breathing. Moonlight muffled by the curtains reflected from the face of the clock set high on the wall: the hands ticked around until midnight. This was officially the middle of the night. It was, therefore, impossible that anyone else might be awake.

Ethan slowly drew back his duvet and tiptoed across the room. The door creaked alarmingly as he inched it open but he slipped through regardless and was free. The landing was buried in gloom. With one hand gripping the banisters for guidance, Ethan crept down the stairs and faced the door to the front room.

In the darkness, it was a featureless black rectangle. He stretched out one hand and his fingers grasped the knob – cold and metallic and sticky, somehow, against his palm. The knob turned and the latch released with a click that echoed and was swallowed by the carpet and the walls.

Ethan stood at the threshold. Perhaps his mother would be inside, thought Ethan, just like usual. Maybe a little tired, as she had been recently, but always ready to welcome him and soothe 'his nerves', as she put it, which seemed always to be poised on the verge of shattering, leaving millions of shards which he worried he would never be able to reassemble himself.

He walked into the room, squinting into the shadows to assure himself that there had been no unexpected changes in its layout. The mantelpiece ran along one wall, coated by a thin film of dust, supporting a familiar row of photos: Ethan alone; Robert alone; Ethan and Robert together; Ethan and Robert and his mother – all poised with dutiful attention to the camera and uncertain smiles. Opposite the mantelpiece, the wall was covered by a large gilt-framed mirror, reflecting only blackness. The window was obscured by a heavy velvet curtain that dragged over the thin carpet.

In the centre of the room was a single armchair and a sofa – remnants of a larger set of furniture, but sufficient for their purposes as, firstly, they rarely had visitors and, secondly, they never used the front room. The armchair was empty.

Ethan had been avoiding looking at the sofa, sneaking glances out of the corner of his eye to take in the scene without staring directly at it. Now he stood in front of it and he could no longer avoid seeing it.

On the sofa was a sheet. Underneath the sheet was ... something. A shape. Ethan strained to avoid making out the details of what might be underneath. A hand reached out – Ethan supposed it was his hand although it did not seem to be listening to his internal demands to stop what it was doing – a hand reached out and pulled back the sheet.

Ethan let out a sigh of relief. It wasn't his mother after all. Underneath the sheet was a small waxy figure in the approximate shape of his mother. The eyes were cloudy and sightless. Its muscles were frozen in a strange parody of expression, the mouth open in an oh of horror and surprise. Clothes hung awkwardly on this figure – the same clothes his mother had been wearing yesterday – like sheets flapping listlessly on a clothes line. Unmoving, lumpen: it had no more presence than a photo of a statue.

Ethan stretched out a finger and touched the face. It was doughy but unyielding. It was cold. His finger rested on the cheek of this figure. Coldness crept up his finger and threatened to infect his arm, burrow its way into the heart of him.

A breath of air on the back of his neck as the door opened and closed. Then a hand on his shoulder. Robert stood next to him, staring down at the sofa in shared contemplation with Ethan.

"Where's mum?" asked Ethan.

"I don't know, Boom," replied Robert, understanding instantly what he meant. "She's not here."

Ethan reached up and took Robert's hand. For once, Robert did not shake it off. Together, they left the room and returned to bed.

"Passport please, sir," asked the man at the booth.

Ethan stared at him, slowly returning back to the present, until the man's expression of boredom was replaced with impatience and a growing wariness. Eventually, Ethan fumbled in his bag and pulled out his passport. The man flipped through it with slightly more attention than average and stared intently at Ethan as he returned it.

"Have a good flight, sir," said the man.

Ethan nodded. This triggered a spike of agony behind his eyes that pulsed and then ebbed away. He took a breath and forced a smile – he liked flying and was anticipating a gentle, uneventful flight.

CHAPTER NINETEEN

June 13

"One final checkthrough," said Argyle.

Ethan nodded. He liked final checkthroughs. In his opinion, the world could do with a lot more of them. Not only was a final checkthrough a calm, predictable procedure, and so worthwhile in itself, it also reduced the chances of anything unpredictable or exciting happening in the future, which was even better.

"I've got the box of spares," said Ethan, pointing at the red box sitting on the floor between them. Once again, they were in the back of a police van, sitting on benches opposite each other. A fluorescent tube ran along the ceiling, illuminating the sparse interior effectively. Argyle was flanked by two other police officers, discreetly conducting their own final checkthroughs while keeping an eye on their boss.

"And remember, you can give that to him – we don't really care – but make sure it's in return for the information we need."

"Yes, the rest of the information to get your money."

"We'll take him in," assured Argyle. "That's priority number two. Priority number one is to get those details. We could get them from him after taking him in, we will if necessary, but if you can wheedle them out of him while you're together, that would be much quicker. And we're in a bit of a hurry, trying to prevent the breakdown of Western civilization, and so on."

"Understood," said Ethan.

"Yes, but is it? You're a bit emotional. Are you going to be able to talk to him? Talk to him calmly, I mean, after his betrayal?"

Argyle stared intently at Ethan.

"No problem. I'm used to him. He is my brother," said Ethan.

"He'll be a bit put off by having Anna there. That was a good idea," said Argyle.

Ethan nodded. It wasn't part of his plan, but if it suited Argyle, that could only help.

"She should be coming round now. Tough lady," said Argyle.

Ethan frowned. "What do you mean?" he said.

"With her condition, her health issues."

"Health issues," Ethan repeated in a neutral tone.

"Meant to be terribly painful, when she has an attack. And having to stay out of the sun all the time, of course."

"Of course," said Ethan. His stomach roiled; his mind lurched – the sudden uncertainty of reaching out for the safety rail and grasping only empty air. Was his face still impassive? Surely Argyle could see that he had crumbled from one moment to the next. Images from his life with Anna popped into his head like bubbles from a submerged diver breaking the surface: Anna chugging her pills every morning; Anna fixing her wide-brimmed hat before creeping out into the daylight from her basement flat; her skin – pale and filigreed with tiny scars. How could he have missed this weakness in her physical make up? How could he have missed the strength it took to keep it from him? Great chunks of memory creaked and shivered and collapsed like rotten stone cliffs falling into foaming waters.

While Ethan tried to think of a way to prod Argyle for more details, the conversation had drifted on. There were more safety reminders. Argyle pushed over a small white tablet and Ethan obediently shoved it into his mouth and swallowed ostentatiously. A waxy transparent earpiece squished uncomfortably into his ear canal; a flesh-coloured plaster was glued gently onto the base of his jaw.

"You can sub-vocalize, we'll still be able to make out what you're saying," said Argyle.

"How do I sub-vocalize?" asked Ethan.

"No idea. But our ops teams are all very keen on it, so it must be useful. Just talk, if you like."

"And you'll hear me."

"Yes, and you'll hear us. The earpiece and mike are good for a few hours before they run out of power. Range isn't great, but we know pretty much exactly where you'll be. We need a code for backup, some sort of emergency signal."

"How about 'spiderman is eating the kryptonite'?"

"I think that may be a little tricky to work into the conversation."

"You haven't heard many conversations between me and my brother."

"Let's go with 'take the lift'."

"Fine. But I'm definitely going to say that by accident."

Argyle smiled and nodded. He could believe that Ethan might do that. He seemed disoriented – not just the scratchy anticipation of being thrust into an unfamiliar adventure. Perhaps it was the prospect of seeing Anna again, his unfortunate girlfriend. In any case, Ethan was only a minor cog in the complex machinery of this operation. As long as he could be trusted to stand up relatively straight long enough to recognize his own brother, he would serve his purpose. Looking at him swaying gently back and forth as though recovering from a punch to the gut, Argyle wasn't sure even that was certain.

As they chugged through the eerily sparse evening rush hour traffic, Argyle cycled once more through the final arrangements. He had all the resources he could wish for – the full apparatus of the state bent on retrieving its money. No doubt there were other similar operations. He had been watching the news: the government was hatching various byzantine financial arrangements, all of which basically involved printing money, and none of which could possibly work, for sound economic reasons that made no sense to him at all.

What he did understand was police work. Finding the thief – finding the stolen money and returning it. That was the simple way to undo a crime. No financial trickery was needed.

The front entrance to University College Hospital stood aloof from the grime and stench of the Marylebone Road, the frontage a single plane of glass reflecting heat and noise and traffic fumes. The car rolled to a halt fifty yards from the main entrance and Ethan emerged from the back seat clutching the red box, glanced furtively in both directions, and tripped over the kerb, so that he was forced to windmill his free arm furiously to keep his balance. So much for an unobtrusive start.

Ethan pushed open the heavy glass door and strode across the lobby to the reception desk. He had no idea whether the receptionist was part of the plan, but she waved him through security suspiciously quickly without even asking him about the red box.

The lift took him up to the ward. The front desk was manned by two nurses – one was the young woman he had met the first time; the other was an elderly male nurse, straggly white hair flopping down over his forehead and down to his shoulders. Distractedly, they pointed him to a room at the far end of the corridor.

"She's on the mend," said the female nurse, "and she's even got her own room, you can go straight in."

It was too easy. The door was on the latch. He opened it to a room dappled in darkness, the blinds drawn, a figure sketched shapelessly beneath the sheets covering the plain hospital bed. Medical machinery was stacked on a table beside the bed – there were a few wires loosely spooled towards the covers. The walls were painted pale green, scuffed and faded with age, no more than a muddy gray in the gloom.

"Anna," said Ethan.

The figure stirred.

"We have a lot to discuss," said Ethan. "And we don't really have any time to do it in."

Anna's head poked out from the crumpled sheets. Dark eyes like two full stops on a page; dirty white sheets mocking her pale pockmarked skin.

"Are you …" she started, and then stopped. Her voice was dry and dusty, squeaking like a gate rusted from disuse. "Did you bring my stuff?"

Ethan held up the bag he was carrying and then placed it ceremoniously on the floor between them. He stood at the foot of the bed, trying unsuccessfully not to loom awkwardly, but unwilling to perch on the edge of the bed. Anna stared up at him, similarly unwilling to break the silence.

"Why?" said Ethan eventually.

Anna looked up at him without speaking.

"I found your diary. I know about you and Robert."

Anna opened her mouth to speak and closed it again. She glanced down at the bag on the floor and back at Ethan, her eyes unreadable.

"It was Robert's idea, you must understand that," she said softly.

Ethan nodded. He knew all about Robert's plans, his intricate self-serving schemes.

"He's always been jealous," Ethan muttered.

"Yes, he was the jealous type. That's it. I met him abroad, on my way to England …"

"In Dahab," interrupted Ethan. He didn't want to hear any more – every word was a cold hook into his intestines, a lurch downwards as the ground was jerked away. Yet he ached to hear the details, to define and somehow circumscribe the extent of their betrayal. He yearned to rationalize, to forgive, and silently implored Anna to offer whatever was the least damaging explanation, to swing her blade so that the wounds were superficial, even though she seemed unaware of the weapon she was wielding, unable to see behind the brittle blankness of his expression.

"Right. Dahab." Anna paused, as if recollecting the baked, dusty streets. "I took quite a circuitous route. I was in Dahab, sorting out a way to get here. Robert helped me. He was part of a hacking collective based in Dahab. He took me under his wing, got the visa through. You must understand, I didn't know anybody, I was lonely. He listened to me."

"But once you got to London, there was something he wanted you to do."

"Yes. Exactly. He went on and on about all the money you earned at the bank. How he just wanted a little bit of it. How they're all thieves, sucking up value without giving anything in return, he didn't see why he shouldn't have some of it himself. But he knew you'd never let him anywhere near your systems, so he came up with this plan. He told me all I had to do was get to know you, tell you about my project, get some time on your systems. It was a great opportunity for me – some real hardware at last."

"And then he gave you some software to add to your project."

227

Anna nodded, then continued before Ethan could say anything else, the words tumbling over each other, a verbal pummeling that almost forced Ethan to take a step back.

"It was just one little gobbet of code. He knew that you'd check everything before it went into First Global Bank's systems, but he said that you wouldn't check my code too closely, because you knew that I couldn't really write anything genuinely harmful, anything that could seriously compromise First Global Bank's systems from the inside. And Robert gave me something plausible, highly obfuscated, a short wrapper with a blob of data that actually decrypted into self-executing code."

"I remember that blob. It was tiny," said Ethan. "Far too small to carry any sort of payload."

"Yes, he was so paranoid. But it was big enough to insert a small routine into the compiler. It invisibly added a new section to any executable code that called out to the malware and inserted it."

"Wow, that's pretty smart, even for Robert."

∞

DCI Argyle took off his headphones and turned to the rest of the room.

"Any idea what he's talking about?" he asked.

The dusty hangar was silent apart from the echoing clack of keyboards, the hush of whispered conversations and the omnipresent grumble of the traffic crawling along the Euston Road. A row of tables piled with cables and equipment ran down the centre of the space. It was flanked by a mix of police officers and soldiers – martial law had eroded the usual boundaries between the two. Broken car and train parts were shoved against the corrugated iron side wall – a legacy of how the space had been used until they had requisitioned it.

One of the soldiers raised her hand. She was squatting next to a bank of monitors that were – if he remembered correctly – monitoring local utilities.

"Yes?" he said.

"Sounds like a variant of what's become known as the Ken Thompson compiler hack. It's a clever exploit, practically invisible once it's been inserted into the compiler, the backdoor ..."

"Alright, I've heard enough," said DCI Argyle, raising one hand in the air. "This is all just chatting. Only harm it's doing is that I'm getting bored out of my mind. Now everyone keep quiet."

He put the headphones back on.

∞

"But what I don't get," Ethan continued, "is why you put yourself in the middle of the experiment. Why did you hook yourself up to your, to that thing?"

"The Transfer Problem?" asked Anna.

"Yes, that, and why would you do that in the first place? What were you trying to achieve, live inside a computer?"

"You're right, we need to fix it. Pass me the bag."

Ethan shifted the bag with one foot, sliding it towards the bed. Anna reached down and snatched it. She sifted through the contents hungrily, muttering to herself. Ethan noticed that she discreetly hoicked up the sheets to cover her arms – there was only a glimpse of pale white flesh.

With swift, precise movements, Anna unplugged all the medical machinery from a bank of sockets next to her bed. She unthreaded various skeins of wires and deftly inserted the corresponding plugs back into the sockets. LEDs blinked red then green; fans whirred and sputtered. Placing the jumble of components on the bed, Anna hummed softly to herself as she sorted through them and started to clip together components.

"That going to fix the damage?" asked Ethan.

"Sure," said Anna, without glancing up.

"Only, I think I got caught in it too," said Ethan.

"I thought you might have. Been having headaches?"

"Could call it that – feels more like a rat scrabbling around inside my head chewing pieces of my brain. Seems to be fading away though."

"The brain is a very adaptable organ, remarkable plasticity."

"I'd rather have the missing bits of my original mind back, if it's all the same."

"A reasonable request," said Anna. "Don't worry, this will suck up your mind and put it back in your brain."

"That probably sounded more encouraging in your head than it does out loud," said Ethan.

∞

"What just happened?" asked DCI Argyle.

"Some sort of problem with the audio. Getting feedback from some power fluctuations."

"Hmmm," said a soldier standing at DCI Argyle's shoulder. His uniform was crisply laundered – even his trousers featured perfectly straight creases – and pinned to his jacket was a cloth badge featuring a row of fearsomely impenetrable symbols sewn in gold thread. The other soldiers treated him as important, although he had no discernible function.

"Yes?" asked Argyle.

"Curious timing," said the soldier.

"Well, it's your military kit that decided to be curious. Perhaps you could give it a kick or something."

"And it's your operation. That is, we're just here in an advisory capacity. Are we missing anything important?"

"So far it's been mainly banter," said Argyle. "Ethan is expressing his profound existential despair at being betrayed by the woman he loves through the medium of slightly annoying comments."

"Yes, our psych people have labelled him as passive-aggressive."

"I don't think I can take much more though. Why can't he just say what he feels?"

"Our troops can be in that room inside sixty seconds. Whenever you say the word."

"Sure, but it's Robert we're waiting for. Let's give it a little longer."

∞

"You're the one who wanted to go first," said Anna.

"I'm not sure about this," said Ethan. He adjusted the spindly silver crown over his head. The latticework of wires pinched over his temples and a metal burr dug into the base of his neck. Coils of insulation spiraled towards a rudimentary control panel that was propped up on the bed in front of Anna.

Ethan shrugged. The cold roiling in his guts threatened to spill acid burning up into his throat. Was it jealousy? Was it the banal reality of betrayal? Anna and Robert, Robert and Anna: with her sitting before him, the stark physical fact of them together clamoured for attention in his mind. Squashing these thoughts, banishing the mental images of them touching, of them laughing, of them naked together, gave fresh impetus to those twisting coils of cold. And yet the impulse he was forced to restrain was not to weep but to laugh: to laugh at the effortless way he maintained a calm, blank exterior, as the fizzing emotions crashed uselessly against his resolve. Was there any point to this superhuman failure to express himself? That thought was simply an emissary of the enemy, to be ignored lest his resolve weaken. The mild, unflappable demeanour he showed to the world was so integral to him that he defended it fiercely and unconditionally.

"You're being a bit quiet, even for you," said Anna.

"I'm fine. Let's get on with it," said Ethan.

"OK," said Anna. "You'll probably feel some tingling. I'll be passing an electric current through your brain. That sounds worse than it is. Well, I think so. That is, don't worry if there are some other transient symptoms, disorientation, paralysis, so on."

Before Ethan could raise some sudden but fairly profound concerns in response to this disclaimer, there was a knock at the door.

"Time for your checks," came a sing-song voice from the corridor. It was the new nurse Ethan had passed on his path through the ward.

"No, wait," said Ethan, "we've got to get this done first before we let him in."

"Him? It's fine. Just some new nurse."

"No, you don't understand," said Ethan. "Tell him to come back later."

"Come in," Anna called towards the door. Then, "Nurse won't have any idea what we're up to anyway," she whispered to Ethan.

Ethan sighed and turned to the door as it opened and a bulky figure shuffled in.

"Hello Robert," he said.

"Hello, Boom," replied Robert.

"He's there, he's there," said yet another soldier sitting in front of a bank of apparatus piled haphazardly on the row of tables running down the centre of the warehouse. To DCI Argyle, they were all starting to blend into one. Calm but staccato voices, a mysterious penchant for saying everything twice, fresh and enthusiastic faces that were vaguely unsettling.

"We can be in there inside sixty seconds," said the soldier standing at his shoulder.

"Yes, I've got that," said Argyle. "Our primary aim is not to capture the targets. We can sweep them up whenever we like. The point of this is to find the money, our money, the country's money. Jesus, I don't know." He turned away in exasperation. When did his job become chasing down some pot of money at the end of the rainbow? Would recovering this unimaginably vast sum really reverse the course of the financial crash, put the pieces of the jigsaw back together again?

"So we hold?" asked the soldier.

"Yes, that's what I said. We've got a tracker on him, he can't sneeze without me getting a full seismographical analysis, let alone get anywhere in Central London. Tell your people to hold."

∞

"I'm scared," said Anna. "What's he doing here? Get him out, Ethan."

Ethan shuffled towards Robert, still framed in the doorway, and then stopped. Robert shrank back.

"What are you doing?" he asked. "Why are you listening to her?"

Ethan shook his head, as if to dispel a swarm of wasps. He turned to Robert and opened his mouth and no noise came out and then he swiveled back to face Anna. Both Anna and Robert stood in silence, fascinated and appalled by Ethan's protracted vacillation.

Anna broke the silence first. "You're right," she said to Ethan, "There's more to it. I haven't been truthful with you."

"Oh, come on," said Robert.

"Shut up," said Ethan quietly.

"Things weren't easy for me, in Russia. My mother, she had health problems. She had a pension from the state, but after the Wall came down, it didn't get paid regularly. It was a disability pension, wasn't meant to ever get cancelled. Some days she couldn't get out of bed, when the pain was bad, and she sent me instead. I'd take her voucher round to the local office of the Ministry of Social Protection – it was a special pension, it had to go through their office – and mostly they would count out the notes and I would take them and go round to the market and get in the line, I had strict instructions from my mum which line to get into, who had the best produce at the cheapest price.

But, sometimes, well, they'd be a few notes short or they wouldn't have anything for me. But I couldn't go straight home. I'd still go to the market and I'd get what I could. I was small, everybody knew me, nobody took any notice of me. So I'd end up with a few cabbages, maybe, even if I could only pay for one."

"Great, we're stealing cabbages, is that it?" said Robert.

"Shut up," said Ethan.

Anna continued as if nobody had interrupted her.

"After she died, I was just a lonely nerdy girl who was always top of her class and who had some highly-developed cabbage-stealing skills. Not much scope to flourish in Moscow. I hitched my way through Europe, ended up in London, enrolled in some computer science courses. No money, bills to pay, I ended up helping out some people with their IT problems, helping them steal some cabbages, if you see what I mean.

"That's how I met Robert. He took me under his wing. He was always going on about you, his younger brother who was raking in all the money in the world working for a bank and didn't have any left over to share with him. He always called you Boom, said you were the lucky one and never thought to share any of that luck with him."

"And that's when he came up with this plan. He was confident he could tunnel out from your systems, and bring some money along with it, but he couldn't get in. He needed you to carry a package inside for him, and he knew you'd never do it. That's when he came up with his idea. My research needed big iron and it was exactly the sort of thing that you'd be interested in. He made a match."

"You know, I'm standing right here," said Robert. "You're talking about me in the third person, like I'm the one in the hospital bed."

"Shut up," said Ethan.

"And it's all bullshit, anyway. You really think it happened like that?"

Ethan strode over to Robert and stood in front of him, his face a few inches from Robert's face, breathing hoarsely but otherwise silent, looming suddenly as for once he unfolded his tall, gangly frame and pulled himself up to his full height. Raising a hand uncertainly, Ethan slowly curled it into a fist and then brought it slowly down and stretched out a single finger and placed it in the centre of Robert's chest.

"You will be silent now," said Ethan, his faint whisper barely carrying over the hiss of the air-conditioning.

Robert shrank back against the wall and nodded hurriedly.

"It's enough," said Ethan. "I don't want to hear any more right now. Robert is going to tell me what I need to know in a minute. First, we get you set up, we fix you."

Anna nodded but Ethan was still facing away from her, staring at Robert. "Yes," she said at last. "I'll show you how to get it ready."

∞

"Hold it, I think we're finally getting somewhere," said Argyle.

The gaggle of soldiers standing anxiously by Argyle had grown steadily, as though they could change his mind by force of numbers. They peered over his shoulder as he consulted the computer screen manned by police officers and soldiers. They nodded sagely as he whispered instructions to other police officers who passed them around the echoing hangar space. And they were waiting for permission to unleash their special forces team who would whisk Robert and Ethan into custody, thereby obviously slicing off the head of the conspiracy that had shattered Britain.

A plangent whine cut across the low hubbub of conversation.

"Getting some interference through," said one soldier wearing a ludicrously oversized pair of headphones plugged into a nearby computer.

"We can still hear what they're saying," said Argyle. "He referred specifically to getting information from Robert, that was meant for us. We can wait while he's fiddling around with all that kit and his girlfriend. Really, I'm not that bothered about that soap opera."

"I think she was also the other brother's girlfriend," said one of the soldiers at Argyle's elbow.

"Yes, I got that bit. Can someone do some research on her, actually? I know she's not going to do much damage sitting in a hospital bed, but, well, I'm sure it will make some interesting reading."

One of the soldiers shuffled off to comply with his request. Two others took his place.

The whine turned into a shriek and then fell silent.

"Interference is still there, we're cancelling it," explained the soldier. "Strange, it seems to be coming through via our network connection. Like some sort of denial of service attack, adding some flows of data that are competing for bandwidth and don't seem to make much sense."

"Keep an eye on it. But our targets are in there, they aren't interfering with us from somewhere outside."

∞

"Ouch," said Anna. She shifted the delicate filigree of wires that was balanced on her head. Various spokes and tendrils poked through her hair or rested on her forehead.

"I think it's meant to feel like that," said Ethan.

"It's fine, just get on with it," said Anna.

"This isn't going to do what you think," said Robert. He stepped forward and then stepped back as Ethan gave him a brutal stare.

"Flick the switch," said Anna. "It's down next to that tangle of ..."

"Yes, I know where it is," said Ethan. He flicked the switch as Anna looked at him uncertainly.

"You don't understand what you're doing," whispered Robert. "It's set the opposite way to what she told you. It won't cancel out what you've already done. It'll send all of the rest of her the same way."

The apparatus sparkled and fizzed. A grating subsonic hum welled up around them. Smelling of ozone, puffs of vapour spurted out from a black box trembling at the heart of the skein of wires gathered on the hospital bed. The lights dimmed and then cut out.

"Goodbye," said Anna. A thin trickle of blood twisted down from her temple where a burr of copper wire had pierced her skin, but her face was set in repose, at peace, a faraway look in her eyes and a rueful smile on her lips. "I'm sorry I hurt you, both of you."

"There, a simple apology. Was that so much to ask for?" said Ethan, turning to face Robert and making no attempt to turn off the machine, which was now rattling as pieces trembled against each other.

"What?" said Anna. Her face twisted. Her eyes opened in alarm, confusion and then understanding. She moaned and swayed on the hospital bed, her head twisting and then arching back.

"You switched it back," said Robert softly. "She switched it to trick you and you switched it back. It was pulling her back after all. It wasn't transferring the rest of her."

With a supreme effort, Anna reached up to wrench the tangle of wires from her head. Scraping along her skin, it buckled and tore and was flung across the room in a final ecstasy of movement. Then Anna slumped across her bed and gathered her head in her hands and wept.

"How ... I mean, just how?" said Robert.

"I'm a slow learner, but I get there in the end. Anna's damsel-in-distress Dahab story – if anyone's doing the manipulating, it's her, not you. Plus, if you steal some money from a bank, that's a good old-fashioned bank robbery. If you steal all the money from all the banks, you haven't really stolen anything of value. You've started a revolution. And you, Robert, are a robber, not a revolutionary."

"And ..." started Robert, but Ethan interrupted him with a wave of his arm. Pointing at the walls and then his ears, he stared fixedly at Robert until Robert acknowledged him with a slow nod.

"You need to tell me that you know all the details from your malware, the bank accounts, where the money has gone, and you're going to tell me them."

"Yes, that's right, I know them all and I'll tell you them."

"And all the codes to access them, any traps that will move or dissipate them."

"Yes, all that."

"OK, write it down here," – he said, handing over a pad of paper and a pen – "and call it out as you write it. I know it will take you a few minutes. Take your time."

∞

236

"Cancel that order," said Argyle.

"The situation is unstable," said the soldier standing at Argyle's shoulder. As he puffed out his chest, the row of golden symbols on his badge glittered ferociously. Apparently, they imbued him with some sort of pre-eminence over the other soldiers; he was their chosen spokesman, imploring Argyle to stop watching and start acting.

"I said the situation is unstable," he repeated. Argyle noted that he still had the soldierly propensity to say everything twice. "We're getting sporadic dropouts across the network. This is a complex environment, we can't completely control it. Our monitoring is suspect, dropouts all over the place, glitches where there shouldn't be glitches. We risk losing the suspects completely unless we go now, right now."

"How many times do I have to say it?" said Argyle. "The target is the account details, not the people. We'll pick them up along the way."

"Sir?" asked a police officer hovering at the edge of their group. She was hopping anxiously from foot to foot, leaning in and holding out a thin manila folder in one extended hand so far that it looked like she might topple over under its weight. "I think you might want to look at this."

"What is it?" asked Argyle, making no move towards the folder.

"It's the background you asked for, on the girl, Anna. The one in the hospital."

"The only one we know for sure isn't going anywhere," said the soldier.

"We're about to move on our targets, the other two," said Argyle.

The officer continued to proffer the folder. Eventually, Argyle took it. He flicked it open and glanced at it. Turning the page, he grunted and looked up sharply at the officer, who nodded as though in reply to a question. Argyle walked to a nearby chair, trailing his entourage, and flopped down in it, spreading the contents of the folder out on the table before him.

"Send them in," he said, "send in the clowns."

"I resent that comment," said the soldier, but he glanced at an assistant who muttered to another even more junior aide who scurried away.

"Tracker still in the room?" asked the soldier.

"Hasn't moved," said Argyle. "Look at this." He pointed at the papers spread out on the table.

Argyle tapped the top piece of paper. "Medical records," he said. "Anna Volkov was born in Japan in 1985. In a small village outside Nagasaki. Father unknown. Mother died in 1994. Leukemia."

"Yes, lots of facts," said the soldier. "And why do I care?"

"Not facts. A story. Her mother would have been a baby, living in Nagasaki at the end of the Second World War, surviving the nuclear bomb. Who knows how her life was blighted by that? She gave birth to Anna, as a single mother, an older mother, and then Anna saw her waste away and die from cancer, probably caused by the American bomb."

"Motive," breathed the soldier softly.

"Exactly. The one thing we've been missing. We've assumed that this was just theft, theft on a large scale. And it was that. But the havoc that it caused, the breakdown in civil order. The collapse in the banks. It wasn't a side-effect, it was what she wanted. Anna is the one we should be examining – she's the only one with a grudge against the entire Western world."

∞

THEY'LL BE HERE SOON, scribbled Ethan on the pad between them.

Robert nodded. "And the access pin for the Zaire deposit account is 3 – 7 – 7 – 0 – 7 – 0 – 4 – 4," he said aloud, continuing to talk in a slow even drawl.

YOU GO, wrote Robert.

TRACKER, wrote Ethan.

Robert laughed and then stopped abruptly to carry on his recitation of account codes. Simultaneously, he held out his hand to Ethan and beckoned.

Ethan coughed and spluttered and put a hand to his mouth and then spread his fingers to present a single, saliva-specked pill lying in the centre of his palm.

FAKE SWALLOW, he wrote.

"Basic technique," said Robert, "I wouldn't expect anything less, would I?"

Then he stared closely at the pill and grabbed the pad and wrote on it: BIO-SENSITIVE.

"Oh dear," said Ethan. He peered at the pill and slowly lifted it back to his mouth. The flecks of saliva were visibly fading from its faintly iridescent surface, the combination of temperature and chemical environment would soon betray that it was no longer inside a human body. Robert grabbed his wrist and took the pill and popped it in his own mouth.

MY TURN, wrote Robert.

WHY?, wrote Ethan.

MY FAULT. YOU RUN NOW.

SORRY, Ethan wrote. Then he underlined it.

GO NOW, BOOM. I'LL WAIT HERE. THAT WILL BUY YOU MORE TIME. RUN FAST.

Ethan ripped the plaster-covered microphone off his neck, scooped out the waxy earpiece, dropped both on the floor and turned to face the door. Anna stood in front of it, one hand leaning against the door handle, propping herself up as though she had just sprinted down the home straight. Her lips were bloodless; a thin streak of blood ran down the side of her face and onto her shapeless pale hospital robe.

"Take me with you, please," she said.

Ethan reached out to brush her aside. She quailed from his grasp and pointed at the foot of her bed.

"Please, you don't understand. I'm ill. I've always been ill. You don't know how I've suffered."

Ethan grabbed Anna's medical chart from the foot of her bed.

"Porphyria? What's that?" he asked.

"It's an inherited condition. Sensitivity to sunlight. Skin problems. And when I have an attack, the pain, it's indescribable. Nothing can control it. My body is a prison, it's a torture."

"And that's why you wanted to escape from it? Of course, that's what made it worthwhile, why you were working to solve the Transfer Problem in the first place. Why it was worth inveigling Robert so you could get to me so you could finally achieve your precious, insane dream. And crashing the whole world's markets, I guess that was just a bonus."

"Please, if you only knew what it felt like. I just wanted to be free of it."

"Well, part of you is free of it," said Ethan, pointing at the ceiling, which was the nearest he could get to pointing at the internet. "And frankly, there are many people who struggle every day with illness and disability who don't turn into cold, murderous psychopaths."

"When did you get so tough, Ethan?"

"Longer ago than you might have realized, Anna." Ethan turned to Robert. "The bad news is, I'm going to have to leave you here with her. The good news is that the police will be here very shortly and then neither of us will ever have to see her again."

∞

"What's happening?" asked the soldier standing next to Argyle.

"Not sure, our audio isn't working at all now," said Argyle. He checked a nearby monitor. "It's OK, he's still there."

"Maintain steady approach," said the soldier. "You have what you need?" he asked.

"Signs are positive. That's what the economists are telling me."

A young woman sitting at one of the banks of monitors turned around to them.

"Still tracing the funds," she said, "but the information we have so far, well, looks like we're going to get about 99% back. They tell us that's enough to stabilize the markets, stabilize the banks."

"99%, you mean practically everything?"

"Yes, all but a few billion."

"A few billion? Hardly worth mentioning then." Argyle chuckled. "ETA?" he asked the soldier.

"Thirty seconds."

"And your target is now all three of them, including Anna."

"Yes, and look, things will be back to normal pretty soon. This is going to be a criminal justice matter, so don't get too, you know, soldierly."

"And the charge is, what, bringing down Western civilization?"

"For the woman, Anna. She was clearly motivated by some sort of animus against a world that had abandoned her and her mother. A world that bombed her mother and killed her of a terrible disease decades later. But still …"

"What?"

"It all seems a bit baroque, a bit complicated. There must have been ways to achieve this result without putting herself in the middle of this experiment, whatever it was, without her ending up in hospital. Maybe if we knew what it was her experiment was actually about, other than just beating the financial markets. For the men, it was theft. For her, it was more complicated."

"Yes, well, you can ask her yourself soon. Hold on, we're going in."

Urgent voices, interspersed with static, scratched at the edge of hearing. A soldier at the table next to them pressed his headphones closer to his ears – the chatter faded to a faint metallic murmur – and squinted, as though blocking out what he could see would increase what he could hear.

"We've got them," said the soldier.

"You've got them?"

"Two of them. Man and a woman."

"No sign of Robert?"

"We've got Robert. Robert and Anna. It's Ethan that's missing. He's not there."

∞

Ethan ran up the stairs, looping around the turn in the stairwell like a stone in a slingshot, one fist wrapped around the bannister. This was the bit he wasn't good at – the heroic running and fighting bit. His breath rasped in his lungs. He headed up the stairs, to the roof, satisfying some primitive instinct to flee to higher ground. But it was also a dead end. He stopped, put his hands on his knees, concentrated on smoothing his breathing, evening out his heartbeat.

Clang, echoing from the top of the stairwell. Muffled footsteps from below. Ethan ducked through a doorway, into a corridor. Dirty white tiles, squeaking of hospital trolley wheels. An orderly strolled around a far corner, whistling. Two doors set into the side wall: toilets. Putting out one hand, Ethan opened the door to the gents, then pulled back, turned, shouldered his way into the ladies.

Fortunately, the ladies was empty. Sinks, a couple of cubicles. Were there voices in the corridor? Into a cubicle, shutting the door. Broken, of course. It banged shut and then creaked slightly ajar.

Standing on the cracked toilet seat, Ethan could reach the ceiling. He punched one of the square plastic ceiling tiles and it rattled, shaking down a shower of dust. With both hands, he levered the tile to one side, grabbed a metal strut and hoicked himself up. Muddied light oozed up from the square hole in the ceiling to reveal a latticework of faded aluminium, branching out from a rectangular grid of steel joists. The ceiling tiles were suspended from the aluminium lattice, about three feet below the real dividing line between floors, a bland concrete slab punctured by a few irregularly spaced, roughly drilled holes. Bundles of cables hung in lazy loops, attached by plastic ties to the steel joists. A film of dust and murk lay over the tiles and the cables and the joists.

The aluminium lattice swayed alarmingly as Ethan crawled above the false ceiling. His back scraped against the concrete above him. He reached a steel joist and lay on top of it, back against the cool metal. Then he reversed the journey, replaced the ceiling tile he had dislodged in its original position, and crawled back to the joist in the gloom.

He was hidden. Safe for a time. But now what? He took his mobile phone out of his pocket, reattached the battery. The screen glowed. A spider froze in the sudden illumination; its shadow was scrawled, giant and distorted, against the concrete. Ethan chuckled and shooed the spider away. It trembled in indecision and then scuttled along the joist and into the gloom.

Ethan cradled the SIM card in his hand. Should he plug it in? It would connect him to IWS. And – unless IWS somehow intervened – it would also betray his location to the police. So, should he scream out his location with the vague hope that a psychotic machine would protect him?

Well, maybe psychotic was a bit harsh. The contradictory messages: instructions that kept him safe; instructions that put him in danger; instructions that sent him round in circles. At first, it had seemed like an insane computer programme shuffling him from place to place with egomaniacal glee. Too easy to slip into the worn familiar tropes of artificial intelligence operating with numbing precision but a deranged lack of strategy.

Of course, it wasn't one psychotic artificial intelligence – it was two. Or, more likely, one artificial intelligence with two different aspects, two sub-personalities. Most of it was Anna, the part of Anna that had been sucked up by her machine and spat out into the internet, the part that had been – in her words – transferred. And her aim, her aim all along, had been to complete the transfer.

The other personality, that was Ethan. A tiny fragment of Ethan. A splinter of his personality, lodged deep inside whatever analogue of a mind constituted IWS. Occasionally, it had broken through, given him some help or at least nudged him away from danger. Competing with the dominant Anna personality and generally failing. Maybe, with some more of Anna's mind transferred back into her body, the Ethan splinter might have a better chance.

Somewhere in there was the spider, the original source of the experiment, the original mental skeleton on which the electronic fragments of Anna and Ethan had been draped. Who could guess what motivated a spider? Scraping together his meagre knowledge of arachnid behavior, Ethan compiled a short list: focus on multiple different targets, predation, visually sophisticated, rapid reactions. Consistent with everything he had seen, but it addressed only the how, not the what and the why. Maybe the spider mind provided only a basic framework. Given that spiders needed little motivation to eat their young, it was difficult to predict what would happen if the spider also contributed its moral outlook.

Maybes piled on top of maybes. Not a strong edifice on which to build a course of action. What had happened to the cautious, painstaking Ethan?

Ethan fingered the SIM chip into its slot and waited while it rebooted. A series of pings signaled incoming messages:

WAIT.

And then:

WAIT A BIT MORE.

And finally:

OK. GO NOW. FOLLOW DIRECTIONS.

Ethan typed out: OK, and started to shuffle towards the originally ceiling tile. The phone instantly pinged again:

STOP SENDING MESSAGES. JUST FOLLOW DIRECTIONS. FOLLOW EXACTLY.

Ethan smiled. He had no doubt which bit of IWS was sending those messages.

CHAPTER TWENTY

June 14

Y ou've got it all figured out," said Robert. He leaned back in his chair. The metal legs scraped against the floor. Turning to the one-way mirror set in the wall, Robert favoured it with a lingering smile. Then, for good measure, he threw in a wink.

"I've got it all figured out," replied DCI Argyle. He scratched carelessly at the notepad on his lap, refusing to look at the one-way mirror or at Robert.

"Yes. You've got me. I stole the money." Robert spread his arms wide to convey the vast scale of his theft.

"You stole the money," said DCI Argyle.

"And now you've got it all back."

"Almost all of it."

"OK, almost all of it."

"We're short about three billion pounds."

"Yes, well, the UK banking industry loses that in a bad weekend, they probably have more than that stuffed down the back of their collective sofas."

"Your hostility to the banking industry is quite deep-seated, isn't it?"

Robert puffed out his cheeks and drummed his fingers on the table. The bare sheet of metal sported a single blank sheet of paper and a bulky black audio recorder, featureless apart from a single small LED flashing red.

"Oh, you're good," said Robert, "you're good at this."

Argyle bowed his head in modest acknowledgement.

"But really, that's all there is to it. You've got your man, well done."

"Ah," said Argyle, looking up at last from his notepad. "It all sounds admirably neat, but I still have a few more questions. Anna, for instance, the conduit that you used to get your brother to install the malware, your back door into the bank. Was she just an innocent in all this? How come she ended up practically killing herself in pursuit of some mad experiment? Did you know that she is in fact a very ill woman, a woman with a grudge?"

"Yes, that is a lot of questions …"

"And then your brother. Your bitter enemy, after you, you and Anna, betrayed him. Yet somehow you ended up with his tracker inside you. And we haven't been able to find him. He's gone, despite, well, despite quite a lot of effort in finding him."

"That's my boy."

"Yes, I'm sure it is, but, you see …"

"Yes, I see, I see. But you have your man, you have your money. And all this fluff about experiments and plots to bring down the Western world, isn't that a little out of scope?"

"You sound just like my boss," said Argyle.

"Thank you," said Robert.

"It wasn't a compliment," said Argyle.

EPILOGUE

Streaks of light filtered through the faded clapboard planks of the wall and dissected the surface of the bar, reflecting off cracked varnish and sticky liquid stains. A yellowed poster was taped to one of the shelves behind the bar. It featured a collage of photos of various drinks rendered in lurid oranges and yellows and greens and a scribbled list of cocktails with imaginative titles.

The door swung open and clanged shut. As it was formed from two sheets of corrugated iron roughly stapled together, this produced a sudden dissonant noise. Aldo paused at the door to savour the drama of his entrance, and then strolled to the bar and swung onto a stool.

"This isn't an easy place to find," he said.

"Hello there, Reginald Oldham-Puckett," said Ethan, who was sitting at the next stool.

Aldo winced. "Please? Can you just use Aldo?"

"You followed my directions, then?" said Ethan, ignoring Aldo's comment.

"Not any other way to get here, is there? We must be about a million miles from the nearest wi-fi."

"Can I buy you a drink?" asked Ethan.

"I'll have" – Aldo squinted at the poster – "let's see, I'll have a Starburst Surprise."

"Hmmm. Good choice."

"Is that what you've got?"

Ethan stared at the liquid confection in front of him. Thick green liquid in a conical glass topped off with not one or two but – in an ecstasy of overenthusiasm – three glacé cherries. A spiral straw completed the ensemble. Ethan sipped from the straw, thoughtfully.

"I'm not sure, actually."

Aldo sighed.

"Look," he said, "do you want to tell me what you called me for? Is it something to do with that girl, Anna? Are you looking for her?"

"In a way – look, I know I'm being vague. I'll tell you the whole story. Then I've got a job for you. It will be … I suppose interesting is the word – and, I promise you this, it comes with the biggest expense account you've ever seen."

Aldo nodded appreciatively and settled into his stool, ready to hear the details.

∞

ACKNOWLEDGEMENTS

Thanks to everyone who worked on my book at Deixis Press, but above all to the inspirational Angel Belsey. Much love and thanks to my family, for indulging my many foibles.

∞

ABOUT THE AUTHOR

Adam Saint's early writing career was hampered by being the last person in his class at primary school allowed to use a pen. He now compiles cryptic crosswords for the Financial Times and writes for various journals on topics including artificial intelligence and bitcoin. His Erdős number is three.

@adamsaint_

∞

ABOUT DEIXIS PRESS

Deixis Press is an independent publisher of fiction, usually with a darker edge. Our aim is to discover, commission, and curate works of literary art. Every book published by Deixis Press is hand-picked and adored from submission to release and beyond.

www.deixis.press

Printed in Great Britain
by Amazon

15739690R00150